The Quiet Neighbours

*To Stella
Enjoy
Linda Sawley*

Linda Sawley

Linric Publishing

Copyright © 2020 Linda Sawley

The right of Linda Sawley to be identified as the author the work has been asserted by her in accordance with the Copyright, Design and Patents Act, 1988

All rights reserved. No part of this publication may be reproduced, stored in or introduced into a retrieval system, or transmitted, in any form, or by any means (electrical, mechanical, photocopying, recording or otherwise) without the prior written permission of the publisher. Any person who does any unauthorised act in relation to this publication may be liable to criminal prosecution and civil claims for damages.

Published in 2020 by Linric Publishing
18 Victoria Lodge
READ, Lancs
BB12 7SZ

British Cataloguing in publication data
Sawley, Linda
The Quiet Neighbours
I. Title
Classification: Romantic Fiction

ISBN 97809534329–7-6

Acknowledgements
Editing and Proof reading by Barbara Schultz

Cover design by Adam Burton

Printed by Sherwood Universal Ltd,
Unit 5 Sherbrook Business Centre, Sherbrook Road,
Daybrook, Nottingham NG5 6AT

Dedicated to the memory of
Richard Bell, founding editor of
'Writing Magazine,'
my mentor and encourager.

Other books by the same author

Everyone Else's Children (autobiography) 1998

A Ring in Time 2002

The Key
(Mitchell's Modes Saga Book 1) 2004

Changes
(Mitchell's Modes Saga Book 2) 2005

New Century: Changed Lives *(Kindle version only)*
(Mitchell's Modes Saga Book 3) 2014

The Survivor 2007

Anna 2010

Joshua and the Horrible History Project 2011
(recommended reading age 7 to 13 years, but enjoyed by 5 to 90 years)

Weaving Through the Years 2012

Linda Sawley's Collection of Short Stories 2014 *(Kindle version only)*

The Rector's Pearl 2016 *(Kindle version only)*

Pemberley in Waiting 2017

Chapter 1
July 2016

Elaine Barnes strode across the university campus car park, dragging her trolley on wheels with one hand and clutching a boxed arrangement of flowers, balanced against her hip, with her other hand. As she walked she couldn't help but grin, and her pace quickened as she got nearer the car. She was free! Free at last to decide what to do with the rest of her life. It was such an exciting time and she was answerable to no one - no husband or parents or children. No job now either. She could please herself and go when and where she wanted. She could live where she wanted also. As from last week she had no home to go to and had spent the last week of her working life living in student accommodation now that the students had left for the summer holidays.

Putting the flowers on top of the car whilst she rooted in the trolley for her handbag and keys, Elaine reflected that it had been a kind gesture on the part of the university. It wasn't her own place of work; she'd taken early retirement from her job officially yesterday, but still had one final engagement today. It was in a Welsh university and they had a tradition on Graduation Day that a visiting speaker gave a lecture on very diverse subjects, depending on who the guest speaker was. It had been an easy lecture for her - 'The effect of the dissolution of the monasteries on the surrounding locality'; the subject that she had studied for her PhD. Usually they just gave a discreet fee, but as they knew that Elaine had retired the day before, they'd given her the flowers too. They were beautiful: roses, gypsophyllia, gerbera and phlox. Elaine wedged the flowers into the back well of the car next to the trolley. Getting in to the car, she took her jacket and high heels off, and put on her driving shoes. They were wrecked old shoes that weren't fit for anything else rather than driving in. It was a relief to get the high heels off, they weren't comfortable wear for all day, and usually she wore much lower heels around the campus. She reserved her heels for high days and special occasions. Pulling the clasp out of her blonde hair, she let her hair fall free, then fastened her seat belt.

Sitting in the car, Elaine still had an enormous grin on her face. There was so much to do and decide, but for the next two weeks at least she was doing nothing and making no decisions. In the car boot were two new books by her favourite authors: Leah Fleming and Santa Montefiore. Having spent all her working life poring over research documents and trying to read medieval manuscripts, when she was not working she liked stories that were easy reads which she could get lost in. Fleming and Montefiore never failed to deliver, and she would start one of them tonight. Elaine was going to her childhood friend's farm for a holiday. It was up in the Trough of Bowland, an area of outstanding natural beauty in the north of England. Gill and Elaine had met at the infant school in the Lancashire town of Ramsbottom. In those days there was no official uniform, but Gill and Elaine both had grey pleated skirts, white blouses and hand knitted cardigans. Their mothers had got talking about knitting in the school yard before the children were called in. The children clung together as they were summoned inside the scary looking large building. That initial bond had stayed ever since, lasting over 50 years, although their lives had taken very different roads.

Elaine set the satnav so that she could get back to the motorway network; after that it was straight up the M6 until she got back to the north of England and more familiar territory. Fortunately, Elaine had begun the journey in late afternoon, so although the first half of the journey was fairly slow, by the time she got near Preston, the M6 was mercifully quiet.
  Taking the exit from the motorway, she also turned off the radio, as she'd had enough of music blaring in her ear. Elaine started thinking about her situation. From having owned three properties a short time ago, she now owned none. It was a very strange, probably scary, but exciting time. Her furniture was all in storage in Manchester, and the boot of her car contained all her documents, passport, and enough clothes to get her through the next few weeks. With it being July, she didn't need much. Winter boots and thick coats wouldn't be necessary for some time yet, and hopefully by then she would be renting somewhere or even have bought something. Where that would be, she had no idea. Over the last few months, whilst she'd been working her notice at Manchester University, Elaine had had several flights of fancy as to where she could live. She had ruled out Manchester, where

she'd lived for almost 40 years since going there to university at the age of 18. And she'd ruled out living in Europe, as now that Britain had just voted to leave the EU, there might be implications for the future. As the rest of the world was probably too hot, she decided to stay in England, or the British Isles, so that she was near enough to visit friends, and for them to visit her. Besides, nobody could beat or even match the British National Health Service, if she ever needed it.

Selling her property in France was a good move as the property market there was a bit up and down, so she was delighted to have got such a good price for it. Mind you, she had extended and improved it over the many years she'd owned it. She had spent many good holidays there, renting it had made her a small income. However, it was time to move on. As well as her own home in Manchester, she'd only just sold the family home in Ramsbottom. Although her mother had gone into a home for the last few months of her life, Elaine hadn't got round to selling the house after she died 18 months ago, but now it had sold. She couldn't believe the price it had sold for remembering how much her parents had paid for it, in the 1960s. But since then Ramsbottom had become a commuter belt for Manchester and prices had soared. Elaine did consider retiring to her childhood home, but decided against it, as all her links with the town were gone. She'd have to make new friends wherever she lived, so she might as well start in a new place. Now with all this property dealing, she had well over a million pounds in the bank, so she could live anywhere. With those happy thoughts, Elaine turned off the main road onto the road leading to Dunsop Bridge and the Trough of Bowland, where Gill lived.

As Elaine got almost into Dunsop Bridge, she saw a 'For Sale' sign on an old church on the side of the road. Elaine slowed down to look at the church. It appeared to be in very poor condition and the windows were boarded up, but the sign said that planning permission had been obtained for it to be converted into a dwelling. Elaine stopped the car and got out. It was almost dark, so she decided she would take another look at it tomorrow in daylight. With her love of history and medieval abbeys, an old church would be a fun place to buy. As Elaine got back in to the car, she laughed to herself at this flight of fancy.

Minutes later, she arrived at Gill Robinson's farmhouse and was greeted by Gill, her three grandchildren and two dogs.

'Get down, Molly, get down, Cassie,' cried Gill. 'Leave Elaine alone.' The dogs slunk away but continued barking, so Gill grabbed hold of Elaine and pulled her inside. Elaine waved to Gill's grandchildren and said she would catch up with them tomorrow, and their mother Liz took them across the farmyard to an adjacent house.

'How was the journey? Are you hungry? How do you feel now you've retired?' asked Gill, all in one sentence. Elaine laughed. Gill never changed, always on to the next question before you'd even thought about an answer to the first question.

'Journey good. Yes, I'm hungry, and I've only been retired for 24 hours so I don't know yet. Will that do? Let me get through the door first before you start your interminable questions, Gill,' laughed Elaine.

'Sorry, you know what I'm like.'

'Yes, I do.' laughed Elaine. 'It's a good job we're such good friends, or I'd have dumped you years ago.' Gill looked crestfallen at that last remark, so Elaine pulled her into her arms for a big hug and got one back.

'It's so good to see you. Come through to the kitchen and I'll get your tea out of the Aga.' The two friends went into the kitchen and Elaine sat at the old pine table that had been there for years, despite the rest of the kitchen being modern and streamlined.

Gill placed a cup of tea before Elaine and a plate of steaming Lancashire Hotpot. 'Thought I'd better remind you of your roots after being down in Wales for the day,' laughed Gill.

'I always love your hotpot; mine never seems as good. You must have a secret ingredient.'

'Yes, it's the Aga. It never fails to make an ordinary meal taste better,' replied Gill. 'Now, tell me your plans.'

'Not until I've finished my meal,' laughed Elaine, and carried on munching. As soon as she'd finished eating her hotpot, Gill produced Elaine's favourite pudding, an Eton Mess. After enjoying every bite, Elaine followed Gill into the lounge and Gill made her sit by the fireplace, as if it was a cold day.

'Now tell me all your news,' started Gill, but before Elaine could reply, the door opened and Gill's second son, Ben, came bounding in.

'Aunty Elaine, great to see you,' he said, enveloping Elaine in a big hug.

'How are you?' asked Elaine. 'Busy as ever?'

'Deffo. We've managed to get two cuts of hay in early this year, so I'm off on building projects next week.'

'You're still doing building then?'

'Yes, whenever I get the work. It helps out, and it stops me from building more units on the farm. I drive Mum and Liz daft when I get my ideas, but I think I've improved the farm over the years.'

'You certainly have,' replied Elaine.

'It's all your fault,' said Gill. 'You bought him that massive Lego set for his fifth birthday and he's never stopped wanting to build ever since.'

'But at least he wants to farm as well, so don't knock it,' replied Elaine. 'He must have saved you a fortune over the years.'

'He has. His Dad was totally against him going to train as a builder, but Ben knew what he was doing, and he never let us down on the farm either. During haymaking, he would bring all his building site mates to help. They loved it and were used to hard work.'

'They loved your food, Mum; that was the attraction. I think they were all a little in love with you, and thought I was the luckiest bloke on earth.'

'Oh, get on with you,' laughed a blushing, but secretly pleased Gill.

'I'll show you round my latest improvements tomorrow, Aunty Elaine, but I'd better get home now, or Liz'll be complaining I'm never at home. See you tomorrow!' and he was gone, as quick as he'd arrived.

'So, tell me all your plans,' said Gill brightly.

'No, you tell me how you are,' replied Elaine. 'Is it getting any easier?'

'Oh, I have good days and bad days, but I think the good days are getting more frequent than the bad days. You don't have much time to grieve when you're running a farm and helping with grandchildren. And it's been just over a year now. Oh, and thank you for the lovely flowers you sent me on the anniversary of John's death.'

'You're welcome. I'm only sorry that I couldn't get over with them and had to rely on the flower shop in Clitheroe to deliver them. Oh no! I've just remembered, they gave me a bunch of flowers today and I've left them in the car. I'd better go and retrieve them before they shrivel.' Elaine jumped up and ran outside to her car, getting the flowers and also a planter, which contained a bright array of summer flowers.

'Flowers and a planter? It must have been a good lecture,' teased Gill.

'No, the flowers are from today, but the planter is part of my retirement present from Manchester. They got a planter rather than cut flowers, so that it would last longer.'

'Very thoughtful,' mused Gill. 'Just a shame you haven't got a house to put it in or outside,' she giggled.

'Well, I can leave it here, I suppose, until I find a house.'

'Certainly. It'll look lovely outside my front door.'

'Have you made any decisions about the future yet?' asked Elaine tentatively.

'Yes, but only just. We had a family conference last week and decided that Ben, Liz and the girls will move into the farmhouse, and I'll take over their bungalow next door. That was the plan when we built it. Ben and Liz were newlyweds and we thought they should have a place of their own, but near to the farm for work. But we always intended that when we got old, we would swap houses.' Gill started looking tearful, so Elaine ran over to her chair and held her tight.

'It was such a shock when he died. I thought we'd have a lot longer yet. He was only 59. And it was so quick. He'd eaten a hearty breakfast at 8am and was dead by 10.'

'I know,' murmured Elaine, stroking her hair, 'but it was the way he would have wanted.'

'That's true. After seeing his father suffer for months with throat cancer, he said he wanted to go quickly and not go through all that suffering and failed treatments. It's just hard for me. I wasn't even with him when he had the heart attack. I didn't get the chance to say goodbye.'

'It must have been,' replied Elaine, 'but Ben was with him. He wasn't alone. When are you planning on moving?'

'Next month, we thought. Whilst it's still summer nights.'

'Well, I've just had a good idea. I'll stay until you're moved in and put off looking for a house until then. And after you are settled, we'll go away for a bit of a holiday. How does that sound?'

'Oh Elaine! You're too good to me. That sounds lovely. As you know, we hardly ever got chance of a holiday. Apart from a few day trips, and the holiday we had for our 30th wedding anniversary, I haven't had a proper holiday away since we went to Benidorm back in the late 70s, when we were about to go to uni,' said Gill, starting to smile again.

'And the less said about that holiday, the better,' quipped Elaine. 'I don't know about you, but I'm ready for bed. It's been a long day.'

'Sorry, I'm keeping you up. I tend to stay up late nowadays, so that I get to sleep when I do go. Otherwise I lie in bed thinking too much.'

'Well, start thinking tonight about where you want to go for your holiday. Your choice of location and my treat. It'll do instead of rent whilst I'm staying here with you. We can go into Clitheroe and book it.'

'I can't wait! Any location, did you say?'

'What have I said? Almost any location then. I don't fancy diving with sharks or anything extreme like that.'

'Okay,' laughed Gill, 'I'll come up with some ideas and run them past you. I'll show you to your room. You're in Tim's old bedroom as usual. Or should I call it the guest room now?'

'Don't get delusions of grandeur, Gill; it's not your style. By the way, I saw Tim two weeks ago. We had lunch in town.'

'He managed to get away from work for a whole lunch break? My, you are honoured. I barely get a phone call from him nowadays.'

'Yes, we were only meeting for a coffee, but a client cancelled just before, so I got him for longer. He looks really well.'

'He's never looked back since he went to that new law firm in Manchester. I can't believe it sometimes, my eldest son, the hot shot lawyer! Sorry, you wanted to go to bed. Come on now, I'll shut up 'til morning.'

Elaine quickly got undressed, put her pyjamas on, and after going to the bathroom, jumped into bed, falling asleep almost as soon as her head hit the pillow. Gill took longer to fall asleep, but she felt more positive about the future and started thinking about a holiday. With a smile on her face, she too eventually fell asleep.

Chapter 2

It was ten o'clock when Elaine woke up, and she hurriedly showered, dressed and went downstairs to find an empty kitchen. She pulled the kettle onto the Aga, which never went out, year in year out. As she was brewing the tea, Gill came into the kitchen.
'Oh, you're awake then, sleepyhead?'
'Morning Gill. I've slept really well. Can't believe it's so late.'
'Easy to tell you don't live on a farm,' laughed Gill. 'Have you any plans for today?'
'Yes, I'll go for a walk round Dunsop Bridge and have a look in the café and say hello. Unless you've any other ideas?'
'No, that sounds good. I've said I'll mind young Kirsty whilst Liz goes into Clitheroe shopping. She's full of cold so hasn't gone to school today. Do you need any shopping?'
'Not that I can think of, but thanks for asking.'
'Well, I'll get round to Liz, then she can get off. I'll see you at lunchtime. What do you fancy eating?'
'Oh, don't bother about me. I'll get something at the café. I'll see you later.'
'Okay then, see you later,' and Gill bustled off out of the door.

As it was getting late, Elaine decided to go for a walk straightaway and have a meal later, skipping breakfast. She rooted her old trainers out of one of her bags and set off, glad that there was a clear blue sky and she didn't need a raincoat or umbrella.
She knew where she was going first as soon as she set off out of the farm, and it wasn't the café. She took the road out of Dunsop Bridge to the old redundant church. It was set back from the road, with a lychgate leading through a large grassy area at the front of the church. To the side there was a graveyard, which still looked to be in use, as there were quite new graves there. Elaine went through the lychgate towards the church, and walked up the path. It was an odd-looking building. Its long length was facing the road and it didn't seem to be of any particular architectural style. There was no entrance on the front of the church and, as she followed the path round, she saw that the large entrance was at the side of the building. Walking round the

back of the building, Elaine couldn't see much else, as all the windows were boarded up. There was a large area of grass at the back of the church, bounded by a row of trees, and there appeared to be large fields behind the trees. Going round to the other side of the church, Elaine noticed that the far end of the church seemed to be all windows as there were multiple boards covering a large area. Its shape was bowed like the front of a stately galleon from many centuries ago. Arriving back at the front of the church, Elaine found an old noticeboard on the floor, which stated the name of the church. 'Saint Gregory and Saint Philip's Church of England'.

Elaine stood and stared at the church, wondering if she could live here. Despite the fact that she could live anywhere in the world, the idea of living in Dunsop Bridge was suddenly very appealing. She would be near her best friend, and one of her two godsons and his family. Taking out her phone, Elaine took a photo of the name of the estate agent who was selling the property, and then tried dialling the number. Typical, she thought, no signal. Could I live in a village where there is often no signal? Brooding over that fact, Elaine set off back towards the village and down the hill to the café.

Julie welcomed her as she opened the door. 'Hi Elaine, here on holiday again?'

'Yes, for a short while. How are you Julie?'

'I'm fine. Have you met the new owners?'

'No, introduce me.'

'This is Erica, and the man in the other room is her husband Paul. This is Elaine, who comes on holiday to stay with the Robinsons at Greenbank Farm.'

'Hello, Elaine, pleased to meet you.'

'When did you take over?'

'Sunday before Easter, you know, during that heatwave. The shop heaved all week, it was a proper baptism of fire. We decided that if we could survive that week, we could survive anything.'

'They were marvellous,' added Julie. 'How long are you here for, Elaine?'

'For a couple of weeks, then Gill and I are going on a holiday, before I decide where I'm going to live.'

'Are you moving? Will it be nearer your work?' asked Erica.

'Work? Certainly not. I've just taken early retirement and I can live anywhere. I just need to decide where,' laughed Elaine.

'It'll do Gill good to go on holiday after the year she's had,' commented Julie.

'It certainly will. I've told her she can choose where we go, but I'm not sure that was a wise thing. Who knows where we'll end up?'

'I'm sure you'll have a good time,' replied Julie. 'I bet she's on the Internet now, searching for an exotic remote holiday.'

Elaine pulled a face. 'She probably is. Mind you, she'll be lucky to get a signal. I couldn't get one this morning.'

'Oh, it's often like that here, but we're supposed to be getting faster broadband soon, so it should be better,' replied Julie. 'When it comes, Erica and Paul are going to get Wi-Fi sorted for the café.'

'Good. Can't live without my phone or the Internet.'

'Better ask that question first before you view any houses,' said Julie.

'Mmm,' replied Elaine thoughtfully, but then changed her manner. 'Now, let's see what I can have to eat. I was up so late I didn't bother with breakfast.'

'What about our famous cheese and onion pie?' suggested Erica.

'Definitely. Just what I fancy, with salad and coleslaw. And a cup of tea.'

The staff bustled away to serve Elaine and she looked thoughtfully at her phone. There was a full signal, but she wasn't going to make a phone call here; she didn't want anyone to know anything at this early stage. After eating her lunch, Elaine was persuaded very easily to have a piece of chocolate cake, which went down very well.

'I think I'd better have a long walk now after all that lunch. I can see I'm going to put on weight if I stay here any longer.'

'Well, Gill is a very good cook, not to mention her daughter-in-law, Liz. One of them always wins the Women's Institute competitions for their cakes,' said Julie.

'I know, they're delicious. Right, I'm off for a walk. Thanks for a lovely lunch,' said Elaine, as she left her money by the till.

Taking the path by the side of the café, Elaine walked to the children's playground and watched three young children playing on the swings, their mums chatting on the bench close by. She kept on walking past the first row of cottages, climbed over the stile, and crossed the wooden bridge over the fast-flowing river. Leaning over the bridge, Elaine watched the busy water for a while before continuing her walk. She stopped at the second row of cottages, which had formerly been homes for the Water Board workers who worked further up the road, who had looked after the water supply for the locality and the pumping station. Looking at her phone, Elaine saw there was a signal. Trying the estate agent's number, she waited but then heard the engaged signal. Typical, she thought to herself, so sat down on a stone by the riverside and waited. She got through at the second attempt.

'Morrison and Stuttard Estate Agents. Skye speaking. How can I help you?'

'Hello, I'm enquiring about the old church in Dunsop Bridge. Is it still for sale?'

'It certainly is. Would you like to view it?'

'Yes please.'

'When would it be convenient? A daytime viewing will be more beneficial, as there is no electricity in the building.'

'No electricity? Has there never been electricity?'

'Oh yes, but the Diocese was advised to disconnect it, to prevent squatters moving in, which is less likely if there is no power.'

'I see. Well, my time's my own. I've just retired, so it's whenever is convenient to you.'

'Mrs Stuttard is out at present, so I'll just check her online diary and see when she's available.' There was a pause, and then Skye returned to speak to Elaine. 'Could you manage this Friday at 11am?'

'Yes, that'll be fine.'

'11am this Friday then. If you meet her at the church gates?'

'Certainly, thank you very much.'

'Could I just take your name and contact details please?'

Elaine gave her the details but hesitated when she asked for an address. 'I currently don't have one. I've just sold my own house and I'm staying with a friend in Dunsop Bridge.'

'I'll leave it at that, then' replied Skye. 'Thank you very much for your call. Goodbye.'

Elaine put her phone back in her pocket and let out a long sigh. She must be mad. She'd probably hate it on sight, and it would cost a fortune to bring it up to modern day standards. But it was so unusual for any property to come up for sale in the area, as most of the buildings and land were owned by the Duchy of Lancaster. Even the café was owned by the Duchy, and the owners amused people by telling them that the Queen was their landlady. But on reflection, it would be so good to already have friends in the village where she lived. It would make it so much easier. One visit to the Women's Institute and she'd make any more friends that she needed. Another thing had just occurred to her. Whalley Abbey was only about 12 miles away. That was the first abbey she had ever visited with her Mum and Dad, and she intended to visit it again shortly, if only to sit on the commemorative bench they had paid for when her Dad died. And that reminded her; she still hadn't added her Mum's name to the plaque on the bench. Well, she would do that soon, she promised herself.

As she was walking back towards the café, her phone rang.
'Hello, Dawn Stuttard here, Morrison and Stuttard Estate Agents.'
'Oh hello, thanks for ringing. Is there a problem with the appointment?'
'Not at all. I'd be delighted to show the property to you, but because of the lack of electricity, could we possibly meet in the café in the centre of Dunsop Bridge? Do you know the place?'
'Yes, of course we can. I know the café very well.'
'Are you from this area?'
'No, but I'm staying here at present.'
'Yes, I'm curious about that. Skye typed "no fixed abode" under the line for address.'
Elaine laughed. 'Well, I do feel like that at the moment. I'll see you on Friday at 11am in the café then?'
'Yes, thank you. We can look at the plans in daylight. It'll make it so much easier to see them before you view the building.'
'Goodbye.'
'Goodbye until Friday.' The phone clicked off. That's it, thought Elaine. I've done it. If she was going to meet Dawn in the café, she'd better tell Gill her plans, before she heard it on the village grapevine.
Over tea that night, Elaine told Gill of her appointment.

'You don't waste much time, do you? But that falling-down old church? Are you mad? Mind you, I'd be delighted if you did settle here.'

'Falling down? Is it?'

'Probably. I don't think anyone's been in it for years.'

'How long has it been empty?'

'Oh, at least five years. It's been for sale for about two years.'

'And has there been no interest in all this time?'

'Well, there was a rush of property developers at first, but no one seemed keen to take it on.'

'Why do you think that was?'

'Not sure. Ben went to have a look, but decided he'd prefer a new tractor to taking on such a massive job. Are you sure about this?'

'No, but if I don't go and look, I might always regret it. I'm not actually buying it on Friday, just having a look.'

'Do you want me to come with you?'

'That's really kind of you, Gill, but if you don't mind, I'd rather go on my own.'

'No, I don't mind. What about Ben then?'

'No, not this time. If I get round to a second viewing, then I promise I'll take Ben. Will that do?'

'Of course. It's your decision anyway. You don't need to consult me or my family.'

'No, but you'll be quite close neighbours, so I don't want to get off on the wrong foot with my new neighbours straightaway,' Elaine giggled.

'Good,' replied Gill, also giggling. 'Now, about this holiday. I looked online last night, and I've got some ideas, but I think I'd prefer to go into Clitheroe to a travel agency. Makes it feel more special somehow.'

The door opened and Ben strode in. 'What are you two giggling about? You're worse than our girls.'

'Planning our holiday,' replied Elaine.

'And the rest of her life,' muttered Gill darkly.

'What do you mean?' asked Ben.

'She's only gone and made an appointment to view the old church on Friday.'

A stunned Ben stared at Elaine and then recovered his voice. 'Are you serious? That old thing?'

'I might be. That's just what your Mum said, by the way.'

'What?'

'That I was mad, and it was falling down.'

'It's not actually falling down, but it needs an awful lot of work doing to make it anywhere near habitable. Shall I come with you?'

'No, thanks. Your Mum offered that, too. If I make it to a second viewing, I'll take you both along with me, for your expert advice; well your advice Ben. I'll only get grief from your Mum.'

'I'm only trying to protect you,' muttered Gill.

'I know, and I appreciate it.'

'So what about this holiday, then?' asked Ben. 'Where are you thinking of going?'

'I've left that up to your Mum.'

'Great. I don't suppose you need me to come along and look after you?'

'No Son, you've a farm to look after. And we're big enough and old enough to look after ourselves. Shouldn't you be milking now?'

'Yes, Mother, I'm going, but Anna's already gone straight there,' he replied as he left the room chuckling.

'Is Anna still determined to be a farmer, then?' asked Elaine when he'd gone.

'Oh yes, I think the farm will be safe in her hands for the future.'

'What about the other two girls?'

'Can't stand any aspect of farming, except the good lifestyle it provides them. Neither Kate nor Kirsty like getting their hands or feet dirty, unless their hands get dirty with flour and baking ingredients.'

'They take after you and their Mum, then.'

'Yes, they both love baking. Kate has just finished at catering college and I think Kirsty will go when she's old enough.'

'Is Anna going to agricultural college?'

'She hasn't decided yet. For now, she's happy to stay on the farm and learn all she can from her Dad. She took it very badly when John died. She was like his shadow, would follow him all over the farm, all day long, if she could. Didn't want to go to school as it interfered with her farming, she said. And that was from about six years old!' Seeing that Gill's eyes were filling up at the mention of John, Elaine decided to change the subject.

'So where are you thinking we should go on this holiday?' asked Elaine.

'I've got a shortlist, but a favourite keeps coming up.'

'Tell me the shortlist first then.'

'A cruise round the Mediterranean, a trip to the Norwegian Fiords, Morocco, Lake Como, Dutch bulb fields, but then I also thought you might like to go back to France?'

'No, I don't want to go back to France. I've spent as long as I want to in France. I want somewhere new. But you can forget Dutch bulb fields if we're going soon, as it's the wrong time of year. So come on, which is your favourite?'

'Lake Como.'

'Really? Why there?'

'Well, you know that I've always loved being beside water, and I saw a documentary on it, and it looked lovely. Well anywhere in Italy, beside a lake would be grand.'

'An Italian lake it is then. We'll go this weekend and have a look.'

'Unless you've bought a house by then,' Gill quipped.

'We'll have to see!' replied Elaine, with a twinkle in her eyes.

Chapter 3

Elaine was awake early on Friday morning. She dressed in clothes that wouldn't matter if they got dirty, but were smart enough to meet a stranger in. She walked down to the café and arrived just before 11, sitting opposite the counter at the back wall of the café. She ordered a cappuccino and had just told Julie that she was meeting someone, when a lady in her mid-40's arrived. She was very smartly dressed, blonde, slim-built like Elaine, carrying sheets of papers under her arm and looking round expectantly until her gaze alighted on Elaine.

'Dawn Stuttard,' she said, to which Elaine replied, 'Elaine Barnes. Shall we go through into the other part of the café so that you can show me the plans?' Dawn nodded, and they went through the arch to the large round table.

'Can I just get some details from you? I've got your name, but not your title. Is it Mrs, Miss, or do you prefer Ms?'

'It's Doctor actually,' replied Elaine, but then seeing the look on Dawn's face, she hurriedly added, 'Not a medical doctor, so don't start giving me all your symptoms. I've got a PhD.'

'I'm so sorry. I shouldn't presume.'

'It's quite all right. I'll probably not use it much anymore as I've just retired, but it's on all my documentation. So, tell me about the property.'

'Of course. It was built in 1777, so it's Georgian in age but not in appearance. In fact, it doesn't really fit into any church architectural era. It's one on its own. It was deconsecrated only two years ago when it was put up for sale, but it hasn't been used as a church for four and a half years.'

'Why the discrepancy?'

'It was hoped that it could be used as a village centre, but they already have a village hall in Dunsop Bridge. They hoped perhaps that another church would take it over.'

'Is it listed?'

'No. It's not of enough architectural interest, but there are some unusual covenants attached to it.'

'Covenants?'

'Yes. There is a beautiful stained-glass window at the east end of the church which must remain. There is also a pulpit near the front of the church which has to stay.'

'Why?'

'The eccentric owner put the covenants in place when he built it, or soon after.'

'So the Church of England didn't build it?'

'No, it was built by a wealthy landowner when he fell out with the vicar in the next village and decided to build his own church here in Dunsop Bridge.'

'And is that all the covenants?'

'Mostly, but there is the graveyard.'

'What about the graveyard?'

'You also own that.'

'Own it?' asked an astounded Elaine.

'Sort of. But it's still consecrated ground, so the church still uses it for burials if requested. You have to maintain it and allow relatives to enter the graveyard at any time.'

'Maintain it? Does that include the gravestones? Some looked a bit decrepit to me.'

'No, not the gravestones. They remain the property of the families and they are responsible for them. But you must pay for the cutting of the grass and any repairs to the walls. And you aren't allowed to sell the two fields behind the church.'

'This is getting worse by the minute. I'm not sure I'm interested anymore,' said Elaine sadly.

'Oh, no, please don't say that. It's a very unique opportunity to purchase land and property in an area which is mainly owned by the Duchy of Lancaster.'

'I know that. I'll reserve judgement until I've seen it.'

'Let me show you the plans, then,' said Dawn, hurrying on to something more positive before she lost all chance of the sale. 'It's got planning permission for a four-bedroomed dwelling. Planning permission for change of use from a church to residential is in place, so that is a major plus and time saver.'

Elaine took a cursory glance at the plans, but without having been inside, they didn't really mean anything to her. 'Well, let's go and have a look then,' Elaine said. Dawn gave an audible sigh, but smiled at Elaine and stood up, gathering the plans together.

They drove round to the church in Dawn's car and she got an enormous key from her handbag, and two large lamps from her boot. She gave one lamp to Elaine and put one on the floor, and, getting the plans in her other hand, jiggled the key in the lock. After a bit of persuasion, the door opened and they went in, turning the lamps on first. The building smelt dusty and damp. They walked slowly into the large room, the lamps only lighting the immediate area where they stood. There were extremely high ceilings, with an upstairs gallery running round two-thirds of the church. Dawn was keeping up a constant flow of chatter about how the place would look when it was converted. Elaine walked ahead of her. She could see the large pulpit and magnificent windows which were divided in to three sections. It was too dark to see the whole of the stained-glass, but it seemed to be a picture of Christ in the central window, and two other figures in the other windows. She presumed that they were St Gregory and St Philip. As she stared at the windows, she became aware of a strange feeling coming over her. She wasn't dizzy or confused, but she felt as if something was washing over her, from her head to her feet, and she felt a great sense of peace. She wanted to be alone with her thoughts, but Dawn was still chattering away.

'I . . . er, could I be alone?' Elaine managed to say.

Dawn stopped mid-sentence and looked at Elaine. 'It's got to you this place, hasn't it? I always feel the same when I come in. I'll go and wait in the car. Come out when you're ready; take your time,' and she quickly left, leaving Elaine to her thoughts. Elaine walked slowly round the building and knew without any shadow of a doubt that she had to have this place, whatever it cost. It was a similar feeling to what she had had when she went to Whalley Abbey for the first time as a small child, with her Mum and Dad. Utter peace.

Elaine wasn't sure how long she spent in the church in her dream-like state, but eventually she tore herself away and went back towards the car. Dawn jumped out and, taking the lamps from her, went to lock the door of the church. They sat in the car together in silence, Dawn having the sense to wait until Elaine was ready to speak.

'I'd like to have a second viewing with my godson, Ben. Is that possible?'

'Of course. When would you like to arrange it?'

'Tomorrow if possible.'

'Tomorrow?' exclaimed Dawn, and then hurriedly recovered. 'Yes, that'll be fine. What time?'

'Probably mid-afternoon would be best. Ben is a farmer so will have to be back for the evening milking.'

'A farmer?'

'Yes, but he's also a builder, and would do the conversion for me, if he thinks it's a good prospect.'

'That's great. Shall we say two o'clock then?' asked Dawn, mentally cancelling her planned shopping trip to Boundary Mill, in the light of this potential sale of a property she never thought she'd sell.

'Yes, two o'clock, thank you,' agreed Elaine. 'I'll leave you now and walk home. See you tomorrow.' She jumped out of the car and rushed away, feeling the urge to cry, and not wanting to make a fool of herself in front of Dawn. It was very strange, she reflected. She'd never felt like this before about any property, not even the house in France, and she'd been pretty stunned by that one. Mind you, it could have been because she was deeply in love at the time.

Although she hadn't told Dawn, she wasn't too keen on the proposed plans that had been given planning permission. Elaine would probably want them changing, but Dawn had let her take a picture of them on her phone so she could look at them at home. She got back to the farm and was pleased that the house was empty. Making herself a cold drink and topping it up with ice, she took it outside to the enclosed rear garden and sat on the garden bench, dreaming, planning, and scheming.

It was Ben who came home first. Rushing towards him, Elaine asked if he was doing anything tomorrow afternoon, as she wanted him to go somewhere with her. It all came out in rather a rush, and Ben stood open-mouthed as he listened to her garbled request. But his sense of humour kicked in and he replied that he hoped Elaine hadn't forgotten that he was a happily married man, and he couldn't promise to go anywhere with her alone.

'You daft thing, I'm not propositioning you. I want you to come and look at a house with me.'

'A house?' Ben asked with disbelief.

'Yes, you know, those things with four walls, a roof and some windows,'

'Yes, yes, I know what a house is, thank you; but where? Didn't you like the church that you went to see today?'

'That's the one. I want you to come and see how much it would cost to renovate.'

'You don't waste time, Aunty Elaine, do you? What time is the viewing?'

'Two o'clock if you can manage it. Please,' she added in a wheedling voice.

'Okay, you win. I still think you're mad, but of course I'll come with you. You sound quite keen if you want a costing doing.'

'I am. There's something about the building that really drew me. I can't fully explain how I felt, but I knew that I wanted it.'

'I bet Mum'll be pleased. She's always saying she wished she saw more of you.'

'I'm sure she will, and that's part of the attraction. I've lived vicariously through your family all these years, so it will be really good to live near you.'

'Talking of building, let me show you round the farm buildings and you can see what I've been doing.'

'Great. I need something to distract me from thinking about this house. It's going to be a long night.'

The two of them set off and Ben showed Elaine that there were now three holiday cottages and three yurts in the next field from the main farmhouse and Ben's bungalow. There was a separate driveway so that the visitors didn't have to cross the farmyard to get to their accommodation, but it was near enough for the family to maintain the accommodation or the visitors to contact them in case of emergencies or queries. Elaine was impressed at the way they had diversified, without losing their dairy animals, sheep, and crops. It was the best of both worlds.

'The cottages and yurts were my inspiration,' said Ben, 'but Liz has got all the hard work of servicing them. Mum also helps out, and we have a cleaner who comes in on changeover days, or any time we need her.'

'Sounds great. Now show me the animals, if you've time.'

'Always got time for you, Aunty Elaine.'

'And always got time to show off your farm,' teased Elaine.

They walked companionably round the farm and he showed her the sheep and lambs up on the higher fields, and the cows in the fields down by the river, and then took her to see the hens, which were Kirsty's responsibility.

'Nobody gets to live for free at a farm; everyone has to work here,' Ben laughed.

'Perhaps you'd better teach me how to milk the cows then.'

'I thought you'd never ask,' he replied. 'Though seriously, I've now got more help in that department, besides Anna. I was approached by Bowland High School to see if I would give work experience to a young man who wants to be a farmer. He's called Daniel. He's what we would have called a bit slow, but in these days of political correctness, he's termed as "with additional needs". But he took to milking and farm work like a duck to water. I don't think he'll ever be able to own a farm, but he can work well once you've explained it carefully to him a few times.'

'So, is he helping you on a regular basis now?'

'Yes, he loved it so much and wouldn't stop talking about it to his parents, so they rang me and asked to come and see me. We've arranged that he'll come and work at weekends and we'll pay him a wage. Then when he leaves school at the end of this month, we'll employ him on a full-time basis. That will free Mum and Liz up from some of the farm work. We can afford some help now we've got the holiday cottages up and running. They're almost fully booked out all this summer and we've got bookings at Christmas and New Year – even for the yurts,' he laughed. 'Wouldn't fancy staying in them in winter, but there's no accounting for taste. But they have got their own log burners, so I suppose they'll be quite warm and toasty.'

'Oh, here's your Mum and Liz coming in now. Looks like they've done a big shop. We'd better go and help them.'

'Put the kettle on, Elaine,' Gill shouted. 'Make yourself useful. Liz likes black weak tea and Ben likes milky coffee.'

'Yes, ma'am, immediately ma'am,' said Elaine, curtseying and pulling her forelock.

'Go on with you,' laughed Gill, staggering in with bags of shopping.

Sitting around the kitchen table, Gill asked if she and Elaine were going to Clitheroe to book their holiday tomorrow. Elaine and Ben looked at each other and hesitated.

Ben was the first to respond. 'Sorry, Mum, Aunty Elaine and I have a secret assignation tomorrow, so she can't come.'

'Oh, yes?' laughed Liz, 'Is this something I should know about?'

'It's something you should all know about,' replied Elaine quietly. 'I went to look at the old church today and I'm very keen on buying it. I've got a second viewing with Ben and the estate agent tomorrow.'

There was a stunned silence, then everyone seemed to speak at once. Gill was the first to be heard.

'What sort of daft idea is this?'

'I thought you'd be thrilled, Gill. You've always said you wanted to see more of me. Well, you would. I'd be a near neighbour,' blurted out Elaine, a little upset.

'Yes, I thought you'd be well up for it, Mum. What's the matter with you?'

'I don't know. I'm sorry. I just thought that you would live far from here, so I could visit you.'

'Oh that's it,' said a laughing Liz; 'she was just wanting cheap holidays. Well, come on, Ben, time we went home before the girls get in.'

Elaine and Gill sat in silence for a while after they'd gone and then Gill said, 'I hope you're not thinking what Liz said. I was just surprised, that's all. It's all happened very quickly.'

'That's all right. I know you better than that. What about coming with us tomorrow and seeing what you think?'

'You didn't want me there today,' replied Gill petulantly.

'No, I didn't want anyone there today. But I want you there tomorrow. Will you come?'

Gill nodded, and after hugging Elaine, set about making the tea. She would reserve her own judgement until she had seen the building.

Chapter 4

Next morning, Elaine was taught how to milk the cows, somewhat erratically at first, but she soon got into the rhythm once Anna helped her; she seemed to have a gentler touch than her father did. Daniel came in from checking the cows and was introduced to Elaine.

'Aunty Elaine's our god-grandmother,' explained Anna.

'What's a god-grandmother?' asked Daniel. 'I haven't heard of one of those before.'

'Well, Aunty Elaine is our Dad's godmother, so we are her god-granddaughters, as she has no children of her own.' Daniel nodded his understanding.

Elaine thought to herself that there was nothing like children to say it out loud and rub in that she had no children, but she'd come to terms with it long ago and gloried in her two godsons and Ben's girls.

'What about I take you girls down to the café for lunch today? Would you like that?' Elaine suggested.

'Great,' said Anna. 'I don't think either of them are going anywhere this afternoon, though I think Kate is out tonight.'

'Will she be getting ready all day then?' asked Elaine, knowing what Kate was like in the bathroom.

'Probably, but I'm sure she'll prefer to come out with you. We haven't seen you for ages. I'll go and ask her.'

'Can I come too?' asked Daniel.

'Certainly not,' replied Anna. 'This is a girly lunch. Aunty Elaine will take you another time, on your own.' At this, Daniel grinned and went back to the cows, whilst Anna shot off to see Kate and Kirsty.

By 12 o'clock they were all ready to walk down to the café. Paul and Erica were there, but not Julie. Instead there was Paul and Erica's eldest son and Louisa, a lady who was also a farmer's wife and had young sons, but worked in the café whenever needed.

'Hi Louisa,' said Elaine. 'Long time, no see.'

'Back on holiday again?'

'Yes, but I'm retired now and might be moving around here. I've sold my house and am looking round.'

'Great news. Now what can I get for you all. No, let me guess. Bacon butties for Kirsty and Anna with chocolate milkshakes, and cheese and onion pie for Kate with a cup of tea. Am I right?' The three girls nodded their heads.

'And what about you, Elaine?'

'I'll have the corned beef hash and a cup of tea please.'

'Right you are. Be with you shortly.'

The girls all chattered about the minutiae of their lives and Elaine revelled in hearing them, marvelling at how grown up they all sounded. Mind you, the last time she'd seen them was immediately after their Grandfather's death, so it was not surprising that she saw a big difference in them, and was pleased at the way their lives seemed to be going. Even though she was newly qualified, Kate already wanted to go into teaching catering eventually, which thrilled Elaine.

Anna was set on staying on the farm, which was a relief for Ben. Having only girls he had worried that the farm would eventually be sold, but not as long as Anna was around, Elaine could see. Kirsty wanted to emulate Kate by going to catering college as soon as she finished at Ribblesdale High School.

Louisa brought their meals and they all tucked in, enjoying the home made food. As soon as they'd finished, Elaine said that she had to leave, as she had to go and see the church again.

'It'll be great if you come and live here,' said Kirsty. 'You could bring us here every Saturday,'

'Don't be cheeky, Kirsty. Aunty Elaine can't do that every week. She'll have her own life,' reproved Kate, but Elaine only laughed.

'We might well do that Kirsty, but next time I'll have to bring Daniel, as I don't think he liked it that he was left out today.'

'All right then, we'll bring Daniel with us next week,' replied Kirsty, not one to miss out on a day trip.

'We'll see,' was all Elaine would say, and the four of them walked companionably back to the farm.

Just before two o'clock, Ben brought the Jeep to the front door and told Elaine and Gill to get in.

'Do we need to drive there?' asked Elaine.

'No, but I want to take some equipment with me.'

'Equipment?'

'Yes, if I'm doing estimates, I want to look everywhere. So, I've brought ladders, lamps and other things with me.'

'Good idea,' said Gill.

Dawn was waiting for them when they got to the church. They all got out of the Jeep and Elaine introduced them. Dawn opened the big door and let them in, bringing her lamps again.

'No need of those; I've brought some powerful lamps so that I can get a good look at it,' said Ben. He connected his lights which provided much better visibility than Dawn's lamps. Dawn tactfully took herself off to her car and left them on their own. Again, Elaine felt the powerfully peaceful feeling coming over her and moved round the room to try and prevent herself from showing emotion.

'You have a look round, Aunty Elaine, and I'll just nip up on the roof,' said Ben. Elaine nodded and went to look at the stained-glass windows. With better lights, they looked incredibly beautiful. There was a figure of Christ in the centre window, with two other saints on the side windows. Now she could see the wording in the glass, her assumption had been correct. It was St Gregory and St Philip represented in the other windows. The figure of Christ was looking straight out into the room, with piercing eyes that held your attention, whilst the two saints were positioned so that they were looking towards Christ. The windows were deeply affecting Elaine. Gill came and stood by Elaine and saw that she was moved.

'Beautiful, aren't they?' Gill said.

Elaine nodded. 'They want this to be the kitchen on the plans. And the upstairs floor would cut the window in half. What a waste.'

'What would you do?'

'I'd leave this full height and make it into the lounge and incorporate the pulpit, which has to stay because of the covenant. The original plans had a massive open plan floor, taking up most of the room. I'd prefer a smaller kitchen-diner in the middle and have all this end of the church as the lounge.'

Ben came in at that point, saying the roof was sound, and Elaine repeated what she had just said about the lounge and the window.

'I agree, it would be criminal to divide this window. I don't know what the architect was thinking.'

'I'd want a downstairs en-suite wet room and bedroom at the front door, too. Future planning for when I can't get upstairs,' laughed Elaine. 'I'd want only three bedrooms upstairs, not four, but all en-suite.'

'Are you thinking of starting a bed and breakfast?' asked Gill.

'I might. Who knows?'

'That makes it easier if you don't have four bedrooms upstairs, if you're planning on having a full height lounge. It'll make more sense. But it'll also keep to the four bedrooms on the plans so won't be a major change. I think the planner would be very sympathetic of keeping the window as it is, even though it isn't listed, so I don't think they'll quibble about the changes.'

'But that's not all I want to change,' said Elaine.

'What else?' asked Ben tentatively.

'I'd want the whole of the side of the church facing the road to be triple glazed bi-fold doors downstairs with a sort of sunroom extension all down the side, so that even in bad weather, I can sit in my sunroom.'

'Sounds great, but expensive,' mused Ben.

'And I want solar panels on the whole roof and underfloor electric heating.'

'That makes sense,' replied Ben, 'as there is no gas here and it would be exorbitantly expensive to put gas pipes in. Are you trying to be eco-friendly?'

'Yes, I want it very well-insulated so that I don't have any electricity bills. Oh, and I want a vegetable plot at the back, so that I can grow my own.'

'When did you have time to think all this through?' asked Gill in amazement.

'I woke up early this morning and looked at the plans in detail and thought about what I wanted in a house. I've already had lots of ideas over the last few months about an ideal home, but with this building I can do just what I want.'

'Sounds like you've been watching too many programmes on TV,' replied Gill.

'Yes, I've become addicted to "Escape to the Country" on catch up,' laughed Elaine. 'And I loved the Sarah Beeny programme about her buying Rise Hall in East Yorkshire and restoring it.'

'Well let's hope that Ribble Valley Council isn't as slow as East Riding Council then,' replied Gill, who'd also watched that programme.

'They're pretty good as a rule,' said Ben. 'Now, what about the Vicar's vestry at the back?'

'I thought that would make a good utility or boot room. There's a door on the outside isn't there? So, I wouldn't have to come all through the house with dirty shoes. And I think I'll need a proper drive to the left of the gate, not just the cart track they've made, so that I can bring the car up to the main entrance when I've been shopping. I might add a garage at a later date, or a carport. I haven't thought that far ahead yet.'

'Thought of everything, haven't you?' asked Ben, secretly impressed by the great ideas he'd heard. At that point, Dawn came in and asked how it was going.

'Great thanks,' replied Elaine. 'I think we've finished now, haven't we Ben?'

'Just the measuring to do and check the gallery, and then that's it,' confirmed Ben. He got his notebook out and his digital tape measure and wrote down all the dimensions. Then he went up into the gallery and checked that. 'That's all, Dawn. Thank you for your patience,' he said with a big grin, and got a big grin back from Dawn.

'I'll be in touch as soon as I can,' Elaine told Dawn.

'You've got my mobile, so ring me any time,' replied Dawn. They all trooped out, she locked the door and they walked down the path together, saying their goodbyes at the lychgate.

Gill, Elaine, and Ben piled into the Jeep and were soon back at the farm, with mugs of tea all round. With pad and paper, Ben was sketching out different ideas for the rooms and said he would do the costings over the weekend. He would have to buy in plumbing, but he was qualified to do the electrics himself. 'I really must train to be a plumber as well, one of these days, then I wouldn't need to buy them in.'

'I'm sure you have contacts from your building friends,' said Elaine.

'Deffo. I know who to use and who not to,' Ben replied, laughing. 'Perhaps I could persuade Kirsty to go in for being a plumber. That would be ace.'

Gill quickly replied. 'Not a chance, Son. You know she doesn't like getting her hands dirty.'

'True, but a man can dream. Right, I'm off. I'll start the costings, whilst Anna and Daniel do the milking tonight. And I'll call in a few favours - tell them it's for my favourite Aunty Elaine.'

'I'm your *only* Aunty Elaine, aren't I?'

'Yes, but you're still my favourite,' he grinned as he left the room quickly, before his mouth got him into more trouble.

Elaine and Gill sat in companionable silence for a while, and then Gill jumped up to start making the tea.

'You sit down,' Elaine said, 'I'll make tea tonight. What do you fancy?'

'We always have easy tea on Saturdays, but I'm making tea for Liz and the girls tonight, as she's been working today.'

'What do you call "easy tea"?'

'We usually have pie, chips and peas. I've already made loads of pies last week. They're in the freezer. I'll get a couple out.'

'Well, I'll peel the potatoes then,' offered Elaine.

'No, I said easy tea. We have oven chips and tinned peas. How lazy is that?'

'Sounds like a tea that I often had on my own. I sometimes went to the chip shop, so that made it even easier.'

'We don't often have a chip shop tea – takes too long to get back from Clitheroe. They've usually gone cold,' laughed Gill. 'You'll have to get used to that if you are serious about living here.'

'Oh, I'm serious. I'm having that church, whatever it costs to refurbish.'

'I'm glad for you. Not just that you'll be near me, but that you're so determined. You've been waffling about your plans for months. I never thought you'd make a decision so quickly.'

'When I saw it, I just knew I had to have it.'

'Good. I'll get those pies out of the freezer before everyone is here for tea and it's not ready.' With that, Gill left the room and Elaine started setting the table, ready for tea.

Chapter 5

After breakfast on the Sunday, Ben came in with a sheaf of papers and diagrams. He spread them all out on the table and called Elaine over to look.

'I've done some rough drawings for you to look at and done the costings. Are you ready for this?'

'Ready as I'll ever be.'

'I reckon I could do it all for just under £183,000, as long as nothing disastrous happens or we find something that I didn't notice. I didn't ask to look at the survey, but I'm sure Dawn will let us have a look. It's so expensive because of all the extra insulation and triple-glazed bi-fold doors you're asking for. Not to mention the sunroom extension, underfloor electric heating and solar panels. But at least your running costs will be lower. Also, all the plumbing and wiring will need replacing. They're probably about 70 years old at the least. So that will mean re-plastering the whole building.'

'I expected all that. That sounds a reasonable figure to me. I thought I wouldn't get much change out of £200,000 actually.'

'You might not if we have to use the contingency money!'

'And can you do it by Christmas?'

'This Christmas?'

'Yes.'

Ben let out a long breath before answering. 'I probably could, depending on the weather, the other trades, the farm and any other of life's problems that occur. Why Christmas?'

'I've spent many of my Christmases at your house with your family and I've always been grateful for that, but I'd love to invite you all this year to my new house.'

'Well, put like that, I'd better get it done for Christmas or else Mum and Liz will have my guts for garters. Christmas it is then.'

'Great. But I won't make you sign a default contract in case you run over. I'm not that cruel, and I know things happen with buildings.'

'Thanks. I appreciate that. It probably puts me under extra pressure to get it done because you're being so reasonable,' Ben laughed.

'That's my strategy rumbled,' laughed Elaine in return, turning as the door opened and Gill walked in.

'What's all the laughter about?' asked Gill.

'My builder has just rumbled my strategy for getting him to do the work on time,' said Elaine.

'I assume the estimate was good then?'

'Yes. Very reasonable. Now I just need to buy the place. I'll ring Dawn in the morning. She'll probably be delighted as it's been on her books for ages.' The door opened again, and Liz arrived.

'I'm glad I've caught you all together. I've had an idea.'

'Oh, no,' groaned Ben. 'How much is it going to cost me then?'

'I don't know what you mean,' protested Liz with feigned indignation.

'It usually costs me. Well, let's hear the worst.'

'I was thinking that as Mum and Aunty Elaine are planning a holiday, why don't we do the big swap of houses whilst they are away? If they pack their things beforehand with labels on the boxes of where stuff should go in the bungalow, we could do the changeover with minimal fuss.'

Ben ran over and kissed Liz soundly. 'That's why I love you, Liz. That's a brilliant idea. What do you think, Mum?'

'But it'll put all the work on you and the girls if we're not here to help,' protested Gill.

'Not really.' replied Liz. 'If you've done your packing properly, we'll just need to plonk the boxes in the right rooms and, apart from making up your two beds, you can sort everything out when you get home.'

'That's true,' added Ben. 'If you need any changes making or redecoration, we can get that done whilst you're away.'

'It doesn't need any redecoration,' replied Gill. 'The bungalow's lovely as it is. Well, if you don't mind then neither do I. Thanks, Liz and Ben. I hope you know what you're doing?'

'It'll be fun,' said Ben. 'We'll get Daniel to help as well. Perhaps even his Dad will come. He loves coming to the farm. And we won't have to do it all on one day like you do with a removal firm. If you're away for two weeks we can just do a little bit each day.'

Anna burst through the door just as Ben had finished. 'Did Gran agree, Mum? Can we move in soon?'

'Yes, Anna,' replied Gill. 'Gran did agree. I hope you'll help your Mum and Dad to move?'

'Course I will. I can't wait to get my own room. You've no idea how awful it is to share a room with Kirsty.'

'Oh, I think I can,' replied Liz. 'I shared a bedroom with two sisters when I was growing up.'

'Yuk. Even worse. Just think! Me, Kate and Kirsty all in one room. Doesn't bear thinking about. I suppose you and Dad'll be having Gran's room, won't you? So, can I have Uncle Tim's room?'

'Anna,' said Ben sternly. 'This is not the appropriate time to be discussing who gets which room. Get back to whatever you were doing and we'll have a family conference tonight over tea.' Anna pulled a face but left the room, leaving the adults shaking their heads and laughing.

'I don't know where Anna gets all these ideas from,' said Gill. 'Although being a combination of Liz and Ben, I suppose I do know.'

'I'm sure by teatime she'll have a master plan of who's going where and will argue that black is white to get her own way,' said Liz.

'And the annoying thing is she'll probably come up with the most sensible plan,' added Ben. 'Come on, Wife, we've stirred things up enough. I think we'd better let Mum and Aunty Elaine have a quiet evening together planning their holiday. I don't suppose you want to take the girls with you as well?' he added hopefully.

'No!' chorused Gill and Elaine together as Ben and Liz left the room, leaving Gill and Elaine chuckling.

'We'd better get on with the holiday tomorrow then,' said Gill.

'No, house purchase first, then holiday. I'll need to be here to sign things so that Ben can get started.'

The evening passed peaceably and they both had an early night after all the excitement of the weekend.

First thing on Monday morning Elaine was on the phone to Dawn. She made an offer £15,000 under the asking price, reminding her that she was a cash buyer, fully expecting an immediate refusal. Dawn said that she would consult with the Diocese who were selling the building. Elaine only had to wait an hour and was told the building was hers. Dawn asked her for the name of her solicitor.

'That'll be my godson . . .' she started but was interrupted by Dawn.

'Not a solicitor as well. First a farmer, then a builder, and now a solicitor. What a skilful man!'

'No, it's his brother, my other godson, Tim. He works in Manchester,' and she gave Dawn the address.

'And have you another godson? Does he work for the Bank of England to get you the money in the first place,' teased Dawn.

'No, no more godsons,' laughed Elaine. 'I do have goddaughters though. One works for ITV.'

'Not the chief executive by any chance?'

'No,' replied Elaine, laughing. 'Katie works in the HR department. And Charlotte, my other goddaughter, is a businesswoman.'

'You have very well-placed godchildren, I must say.'

'I like to think so. Now, how long do you think it will be to completion, because I'm going on holiday as soon as I've signed the contract?'

'It's as fast as your solicitor works, especially as there is no mortgage company involved.'

'Then I'll make sure it's quick,' replied Elaine. 'I'll pop into your office tomorrow to sign the preliminary contracts and pay a deposit, and to pick up a copy of the survey. Will 11 o'clock be convenient?'

'Yes, that's great. I'll see you then.'

Both ladies said goodbye and then Elaine went in search of Gill.

'What's your plan for tomorrow morning?'

'Nothing that won't wait. Why?'

'I'm going to Clitheroe to buy a house and then we're going to book a holiday. And I'll need to go to the bank first to transfer some funds over so that I can pay the deposit on the church.'

'Sounds good to me. Afterwards we can go to Blueberries near the market for lunch. Then go and get cheese from Gradwell's cheese stall. And we could have a mooch round Dawson's department store, and the sale is on at Beryl's shoe shop.'

'Enough!' cried Elaine. 'I want to be back on the same day, not next week.'

'Sorry,' said a somewhat shame-faced Gill. 'I love going to Clitheroe and I don't make enough time to look round the shops. It's usually straight to the supermarket or market and then straight home again.'

'We'll see where we get up to. We can always go again. My time's my own, even if yours isn't.'

They had a great time. Dawn had everything in place for signing, the money for the deposit was transferred, then paid to Dawn, and then they were off to the travel shop on Castle Street. After much debating and spending ages over the holidays on offer, they chose a 15-day coach tour of Italy, staying at many places along the way and taking in most of the northern lakes in the itinerary. They also decided to have a couple of days in London to see a show before they picked up the coach at Folkestone. They would be away for nearly three weeks. The holiday was booked for the third week of August, four weeks away, hopefully enough time to sign the final contracts for the church building.

By then they were both hungry so went to Blueberries for a lovely homemade lunch with pudding, followed by a trip to the market, enjoying the cheeky banter of Stuart at the cheese stall and chatting to his long-suffering wife. Afterwards they went to Dawson's where Elaine bought a tea pot that took her fancy and Gill bought rather more mundane tea towels. Then they were off to Beryl's shoe shop, both buying a pair of summer sandals, telling themselves that they needed them as they were suitable for wearing on a coach holiday in Italy. Then they called in at Style Boutique just above Beryl's as they saw that they also had a sale on. Elaine bought some crop pants and Gill a floaty skirt, both useful items for their holiday. Fully laden, they decided it was time for home and they were both glad to get the weight off their feet and have a cup of tea. By teatime neither of them felt like an evening meal, so they settled for a sandwich in the kitchen.

The next four weeks passed quickly as Elaine helped Gill to pack up all her belongings, making many trips to the tip and the charity shops, taking Liz and Ben's old belongings too. After three weeks, all Gill's possessions were boxed up and labelled. Kirsty and Anna were all packed up too and couldn't wait to move into the farmhouse.

Tim pulled his finger out and managed to get the contracts ready for signing three days before they were going on holiday. Dawn handed over the key to the church to Elaine and wished her well.

'I'll let you know when the housewarming party is,' promised Elaine.

'Make sure you do,' laughed Dawn. They shook hands and Elaine came out

of the office smiling to herself, the big key weighing heavily in her handbag. As soon as she got back to the farm, she found Ben and gave him the key.
'You can start tomorrow now,' she quipped.

'I'll leave the key on the big key hook in the farmhouse as you might want to go down before you leave.'

'Good idea. In fact, I think I'll go in the morning.'

'By the way, the plans are back from the new architect. She's taken them to the planning office, and they don't need to go to the planning committee again as there is no change in the number of bedrooms and the planning officer is happy with the alterations. In fact, she thinks they are an improvement from the original plans.'

'Great. You can get stuck in whilst I'm away.'

'Do you mean before or after I've finished moving two households?'

'Piece of cake to a man like you, Ben. I've every faith in you.' Ben just groaned and shook his head.

'Thanks for recommending Jennie Calvert as architect. She's been superb. She seemed to know just what I wanted.'

'It's a pleasure. I'll use her myself if we ever think of building anything else. She's a Lancashire lass who's been working in London for the last four years and has only just returned north.'

'I love how she's incorporated the pulpit into the lounge. It's a separate area for reading now and I know I'll love to climb the stairs and sit in that place, especially in an evening. I love the idea of having bookshelves on the wall behind the pulpit. It'll keep all my books tidy. Well, some of them. They'll still be littered all over the house probably.'

'I can always build extra bookshelves at any time later.'

'Good. I'll hold you to that.'

Ben hurried out of the door before she could think of anything else to add to the long list of jobs he had to do in the next five months.

Next morning, Elaine walked down to the church and let herself in. It felt totally different today as she now knew that it belonged to her. She took a closer look at the pulpit with her phone torch. It was uniquely beautiful. It had three small steps leading up to the platform which seemed quite large for the vicar just to stand there, but that was an advantage now that it was going to be transformed into her reading and computer area. But it was the exquisite carving that held her attention for a long time. It was worked in panels and seemed to represent different occupations and crafts that were part of the local area. There were sheep and cows, farmers haymaking, the river running through a meadow, corn dollies, harvest bread, and fields of corn. But what puzzled her was a carving of miners coming out of a mine shaft with winding gear in the background. Elaine wasn't aware of any mining in the area, so she must remember to ask someone.

Leaving the pulpit, Elaine looked slowly round the rest of the room, imagining how it would be with all her furniture in place and her long sunroom all down the side. Again, that feeling of great peace came over her and she knew she would be happy here.

After securing the door, Elaine decided to look at the graveyard. Ben had said that the walls were in good condition round the graveyard and she was thankful for that. There was a separate entrance to the graveyard through a different lychgate. The first grave she stopped at was a modern one, by the side of the front wall near the lychgate. The grave was obviously well cared for so perhaps it was a local family, Elaine surmised. But on reading the gravestone, she realised the tragedy that must have befallen one family. It only had one date but there were several inscriptions.

31st July 2015
In loving memory of
Mary Baxter, aged 65 years
loving wife to Frederick Baxter.
Also their daughter,
Amanda Tattersall, aged 38 years
and son-in-law
Jason Tattersall, aged 41 years.
Also their granddaughter
Freya Tattersall, aged 14 years.
Rest in peace.

What an odd gravestone, thought Elaine. Does this mean they all died together on the same day? There must have been some tragic accident. It sounded like almost the whole family were wiped out. Perhaps Gill would know more, she decided, and moved on to the next grave. This was a much older one and the writing was worn away. Elaine could just make out the date 1813 but not the names. So much for Dawn saying the people are responsible for the graves, Elaine pondered. it didn't look like anyone had been to this grave for decades, if not centuries. There seemed to be no pattern to the graves; old were next to new, unlike cemeteries where newer graves were all together.

Some of the graves were just marked by a cross made of wood; others were neatly tended, more modern graves. Right in the centre of the graveyard was a large stone edifice that looked possibly early Victorian in age. It was in the form of a large column with an urn on top, with stone leaves draped from the top of the urn down the sides of the column. Elaine looked at the inscription. It started with a text:

The Lord Giveth and the Lord Taketh Away
Blessed be the Name of the Lord
Erected to the Glory of God
and in memory of Margaret Ann
beloved and loving wife of John James Talbot
died 30 June 1802 aged 36 years.
Also of their children
Joshua died 1 January 1786 aged 2 months
Mary died 2 February 1790 aged 3 years
Martha died 2 February 1790 aged 2 years.
Jeremiah died 3 February 1790 aged 6 weeks.
Henry died April 30 1793 aged 1 year
William died October 15 1795 aged 9 years
Elizabeth died at birth 30 June 1802

Also John James Talbot, founder of this church
died 2 April 1819 aged 69 years

Also James John Talbot, son of the above
died March 13 1850 aged 65 years

Also Miriam, wife of James John Talbot
died July 7 1871 aged 83 years

Elaine stared long and hard at this gravestone. This poor family. Losing all but one of their children by the look of it. It didn't bear thinking about. And the poor wife dying in childbirth probably, and her child with her. How that man ever carried on she couldn't imagine. She moved quickly on and was relieved to find some graves that held long-lived occupants, but also some other older graves that told the story of parents losing their children. Feeling thoroughly miserable by then, Elaine wondered what she had taken on with these graves, but it was too late now. They were 'hers'. And she would do her best to keep the rest of the graveyard in good order so that it enhanced their last resting place. But she would look at the other graves another day.

Walking back to the farm, she decided to do a detour to the café. She had never needed a cappuccino and a piece of cake as much in her entire life. It was a good job that she never put weight on and had stayed slim, she reflected, as she tucked into her cake, already feeling better.

Chapter 6

It was soon time for Elaine and Gill to go on holiday. They'd had great fun trying to pack all their belongings into a wheeled trolley and one small bag each, but had managed to do it. All they would need was shorts, t-shirts, swimwear, some summer dresses and a couple of smarter dresses, for evening meals.

Kate agreed to take them to the train station so that they didn't have to take a car themselves or have to negotiate traffic in London. As they passed the old church Elaine noticed that Ben had already put up wire fencing all around the church and had installed the essential worker's temporary toilet near the side door of the church. Elaine and Gill looked at each other but said nothing, Elaine too excited to make a comment in case she started with tears. She wasn't sure why she was so emotional about the church, but didn't want to start the holiday off with tears.

Waving them off at the station, Kate left them saying she had to sort out her bedroom before the Big Move started, which made them all laugh.
Kirsty and Anna had sorted out their bedrooms the day after it was planned weeks ago.

Some of the train connections were dire but because there were the two of them, they chatted away and didn't let frustration get the better of them, drinking lots of cups of coffee in varying cost and taste. They had found a reasonable bed and breakfast in London and managed to see a show and a play before heading off to Folkestone on the train.

After a few false starts, they found the correct coach trip and bagged seats near the front. They would be on the same coach for two weeks, so were glad they'd arrived early enough to get good seats. The other occupants were nearly all middle-aged like themselves, mainly couples, but several people travelling alone, both men and women, but no children.

'Probably because it wasn't the sort of holiday children would like,' surmised Gill, to which Elaine agreed.

The ferry crossing was on time and they arrived in Calais and continued motoring through France, then Switzerland. before arriving in Italy.

Eventually they arrived at an hotel outside Milan, where they were going to stay.

A pre-dinner drinks party had been arranged by the coach tour and Gill and Elaine got to know some of their fellow passengers. The first lady they met was Phyllis who obviously spent a lot of time on coach holidays. Before the end of the evening she had everyone on the tour weighed up. Who was married, who was on their own, who were with friends, who were looking for romance, who were gay, who were mothers and daughters. She seemed to latch on to Gill and Elaine and it was all they could do not to burst out laughing all the time. She had Elaine and Gill down as two single ladies, looking for romance, despite their protestation of not looking for anyone, nor being gay.

At breakfast next morning, a single unattached elderly man asked if he could join them. It was obvious he liked the look of Gill, but she wouldn't entertain him. He was newly widowed and initially Gill made the mistake of telling him that she was too. He was obviously looking for wife number two, so Elaine and Gill had to make good excuses to get rid of him as the day progressed. Thankfully, he latched onto another single lady who was very impressed by his overtures. Elaine teased Gill that she had made a quick escape.

Phyllis kept the tour group entertained with her tales of other holidays she'd been on and was obviously a busybody and a matchmaker all rolled into one. Where possible, Gill and Elaine stayed well clear of her, although they both had to admit she was harmless enough - somewhat irritating but quite amusing at times.

The holiday gave Elaine and Gill plenty of time to talk about their past and their futures. They reminisced about their primary schooldays, the teachers they'd liked and the teachers they'd been a little frightened of. Both being bright students, they'd passed the 11-plus examination and were admitted to Bury Grammar School for Girls, travelling together on the bus each day. They stayed until they were eighteen and ready for university. From there they had taken different paths, Gill to do teacher training at Charlotte Mason College in Ambleside and Elaine to go to Manchester University to read History. They swopped stories of their differing student days and early romances that never came to anything. Gill had qualified in 1979 and was one of the first students at Charlotte Mason to receive a degree as well as a teaching certificate from Lancaster University. On finishing there, Gill had obtained a post at Clitheroe Grammar School, joined the Young Farmers Association, of which she'd been a member at Ambleside, and met John. 'And the rest is history,' Elaine added.

That night Elaine couldn't sleep and sat quietly on the verandah so as not to disturb Gill, thinking about her university days. At first, she had felt overwhelmed by the sheer size of the campus and, missing Gill acutely, she took time to make friends. Eventually she decided to go to the Students' Union as they were holding a disco that night. At least she knew how to dance, and modern dancing didn't need a partner like it used to do in her parents' days. Entering quietly, she wasn't looking where she was going, too busy taking in all the sights around her, when she tripped up and fell over a young man's foot. He instantly picked her up, but his friends interrupted.

'Hey, Peter, leave her alone. It's not good manners to harm the Freshers.'

'I can't help it if they throw themselves at my feet now, can I?' Peter laughed in return. Elaine was mortified, to be singled out like this, but also that they knew she was a Fresher. But Peter was having none of his friends' teasing. He gently kept hold of Elaine and drew her away from his friends, and sat her down at a table at the far end of the room and bought her a drink.

'I've got you a gin and tonic. Most of the girls seem to like them,' he added.

Elaine muttered her thanks, sipping the drink, but not liking to tell him that she didn't like it. 'I'm Peter Greenhough, by the way.'

'Elaine Barnes.'

'Are you a Fresher? It's just that I haven't seen you around before.'

'Yes, I've just started. I'm reading History. Are you in your final year?'

Peter laughed. 'No, just a Fresher like you. Some of my friends are in their second year, I was at Manchester Grammar with them. But I had a year off before I started here, so I'm a year behind them. I'm reading business and French. I spent my last year in France working in hotels and vineyards generally. Having a good time mostly,' he laughed. Elaine looked at him and realised how good looking he was and wondered why he was bothering talking to her. She'd had a few boyfriends before but not many of them seemed to stay. She also noticed that he spoke with a very cultured accent;

definitely not from Manchester, she thought.

'What about you? Where are you from?' Elaine jumped from her reverie and realised that Peter was speaking to her.

'Oh, I'm from Ramsbottom, near Bury.'

'Yes, I know it. We went walking up Holcombe Hill one Easter and went into Ramsbottom afterwards to get a drink and something to eat.'

'Where are you from?' asked Elaine. 'You don't sound like you come from Manchester.'

Peter laughed. 'No, I come from another Bury – Bury St Edmunds in Suffolk. I went to school in Stowe until I was 16 but wanted a complete change. My parents decided to move to Cheshire where my maternal grandparents live, so I went to Manchester Grammar School for my sixth form, and then here. Would you like another drink? Same again?'

'No, thank you,' replied Elaine rather too quickly.

'Which one? You don't want a drink, or you don't want the same?'

'I'd rather have a Coke if I could? I'm not a keen drinker.'

'Okay,' he replied, and went to the bar. That's probably ruined a nice conversation, thought Elaine. He probably won't be interested now because I don't like a lot to drink. But when he came back, he seemed keen to continue talking. And talk they did, despite his friends calling for him until long after everyone had left. They were inseparable from that first night and spent all their spare time together. Very often they would go and visit friends in France. When it was his 21st birthday in their second year, he asked her to pack a weekend bag and come with him to France. First, they had to go to a very formal dinner in an elegant restaurant in Manchester with all his family and friends. He'd warned her that it was a black-tie event, so her mother bought her a formal evening gown for her own 20th birthday present. The party had been an eye-opener for Elaine, as she realised just how rich Peter's parents and relatives were and, once again, she couldn't understand what he saw in her.

Previously, they had flown to Paris for the weekend and that's where she assumed they were going again. So, she was surprised when he picked her up in a smart MG Tourer sports car. They crossed on the ferry and he drove down to the town of Limoux in the vine-growing region of France. Stopping outside some large gates, Peter got out and took a key out of his pocket, opened the gates, and drove through. It was a very dilapidated, large villa, surrounded by fields of vines as far as the eye could see.

'What do you think? Do you like it?' asked an excited Peter.

'It looks like it needs some modernising,' replied Elaine cautiously.

'I know that, but do you like it? It's got a swimming pool at the back, too.'

'It's lovely, but is it open?'

'Open? No! It's not a hotel. It's mine. My parents have bought it for me for my 21st birthday. I can't wait to show you inside.' He grabbed her hand and showed her through the enormous villa with six bedrooms upstairs and several large sitting rooms downstairs. 'I'm going to spend all the summer holidays doing it up. Will you come and help me?'

'Yes, of course, however I'll probably have to get a job for the summer holidays, but I'll come out when I can.'

'I've got lots of plans and I've been finding out local tradesmen so that I can get started soon. Are you too tired to go out tonight?'

'Yes, I want a bath and bed,' she moaned.

'Not very romantic for my birthday party,' Peter frowned.

'Okay, then. I'll get freshened up and we'll go out.'

'Wear something special,' he said.

After a quick wash and change Elaine did feel better and was glad she'd made the effort. He took her to a restaurant in the nearest town where he was obviously well known. Elaine admired how he spoke to everyone in flawless French and ordered different wines to suit each course. She only sipped hers, but he seemed able to hold vast quantities of wine, as all his family could, without seeming to get drunk. At the end of the meal he took her onto the terrace outside and promptly proposed to her, producing a large solitaire diamond ring. Elaine was so overwhelmed that she didn't answer until she saw that Peter was looking worried. So, she nodded her head and held him close.

Suddenly, the waiters appeared on the terrace, bringing a tray with champagne to toast the couple. Elaine was amazed. He must have planned all this beforehand and never let on to her. She already loved him totally, but now she felt she loved him even more. She was so blissfully happy she thought she would burst. Peter had even asked her father's permission before they'd come away, which astounded Elaine, as neither her mother nor father had said anything to her before she left.

It was a short engagement, and they married at Ramsbottom Methodist church during their final year at university. Peter's parents overwhelmed Elaine again by buying them a large detached house in Manchester so that they could both continue their careers once they graduated. Elaine got a job at Manchester University as a part-time lecturer and began a doctorate course. Peter got a job at a business that imported wine from France and sold it to all the prestigious restaurants in the North of England and the Lake Distract.

They were blissfully happy. Peter spent a lot of time travelling both in England and in France for work, but he also spent every spare moment doing up the villa he owned. Elaine would travel with him and she would spend the time doing her PhD research whilst he was working at the villa. Very often they would go to the nearest vineyard two miles away. It was owned by an elderly couple who had three daughters, but only the youngest one was interested in the business. The other daughters had married and left. Peter was able to help them out at times and he bought wines from them, both for his work but also for his family and friends.

Sometimes Elaine was so tired that she didn't make the journey to France and Peter was happy to go alone. Elaine started to question whether her marriage was not as it should be. Peter was spending nearly every weekend in France and even discouraged her from going at times. He was also making love to her a lot less frequently nowadays. But it was still a shock when he announced that he wanted a divorce as he had fallen in love with the daughter of the local vineyard owner. There were tears and remonstrations from both Peter and Elaine and from Peter's parents, who were horrified at his behaviour. But Peter was adamant. He was going. He resigned from his job and moved into the vineyard with Chantelle and her parents. Her parents were delighted. They had got a longed-for son to run the vineyard at last.

Peter's parents were insistent that Elaine was not left financially embarrassed by the divorce and were totally on her side. Peter was made to sign over the deeds of the house in France and the house in Manchester to Elaine. She wasn't sure about keeping the house in France as it was so near to Peter's new home at the vineyard, but they had done so much to it, so she decided to keep it for the time being. However she came to love going there and taking friends for holidays, so she'd kept it until last year. Elaine eventually sold the house in Manchester and bought a similar house further out in the suburbs.

After the divorce, Elaine changed her name back to her maiden name and threw herself into finishing her doctorate. Although it made her mother and her bosses proud, it seemed a hollow victory for Elaine without Peter to share it with. The niggling doubt was that perhaps she had spent too much time on her research and not enough on her marriage. Her mother bought her a set of Doctorate gown and cap even though Elaine said it wasn't necessary. She would only wear them at graduations and the university would hire them for her. But it pleased her mother and she said that she was sure it was what her father, who had just died, would have wanted to do. When she brought her father into the equation, Elaine gave in and agreed to having them. She didn't want to upset her mother so soon after her father's death. Elaine was only sorry that he hadn't lived to see her achieve her doctorate. He would have been so proud.

Wiping away her tears, Elaine looked at the clock in the bedroom and decided that it was time to go to bed. Even if she couldn't sleep, she would lie still and relax, but as soon as she got to bed she fell asleep.

Over breakfast, Elaine was a bit groggy but told Gill not to fuss; she'd only been remembering her past life, due to being unable to sleep.

'What set that off?' asked Gill.

'I think it was talking about our childhood and going away to university. It set me off thinking about Peter.'

'Do you still miss him? I know how devastated you were when you divorced.'

'No, not now. I did for a long time. But we've stayed friends and I like Chantelle and her parents. And their three children are delightful.'

'All boys, aren't they?'

'Yes, the grandparents were very pleased.'

'Do you regret not having children?'

'Sometimes. When I see your grandchildren I think, "What if?" occasionally.'

'At least you didn't have any children when you broke up with Peter.'

'At the time I wished that I'd had one because then I'd have something of him to remember him by and keep us in touch.'

'Had you and Peter intended to have children?'

'Yes, we planned to have a family immediately after I completed the doctorate, but we were a bit slapdash with contraception and I did conceive once.'

'You never said? What happened?'

'I lost it quite early on, so we never got round to telling anyone. Besides, you'd just had Ben, so I didn't say anything.'

'That must have been extremely hard for you. Especially when we asked you to be godmother.'

'It was, but I was thrilled for you. Now enough of this maudlin talk. Where are we going today?' Elaine jumped up from the table and went back to the bedroom to get her things for the day trip, leaving Gill thinking about what she'd said.

Chapter 7

Gill and Elaine made friends with a married couple on the coach trip and often sat with them for meals. They had just sold their business, retired, and were taking time out to decide where to live, so Elaine had a lot in common with them. It turned out that the lady, Maureen, had been brought up on a farm and she was very interested in how Ben was making the most of farming and diversity. Maureen and Ray Vaughton took Gill's business card and said that they would like to come and visit their holiday cottages, as they often holidayed in the Lake District.

When they were on their own, Elaine teased Gill about having given out her business card, saying that even on holiday her mind was back on the farm and business. Gill ruefully agreed, as she was often wondering how the move was going ahead and was grateful that it was occurring whilst she was away. It would have been upsetting to hear the children arguing over the rooms which had been hers and John's home.

But there was no time to be sad, between viewing all the Northern Lakes, eating too much, drinking too much, warding off Lotharios and fortune seekers, and lots of shopping. Elaine liked the lakeside town of Bellagio on Lake Como the best. Gill teased her that it was because she liked the expensive shops. But Gill preferred the town of Sirmione at Lake Garda. They both agreed that the holiday had been perfect and just what they needed. Promising to keep in touch with Maureen and Ray, they were soon heading back to Folkestone. After many delays on the rail network they eventually arrived back at Whalley station to find Liz waiting for them; apparently Kate was out with her boyfriend.

'Have you had a good holiday?' Liz asked them.

'Brilliant!' said Gill.

'Fantastic!' said Elaine.

'Did you manage to get everyone moved?' asked Gill tentatively.

'Oh yes, Anna had it organised like a military operation. I hope you'll like what we've done.'

'What you've done? I thought you were just going to dump the boxes in the rooms and leave it to us to sort out?' asked Gill.

'Anna had other ideas, I'm afraid. But I'm not saying anything until we get home.'

Elaine closed her eyes for the journey home, but Gill was worried about what she'd find. They drew up into the farmyard to find Ben, Daniel, Anna, and Kirsty all waiting for them. After saying hellos and asking after the holiday, Gill could see that Anna was bursting to show them the houses.

'Are we going to get a guided tour then, Anna?' asked Gill.

'No,' replied Liz instead. 'We're all going to have a drink in the farmhouse and look round later. Anna, put the kettle on.' Although Anna was obviously not best pleased about the delay, she pulled the kettle over on to the Aga and set about organising the orders of tea and coffee.

As soon as they'd finished, Anna was obviously itching to show them round, so Gill and Elaine were taken upstairs to start the grand tour. First, they looked at Gill's old room.

'This is Mum and Dad's room now. We haven't done much in here 'cos Mum liked your décor, so we just moved their things in.'

'Very nice,' said Gill, secretly thrilled that they had liked her décor.

'And this is my room,' Anna said proudly. It was Tim's old bedroom, so Anna had got her wish, thought Gill, but it was smaller than it used to be.

'It looks smaller,' Gill commented.

'Yes,' said Anna, 'that's because of the en-suite between my room and Kirsty's room. Dad took a bit off each room and put this shared bathroom between the bedrooms.'

They all inspected the bathroom, approving the fittings and colour scheme. Kirsty's bedroom was next on the tour and it was a riot of pink, still her favourite colour. It was Ben's old childhood bedroom. Finally, they looked at Kate's room which was on the top floor of the house. They'd put a bathroom up there as well, with a small study area that could be used by any of the girls.

Gill and Elaine both showed their approval of the changes and marvelled at how quickly they'd managed to get all the plumbing done.

'Looks like you've found yourself a plumber, Ben,' remarked Gill. Elaine was secretly thinking that nothing would have been done to her house during the holiday if all this work had been done in the farmhouse. And they hadn't seen the bungalow yet.

'Yes, I've found an excellent plumber: Daniel's dad, Martin,' replied Ben. 'I was asking him to help with the removal and said that I needed a good plumber. He said that he was a plumber and had booked the next two weeks off work so that he and his wife Helen could go touring in their camper van in Scotland. Not many people want things doing during the school holidays, so he always takes his time-off, then. Well, in the end, they brought the camper van here and parked on the field near the yurts. Helen said she was happy to spend her holiday in Dunsop Bridge because all they do is read a lot, walk a lot and go out for meals, and they could do all that in Dunsop Bridge just as easily as in Scotland.'

'You don't half land on your feet, Ben,' laughed Elaine.

'Well, it's going to help you as well, Aunty Elaine, 'cos he's said he'll do all the plumbing in your house. If you let them park the camper van in your garden, he'll give you "mates rates".'

'They'd be very welcome,' replied Elaine.

'It'll mean Martin not being away from home for big jobs when he's working here, especially with all the ensuites you've ordered. Helen can come too,' added Ben.

'Sounds perfect.'

'Now I want to see my new bungalow,' demanded Gill.

'Okay, Gran, I hope you like it,' said Anna, suppressing a smile.

'Lead the way, then,' replied Gill. They all walked across the farmyard to the bungalow and Gill opened the door, heading straight for the kitchen.

'Nothing changed in here, then,' commented Gill.

'No, we left it because you helped Mum design it only two years ago,' replied Anna. But then Gill realised that all her own pots and pans were in place, even her new tea towels that she'd bought at Dawson's.

'I thought you were going to just leave boxes everywhere?' asked Gill.

'We thought you'd be too tired to do anything after your holiday and we wanted it to be ready to move into,' said Liz. 'We've left the lounge as it was; come and see in there.' The décor was just the same, but all Gill's furniture was now in place. A large bunch of roses, Gill's favourites, were on the dining room table scenting the whole room. Gill nodded her approval.

'Come and see the bedrooms,' said an excited Kirsty.

They went into the largest bedroom which had belonged to Ben and Liz and Gill gasped as she went in. It had been re-decorated with the same paper that she'd had in her old bedroom, but there was all new bedding and curtains, which complemented the new paper. Gill hadn't got round to buying any new things when she'd had the old room decorated, so was very pleased by this thoughtful touch.

'Oh, I love it! It's just how I imagined my bedroom would be when I got round to finishing it,' Gill said. 'Thank you, all of you.'

'Actually,' replied Liz, 'it was Kate's idea to buy the wallpaper, accessories and bedding.'

'Well, I'll thank her when she gets home. Can we look at the other two bedrooms?' The family all moved into the next bedroom. Elaine's belongings had been placed on the bed whereas Gill's had been put away in the cupboards and drawers. Elaine thought that was very tactful of the family so that they didn't appear to be rooting through her things. The strong pink colours that had been Kirsty and Anna's bedroom were gone and a pale grey theme was evident. It was very restful, with lilac accessories and bedding. Elaine nodded her approval. The next bedroom had also been re-decorated in neutral colours. The very large bathroom had gone and in its place were two small bathrooms: one with a bath and one with a shower.

'Goodness,' said Gill, 'you have been keeping Martin busy.'

'Well, we knew you like baths and Aunty Elaine likes showers, so we put both in,' laughed Ben.

'Hopefully I won't be here for all that long,' replied Elaine.

'Hopefully not,' said Ben. 'It's too late to show you the church today, but if you come down there tomorrow I'll show you round.'

'I'm surprised you've done anything at the church with all the work that's been done here,' teased Elaine.

'It won't look much to you. No new bathrooms gone in yet; Martin has been too busy,' laughed Ben.

'So I can see,' replied Elaine.

'Come on, all of you, let Gran and Aunty Elaine get to bed; they'll be tired out after all that travelling,' said Liz and, after saying goodnight, the family all went back to the farmhouse. After putting their holiday bags in the hall, Gill and Elaine decided that an early night would be a good idea and they went straight to bed, both asleep as soon as they lay down.

Elaine was up early next morning and couldn't wait to go and have a look at the progress on her new house. Gill was out somewhere on the farm so, Elaine left her a note and set off. As she walked into the church grounds, she saw there was a hive of activity. Scaffolding was up all round the church and there was the sound of banging and hammering inside. Elaine cautiously entered the church, calling out to Ben, but it was a stranger who answered.

'Hard hat area, missus,' the man cheerfully called, bending down for a safety hat and handing it to Elaine. 'I assume you're Aunty Elaine,' he said, 'I'm Jake.'

'Yes,' laughed Elaine, 'I'm Aunty Elaine, but just drop the "aunty" bit. It makes me feel old when Ben still calls me that.'

'Okay, Elaine it is. Ben's gone to the auction mart with Anna so it's only me at present. Do you want me to show you round or do you want to wait for Ben?'

'No, I'd like you to show me round, although I know it won't look like much yet.'

'Certainly not ready to move into yet,' Jake laughed. 'But a lot of preliminary work is going on. The roofers are coming tomorrow.'

'Is there a problem with the roof?'

'No, but Ben's having it all checked out and some slates replaced to make it ready for the solar panels going on. Easier to do it before than after,' he quipped.

'True,' replied Elaine. 'Now what's happened to the windows?' Elaine had noticed that the stained-glass windows had all been boarded on the inside as well as outside.

'That's to protect the windows during all the building work. A stained-glass expert is coming out to do minor repairs when we've nearly finished, and it was his suggestion. We've covered the pulpit up too.'

'Good. I wouldn't want either the windows or the pulpit to get damaged. Are you local, Jake?'

'Used to be. Live in Clitheroe now. Moved there when I left the army. There's no jobs in Dunsop Bridge,' he laughed.

'I was wondering if you knew about any history of mining in the area?'

'Yes, it was just down the road. The chap who built this church was a mine owner. Why do you ask?'

'The pulpit carving. It shows pictures of local activities such as farming and corn dollies, but it also shows a mine entrance with mine workers and winding gear. I didn't understand that.'

'Chap who built this lived down the road and had some workers' cottages for his miners. They've all gone now and the mine closed shortly after the man died. The seam was empty by then so no longer viable. The big house where the man lived has also gone. Too dangerous with mining subsidence. Such a shame. He was like the local squire and was a particularly good landowner and employer. You knew if he gave you a job, you'd got it for life. And a cottage to boot. Not like today with zero contracts.'

'Was it John Talbot?'

'Yes, how did you know?'

'I've been reading the gravestones. So I know who built the church. Such a tragic life.'

'Yes, only one child survived childhood.'

'Do the family still live in Dunsop Bridge?'

'No, the surviving son left when he went to live in London with his wife's family.'

'But he got buried here?'

'Yes, he often visited, I believe. Long before my time though!' laughed Jake. 'Now let me show you what's been done.'

Jake showed Elaine where the plaster had been ripped off all the inside walls, and steels had been put in so that it could strengthen the upper gallery floor and hold the weight of a whole new upstairs area. Outside, footings had been dug to prepare for building the sunroom extension all down the side wall of the church facing the main road.

'Hi, Aunty Elaine,' shouted Ben, as he walked in through the door. 'Has Jake been driving you daft with all his talking? He never shuts up, but he's a good worker so I have to put up with it.' Jake cuffed Ben round the head and they started fighting like schoolboys.

'Leave him alone Ben,' Elaine interjected. 'He's been a mine of information about the village and answered something that was puzzling me.'

'And what was that? said Ben. 'What would this dim lad know that I didn't?'

'Why there was mining depicted on the pulpit. It didn't make sense.'

'And does it now?'

'Of course, the church builder was a mine owner. I didn't know that.'

'And neither did Ben,' chipped in Jake. 'He hated history at school. He knows nothing about the village's history.'

'True,' said Ben sheepishly. 'You're right, he did know something I didn't. But don't get big-headed, Jake or I'll have to cut your wages.'

'And I'll have to find another job to work on and leave you in the lurch,' replied Jake.

'Okay, leave the arguing for another day. I'm going,' said Elaine, laughing as she took off her hard hat.

'If you're going now, I've got some stuff for you, Aunty Elaine.'

'Some stuff?'

'Well, it's two boxes, actually. In fact, I'd better give you a lift home with them as they're quite heavy.' Ben went into the vestry and brought out two large dusty boxes, one by one. He loaded them up by the door and told Jake that he wouldn't be long. Jake replied that he'd been out all day, only been back for five minutes and was going off again. What sort of boss was he? Elaine could see that they were going to start arguing again, so pushed Ben towards the door, picking one box up herself.

Once the boxes were safely installed in the Jeep, Ben drove Elaine back to the bungalow and put the boxes in the hallway.

'Are you and Jake always like that?' asked Elaine.

'Yes, I've known him for years. He drives me daft with all his talking, but he gets the job done even whilst he's talking,' Ben laughed. 'I'd best get back to him before he kicks off again.'

'Thanks for the lift and the boxes. Where were they?'

'In the vestry cupboard. There was a locked cupboard and I rang Dawn to ask for the key but nobody seemed to have one, so we had to force the lock. There's a safe in there as well, which might come in handy for storing the family jewels.'

'Yes, when I get some, I'll keep them in there,' laughed Elaine.

'Seriously though, it would be good to keep things like your deeds and important documents in there as it's fireproof.'

'Good idea. Well, these boxes can be tonight's entertainment.'

'By the way, the grass man came earlier. Have you met him?'

'The grass man? I don't think so.'

'He really belongs to St Hubert's church but he's been cutting the grass in your graveyard and church since the church closed.'

'And who's been paying him?'

'Dunno. St Hubert's, I suppose. He was asking if the new owner wanted him to carry on cutting the grass.'

'Yes, the new owner does. What's his name?'

'Frank. He lives in the village. Shall I tell him to call in at the farm and you can talk to him?'

'Yes, please, and I must find out if I owe St Hubert's any money. I'll start paying from now.'

'OK. Enjoy the boxes! Bye,' said Ben as he left the room.

Elaine looked at the boxes, but decided to save them until after tea before looking at the contents.

Chapter 8

After tea, Elaine settled down by the fire and opened the first box.

'Oh look, Gill, these are old leaflets from the church.' Gill crossed over to have a look.

'Here's a brief history of the church which will come in handy,' commented Gill.

'Yes but look at these other leaflets. They're advertisements or hymn sheets for special services that took place here over the years. Look, here's the Harvest Festival hymn sheet for 1886. And Easter Sunday 1904.'

'They did Handel's "Messiah" in 1864,' said Gill. 'The choir of Clitheroe St Mary's church performed, with soloists Hilary and William Ashton, Jack Bowtell, and Olwyn Pierce. I love the "Messiah". Especially the "Hallelujah" chorus.'

'It must have been quite amazing to hear it in this church,' agreed Elaine. 'Shame it's shut down; we could have had another concert this Christmas.'

'As long as I didn't have to sing,' added Gill.

Elaine pulled a face. 'Me neither,' she added, and they both laughed. They spent a pleasant hour looking at all the different leaflets and putting them in date order. Gill teased Elaine that it was because of her analytical mind that she'd put them all in order and reminded her that she wasn't at work anymore. 'You could catalogue them all and put them in your new bookcases by the pulpit,' suggested Gill.

'Good idea,' Elaine replied. 'I might have them bound so that I have a permanent record. Hey, look at the time! I'm going to bed and leaving the other box for another day. Night-night,' she said, yawning on her way to bed. Gill wasn't far behind.

The next day, Elaine decided it was time to go and visit Whalley Abbey. As she drove past her church, she noticed a boy working at the newest grave, so stopped the car to speak to him. But as soon as he saw her, he ran off, despite her calling him. Getting back in the car, Elaine was upset that she hadn't had chance to speak to him but wasn't sure how to deal with it. She decided that she might as well carry on with her journey to Whalley Abbey. After parking up in the abbey grounds Elaine found a lady sitting in the admission kiosk.

'Hello, do you want to go round the grounds?'
'Yes please,' said Elaine.
'Have you been here before?'
'Yes, many times. I first started coming with my parents as a small child.'
'Are you a Friend of Whalley Abbey then?'
'A friend? No, I didn't know there were friends. I'm Elaine, by the way.'
'I'm Alia. It's £2 to go into the abbey grounds each visit, but if you join the "Friends", you can go in free at any time.' Alia showed her the leaflet.
'Two pounds per visit? That's a bargain. And £10 a year is even better. I'm moving to the area so will probably come quite a lot now.'
'If you're not in a rush there's a tour of the grounds by one of our guides at two o'clock,' said Alia. 'Why don't you join them? You could kill time by having your lunch in the Autisan café. It's run by the Autistic Society; they use it as a training facility for people who have autism and probably wouldn't get the chance of another job.'
'Sounds good. I think I'll give it a try. But first I need to go and check up on my father's memorial bench.' Elaine told Alia her brief story of being brought by her parents, which resulted in her career related to history and monasteries. Now that her mother had died, she wanted to order a new bench plaque adding her mother's name.
After becoming a member of the Friends of Whalley Abbey, Elaine set off in search of the bench but couldn't find it. She eventually found the gardener and asked him about it. He said that the bench was in the shed, as it was in a bad condition due to vandalism.
'Vandalism? In a place like this?' asked Elaine.
'I'm afraid so. Kids come in at night and cause havoc sometimes.'
'How bad is it?'
'Not good. I don't know whether it's worth preserving, to be honest. I'm so sorry.'
'Don't worry. I think I'll replace it anyway. It must be about 30 years old. I intend getting a new plaque as my mother has died now. So I might as well get a new bench. Where would you recommend?'
'There's a man in the village who makes very sturdy benches. He's on King Street. If you go and see Christine in the Conference House, she could help you get it organised and let you know where to get the plaques.'

'Thanks. My mother sorted it out last time, so I've no idea. I'll leave you to get on with your work. Bye.' The gardener nodded his reply and got on with his weeding.

Elaine wandered round the grounds, reminiscing about her previous visits as a child. She'd had a good childhood. Her parents, Tom and Kath, thought they weren't going to have any children and her mum had stayed at work as a primary school teacher. Her dad was a part-time accountant in a large mill, but also had his own business: the best of both worlds he would tell people. They'd bought a large house set back off the main road on the outskirts of Ramsbottom going out towards Bolton. They had a good marriage and a happy life together taking frequent holidays touring all the ancient churches and monasteries in both England and occasionally abroad. Then when she thought she was going through an early change at 44 years old, Kath found out that she was pregnant. It was a shock to both of them and Tom insisted that she gave up work immediately; he wasn't taking any chances. Elaine had been born on Remembrance Day, November 11th, 1958, so they gave her Poppy as a middle name, in honour of all the men and women who had given their lives in both the Great War and World War II.

Tom had no brothers or sisters, just a few cousins who all lived away, so Elaine rarely saw them. Kath had two sisters who were much older and had left home by the time Kath went to High School, so they were not very close. So Elaine did have some distant cousins in Hereford and Cheshire, but she didn't really keep in contact with them, as they were nearer her mother's age than hers and most of them had died.

Her childhood had been mainly just the three of them, although they had many friends and people whom she called aunty and uncle. Then there had been Gill and her parents of course. Holidays were spent going round monasteries, which had been such a passion with her father. Fortunately, her mother was interested in history as well. Part of the fun was in the planning. They would decide on the monastery first, then do the research all about it, before booking a holiday nearby. In pre-Internet days, Elaine reflected, it meant a lot of painstaking research at the library or in her dad's massive store of books on the subject; books that she still owned.

It was no great surprise that when she decided to do history at university, she specialised in the medieval period. She reflected sadly that her father didn't see her graduate with her doctorate. His death had been sudden; he was 70 years old and had only retired the month before. Fortunately, he had sold the business, so left Kath well provided for. At first Kath was going to sell the house as it was too large for her but decided that she didn't want to live anywhere else as it had so many memories. And so she'd stayed, right up until her late 90s. By then, she was living downstairs with a live-in helper, Marjorie, who was marvellous. Her mum never lost her sense of humour or her memory, staying bright and alert to her death.

However, after a fall that resulted in a broken hip, Kath had to go into a care home for the last few months of her life. She even had a hip replacement in her late 90s, gladly telling everyone that anything the Queen Mother could do, she could do better! She had died in her sleep the day after her birthday, and Elaine was grateful that she'd not suffered a long and lingering illness at the end. It was the way she would have wanted to go. Elaine's only regret was that she wasn't there when her mum died, but she'd spent the day before with her enjoying the birthday party, so had to be content with that.

Marjorie had stayed on in the house as housekeeper for a couple of years, happy to live there rent-free in return for light housekeeping. It was a convenient arrangement for Elaine, until she decided what to do with the house. As it happened, Marjorie's son decided to move away and asked her to go and live in a granny annexe with them. That was partly what prompted Elaine to think about selling the house. She hadn't wanted to turn Marjorie out beforehand, although Marjorie wouldn't have bothered, as she had a widowed sister living nearby.

All this reminiscing made Elaine feel hungry and so she went to the café for her lunch. Alia had not been wrong. The food was delicious and in large portions and the café was obviously very popular. Elaine had a lovely chat with a young man called Daniel, who served her food. After lunch, Elaine waited by the side of the Conference House for the tour. A lady dressed in monk's robes approached and smiled a hello.

'I'm Beryl. I'm your guide for today,' she said.

'Elaine Barnes. You don't mind me coming on your tour?'

'Not at all, it's just a small party of Women's Institute members from Lund. The more the merrier,' laughed Beryl. At that point, a small minibus arrived, and the ladies all disembarked, then dashed off to the toilets before joining Beryl and Elaine. The tour went well and Elaine really enjoyed hearing about the history of the abbey from Beryl. Afterwards, the WI ladies went for a cup of tea and cake in the café, leaving Beryl and Elaine talking together, and Elaine complimented Beryl on her knowledge. In the end, Elaine said that she had to leave, but not before Beryl had put the idea in her mind about becoming a guide at Whalley Abbey. There was only one more guide besides Beryl, so they could do with help. Elaine said she would think about it and took Beryl's email address. Returning to the café to have a piece of homemade cake this time, Elaine reflected that being a guide was the sort of thing she could easily do now she was retired, yet making use of her expertise in history and especially monasteries. She could also do some stints on the admission kiosk like Alia. Yes, she thought, I've got a lot sorted out today and this is something I'll take on. I'll email Beryl tonight, if I can get any signal, she added ruefully to herself. After managing to get a signal that evening, Elaine emailed Beryl and said she was interested in becoming a guide. She then told Gill all about her day.

'I'm glad you're going to get involved locally. It'll be good for you, and for the abbey, with all your knowledge.'

'Yes, from what I hear about other people who've retired, I'll soon be so busy that I won't know how I found time to work,' she laughed. 'But it's important to me that I am busy. I know I love my own company, but I don't want to sit at home all day with nothing to do. My brain's too active for that.'

'At least you've got me nearby,' commented Gill.

'Yes, and I'm really glad about that, but you are busy with the farm and the family so I need other things too. Oh, I saw a sign for a tennis club in Whalley, so I need to follow that up soon or I'll have forgotten how to play.'

'You spent so much time playing tennis in Manchester, I'm surprised you haven't taken it up here yet.'

'All in good time. I will contact them soon.'

'As long as you don't want me to join, too.'

'No chance of that. You've always hated tennis.'

They sat in silence for a while, then Gill spoke again.

'What about a man in your life?'

'What about a man?' asked Elaine. 'I haven't got a good track record so far, have I? And if the men we met on holiday are anything to go by, I'm better off on my own.' This set Gill off giggling.

'And anyway, what about you? What about a man in your life?' asked Elaine, turning the tables on Gill.

'No, I'm not ready yet. I don't know whether I ever will be. I was so happy with John. But I won't say never. You can't foresee what might happen.'

'You could be swept off your feet tomorrow by the milk collection man and whisked off into the sunset leaving me here all by myself,' teased Elaine, but was surprised by the outbreak of near hysteria from Gill.

'I don't think so. Have you seen the milk collection man? He's about our age, bald, but with a big beer belly and wears shorts all year round. And he has an awful leering laugh. Not a good prospect,' she laughed.

'Well, he can't be worse than some of my men over the years. He might have hidden talents we don't know about.'

'I don't want to discover anything hidden about him, I can assure you.'

'Do you remember Max? I thought I'd found the perfect man with him,' said Elaine. 'He was so attentive and always held the doors open for me and was so polite and patient.'

'I reckon he was gay, you know,' Gill replied. 'I mean; he didn't even hold your hand for about a month.'

'I think you're probably right. He never did admit it, but he's never married either. His mum was so desperate to get him married off and out of her hair. I think he was dating me just to please her. He'd have probably married me as well, just to please her. But he was such a refreshing change after Greasy Gary. I felt valued and precious as a person with Max and not just for sex.'

'Oh, Greasy Gary. He was awful. I never understood what you saw in him!'

'Oh, he did have his talents, but shall I say they were all physical; he had no conversation at all. I think it kept going longer because he loved the villa in France and would do all sorts of jobs for me out there when we went to stay, so he had his uses for a time. But it soon fizzled out.'

'Thank goodness. Then there was Matthew. What went wrong there?'

'Ruled by his mother. Unlike Max's mother, she didn't want him to leave home. Every time we suggested going away together, she would have an illness and I'd either end up cancelling it or going with a work friend. It didn't matter when we were going to the villa; it was only the flights that were a problem. However, if we tried to book any other holiday there were always difficulties. He hardly ever stayed over. He used to creep home about midnight like he was married and had to get home.'

'He was married. To his mother!' laughed Gill.

'He did marry eventually, weeks after she died. A real flighty woman. His mother must be turning in her grave because they stayed in her house.'

'What about Derek?'

'Oh, I was well out of that relationship. He saw that I had a nice house, a villa, and an elderly mum with a nice house. He saw the pound signs, I think. He moved in with me but soon lost his job as foreman on a building site. He didn't seem to make any effort to get another job and kept saying we could go and live in France. He even suggested us getting married and wanted a pre-nuptial agreement. All in his favour, of course. I think he was just taking me for a ride.'

'I'm sure he was, and I was glad that you saw through him in time. And then there was that widower. What was his name?'

'Jeremy? Yes, he was a work colleague's husband. It was so sad when she got cancer and died, leaving four children all under 14. I tried to support him through his early grieving, as I was his wife's boss, but I came to see that he was just looking for another mother for his children. And I don't think he was bothered about how the children felt or how the new mother would feel. It only mattered that he had someone to look after them, so that he could concentrate on his career. I was well out of that one, but it left me emotionally drained and I felt guilty for years afterwards. I still send the children birthday cards.'

'Did he remarry then?'

'Oh, yes, another of my work colleagues. They didn't have any more children and she has had a hard life bringing up his traumatised children with little or no input from him.'

'Another narrow escape. Perhaps you are better off on your own. You don't have much luck with men.'

'Thanks! I don't need you to tell me that. I don't like to think there will never be anyone special in my life, but I'll be very hesitant in the future. No, I'll say the same as you, Gill. Never say never. But who knows what may happen? And now I'm going to bed. Perhaps to dream of my next disaster boyfriend,' Elaine laughed. Gill said goodnight and it wasn't long before she too went up to bed.

Next day Elaine went for a walk round the graveyard again and went over to the far side, waving hello to Ben and Jake as she passed. She'd noticed five white war graves on the far wall. She bent down to read the inscription on the first grave.

Private Thomas Farnworth
East Lancs Regiment.
Died February 28 1915
Aged 19 years

Corporal William Farnworth
East Lancs Regiment.
Died December 10 1915
Aged 25 years

Corporal Ronald Farnworth
East Lancs Regiment.
Died January 30 1917
Aged 24 years

Sergeant John Farnworth
East Lancs Regiment.
Died November 11 1918
Aged 23 years

Elaine reeled backwards as she read this. Four sons all killed during one war. And one on the last day of the war as the Armistice was being signed. How awful for the parents to cope with. She wondered if there were any other children in the family. She sincerely hoped so. Perhaps there were younger sons who were too young to fight and daughters that would comfort them. When she got home, she would Google their names and dates of death and see if she could find out anything about them. Rooting in her haversack for a pen and a piece of paper, Elaine noticed a sudden movement at the front of the graveyard. The young boy was bending down near the grave at the side of the front wall.

'Hello,' Elaine called out, but the boy took flight, leaving his flowers strewn across the grave. Elaine ran after him but he'd disappeared. She went back to the grave and picked up the flowers the boy had dropped, placing them in the urn on the grave, after checking that there was enough water in. Fortunately, the graveyard had a water tap so that visitors could use it for their floral offerings. Elaine decided that she would provide a bench as well with a few urns on, so that if people came unprepared there would be enough urns to share. The grave was immaculately cared for with lots of bulbs and shrubs planted around it. It was the grave where a whole family had seemed to die on the same day. Perhaps it was his family, thought Elaine. Sadly, she turned back to the white war grave and wrote down the names of the men who had died. She needed to know more about all the owners of the graves. Perhaps she had better start Googling tonight.

But before she could start the laptop up when she got back to the farm, there was a knock at the door. When Elaine opened the door, a small, weather-beaten man, probably in his 70s, was standing there, twisting his hat in his hands.

'Hello, missus, I'm Frank.'

Elaine looked at him blankly and then remembered.

'Oh, you're the grass cutter.'

'Yes.'

'Ben tells me that you're happy to go on cutting the grass for me in the graveyard.'

'Yes.'

'Have you been paid for doing this for the last couple of years.'

'No.' Obviously a man of few words, thought Elaine.

'What made you do it then?' Elaine couldn't help asking.

'Needed cutting. Came here as a kid.'

'What? To the church?'

'Yes. Parents got married here. Both buried here.'

'Well, I need to thank you for all you've done. You keep the graveyard in excellent condition. Do you use your own lawnmower?'

'Yes.'

'How often do you cut the grass?'

'Every two weeks. Spring to October.'

'And can you cut the grass in my part of the garden as well, in front and at the back of the church? I'll pay extra obviously.'

'Yes.'

'How do you want me to pay you? Every time you cut the grass?'

'No. Once at end of October. Feels more then.'

'Right,' said Elaine, rooting in her purse, 'here's £50 to be going on with for the last two years. It's all I have in my purse.'

'Thanks.'

'I'll probably see you around in the graveyard, but if not, come to me here to get paid or leave me a bill.'

'No bill. I'll just tell you,' and with that, Frank turned on his heel and walked away, leaving Elaine amazed at such a taciturn man. She must remember to get some more money for him. To keep cutting the grass with no remuneration was saintly and needed rewarding.

After tea, she Googled all the names of the Farnworth men who'd been killed in the war, but apart from brief details about their births, service record, and time, cause, date and place of death, there was no other information to be found. It was very frustrating. Perhaps she could Google other members of the family, but as most of it happened after the 1911 census, she'd have to wait another few years before the 1921 census was available. For 1911 there was just a list of the family names, only mentioning parents and four sons. There were no younger sons or daughters. So, it looked like they lost all their children in the war. Perhaps the 1921 census would reveal new children born after the war but Elaine doubted it. The parents would probably be middle-aged by the end of the war, although she had heard of parents having more children later in life after they'd lost all their children. She felt sad for them.

When Elaine Googled the names of the modern family who all died on the same day, she was horrified. They had all been caught up in a terrorist plot. Their plane was blown up just after leaving the airport on the return journey, with no survivors. So, who was this young boy? Was he a relative? Was he related at all? Perhaps he was a friend of the daughter who died? He looked to be in his mid-teens, she thought, but it was hard to tell. Thoroughly saddened by her find, Elaine decided that she was investigating no more for now. It was too sad. She would ask around in the village to see if anyone knew the boy, or the Farnworth family. But for now, she was going to bed with a novel that would take her mind off all the sadness.

Chapter 9

August 1914

'Jeremiah? Is that you?' shouted Hilda Farnworth.
'Who else were you expecting?' shouted a grumpy Jeremiah Farnworth, Hilda's husband.
'Are those lads of ours coming home tonight?'
'No, they're staying at their brother William's in Clitheroe.'
'That poor wife of his,' replied Hilda. 'How she puts up with all them great lads in their little house, I'll never know. I bet they wake up the little 'un as well.'
'Well, I'd rather they stay there than come back here full of beer and talking nonsense like they usually do,' muttered Jeremiah.
'I'll lock up for the night then,' said Hilda. 'At least we can have a bit of peace tonight.'
'Aye,' replied Jeremiah. 'But they'd better be back for milking tomorrow night. I 'spose I'll have to do the morning milking on my own.'
'I'll give you a hand,' promised Hilda, sighing. It was a bad time for everyone in the country just now. War had been declared and, although her boys would be safe from fighting because of being farmers, a lot of women were going to lose their husbands, fathers, and sons. Her eldest son William might be at risk of being called up to fight, as he had moved to live in Clitheroe, having no interest in farming like his younger brothers. But as a married man he would be safe, Hilda reassured herself. She couldn't say anything to Jeremiah about this, as he would always refuse to discuss things that hinted at emotions. Sighing again, Hilda went up to bed, blowing out the candle and saying a silent prayer for the safety of her sons.

The boys arrived home in the pony and trap, laughing and carrying on with each other about an hour after noon next day. When Hilda berated them for being late, they all looked at her sheepishly and went silent.

'What's the matter with you lot? What are you all grinning at?' Nobody spoke. 'Come on, I'm waiting. You're not too old for me to go and get the strap down from the back of the door.' At this, the lads laughed. They were all tall and their mother was little more than five feet. 'And don't think I won't,' she added fiercely.

'We've joined up,' said Tommy, the youngest, a big grin on his face.

'What do you mean, you've joined up?'

'We're soldiers now. In the army. We're going to war,' said Ronnie, the second eldest.

'You can't have, you are all farmers,' gasped Hilda, clutching her chest.

'Well, we have, all of us,' added John. 'See, here's our papers,' as he thrust a sheaf of documents at her.

'Yes, the recruiting officer said we'll all be in the same regiment so that we can be company for each other,' said Ronnie.

'And all get shot together, I suppose?' added Hilda bitterly.

'Don't be daft, Mum, we'll be fine. We'll be able to look after each other,' said Tommy.

'And have you thought how your Dad's going to manage on the farm? No, I don't suppose you have. Probably had a belly full of beer last night and still stupid this morning. I don't know what your Dad's going to say about this.'

'Say about what?' asked Jeremiah as he came through the door.

'Your stupid sons have all joined the army this morning. Well, these three have anyway,' shouted Hilda.

'Nay, what did you do that for, lads? How are we going to manage on the farm? I'll have to see if our William will come back to work here for the duration.'

There was silence. And then John said in a quiet voice, 'Our William joined up as well, Dad.'

'Our William?' shrieked Hilda. 'What about his wife and child? Does she know, our Betsy?'

The boys all nodded miserably; their joyous, proud attitude shrivelled and gone.

'What did she say?' asked Hilda.

'We left them to it. You could say she wasn't best pleased,' said Ronnie quietly.

'And no wonder. I don't know what the world's coming to. Married men leaving home all for a bit of fuss.'

'It's not a bit of fuss, Mum, it's war. We've got to show those Hun what we're about. We have to protect all you lot left at home.'

'That's brave words, our Tommy,' said his mum bitterly. 'I'll remind you of that when you've been to war.'

'Don't go on, Mum. It says in the papers that it'll all be over by Christmas, so stop worrying. We'll be back to annoy you for Christmas dinner,' Ronnie grinned.

But they weren't. Hilda had to watch as all her sons went away to training camp first of all, although soon enough they were home for a brief time on embarkation leave. They'd learnt not to say too much when Hilda was around as she got very upset, but she overheard them anyway, boasting with their mates and their dad about how they couldn't wait to go to France 'cos who in their school or village had ever been to France? As it turned out, quite a lot of their school mates ended up in France, or Belgium, or Egypt, but at war wherever they were. William's wife, Betsy, and their son Samuel, came to live on the farm during the war and, although Betsy wasn't from a farming background, she mucked in with the other older workers who had come out of retirement to help Jeremiah run the farm.

At first the letters home were buoyant and full of little jokes and anecdotes about army life, but once the boys were sent abroad the letters became terse and not saying much at all, not only because of the censorship. The only bright spot was the first Christmas when they reported that they'd had a cease fire on Christmas Day and had ended up playing football with the Hun after singing 'Silent Night'. Hilda couldn't believe it, but she supposed that the Hun were only young men like her lads and were sorry to be away from home at this special time of year, missing their families. Well, for all she cared, they could all go home again. If the leaders of the countries got their act together and sorted out their differences, then all her boys could come home again. If only women were in charge, it would have been sorted out long since, thought Hilda, especially some of those Suffragettes. They'd have taught the Hun a thing or two. And now some of them were driving ambulances or being nurses in France and doing men's jobs. Good for them, thought Hilda.

For the next few years Hilda constantly worried about her sons and dreaded anyone knocking on the door in case it was bad news. She hardly ate and became even thinner than she was before. Jeremiah worried for her but said nothing, as he knew that she would only shout at him, as if it was all his idea that the lads had gone to war. She became one of the most regular people at the church of St Gregory and St Philip's, praying desperately that her sons would survive. But it wasn't to be. Eventually, in early 1915, the dreaded telegram came to Greenbank Farm. It said that her son Tommy had been killed in action. Hilda was beside herself with grief and Jeremiah couldn't help her, as he too was burdened by grief. Each was unable to help the other, both heartbroken but not able to share their burden, grieving in different ways. Meals became silent affairs. Young Samuel learned to eat quickly and get back out on the farm, finding a friend in one of the farm workers who was unfit to go to war. Samuel followed the man around all the time and it made things easier for him, to take his mind off all the misery in his grandparent's farmhouse. He was too young to really understand where his daddy was and only knew that his mummy kept getting upset. Neither did he understand why his Uncle Tommy wasn't ever coming back.

Hilda was cross with the authorities that her son couldn't be returned for a funeral or that his brothers weren't allowed time off to mourn their brother. Although Jeremiah tried to explain how many other sons had died and they couldn't bring them all back, Hilda was having none of it. She didn't care about the other people's sons, only her own.

But worse was to come. William was the next to be killed, near the end of 1915, but it took a while for the news to come through, as the telegram went to their old house in Clitheroe. Samuel was totally bewildered by this news and again didn't understand it. He only knew that both his mummy and granny were forever crying and both grabbing him and holding him so tight that it frightened him and sometimes hurt. He just kept escaping and telling the farm animals how unhappy he was.

Throughout 1916 the war dragged on, but both Hilda's remaining sons survived, even managing to get home for a brief period, although not at the same time. Hilda was shocked at how thin they both were and how nervous and twitchy they were whenever there was a loud noise. They seemed to have lost their lively sense of humour and their constant joking with everyone around. It was hard to let them go away again, but she knew she had to. She wasn't the only mother who was suffering. Soon it would all end, please God, she said each night as she prayed for them.

In early 1917, Ronnie was invalided back to England to a hospital down south. He'd lost a leg during a battle and they were bringing him back to recuperate before returning home. Hilda thanked God that he was out of the fighting and soon he would be back home to her, where she could feed him up and lavish her motherly care on him; not that he'd like it, she laughed to herself. But before she could even get a bed downstairs for his homecoming, a telegram arrived to say that he'd succumbed to infection in the hospital and had died that day.

Again the grief was overwhelming. How could three of her sons be lost to her forever? Only John remained of all her sons. She was grateful that Samuel was around, as it forced her to make meals for the family and farm workers and try to keep up an appearance of normality, but it was extremely hard. And it wasn't just their house that was affected. News came through that many of her sons' friends had been killed in action too.

Eventually, gradually, the war seemed to be turning round and victory was in sight. But just one week before the Armistice, news came that John was missing in action. Hilda couldn't believe the telegram. Surely this son was spared to her? She thought of all the possibilities that might have happened. He was lost and couldn't get back to his unit. He had a head injury and couldn't remember his name. He had been taken prisoner. He'd broken a leg and couldn't walk. But on the day of the Armistice came the news that he was dead, not just missing. There was no joy at the ceasing of hostilities at Greenbank Farm. How could Hilda and Jeremiah ever feel joy again when all their four sons had died?

Slowly, they tried to carry on with the farm, but all the joy had gone out of it now there were no sons to leave it to. Hilda said to Jeremiah that she would never feel normal again, but he just nodded and said nothing. They were still grieving separately. Betsy had gone back to Clitheroe, taking little Samuel with her as he was getting too upset by the sad atmosphere at the farm. Eventually Hilda and Jeremiah decided to sell the farm and move to Clitheroe themselves, nearer to Samuel and Betsy. Jacob Robinson was glad to buy the farm and gave them a good price, so that the Farnworths could buy a house in Clitheroe and have enough to live on. Jacob Robinson hadn't lost any sons in the war; they were too young to fight. He was lucky, thought Hilda and

Jeremiah bitterly. He'd have sons to leave the farm to when the time came. Jeremiah and Hilda turned their faces resolutely towards Clitheroe, only ever returning to Dunsop Bridge to see the white war grave for their precious sons in St Gregory and St Philip's graveyard. But even though there were four names on the white war grave, only Ronnie was buried there as he'd died in England. They did not know where their other sons were buried and no longer had the energy to find out. The war had beaten them.

Chapter 10

October 2016

Elaine decided that it was time to look up the two saints in the church name. She looked up St Gregory first and was amazed to find that not only was he a saint, but he was also the Pope and was known as Gregory the Great. That surprised Elaine, as she knew that the builder of her church, John Talbot, had been no friend of Catholics, and wondered why he'd chosen this saint. St Gregory had lived to the age of 64, from AD 540 to 604, and was known for reforming a lot of the liturgy. The website said that St Gregory was the patron saint of musicians, singers, students, and teachers. Now Elaine could see how the church came to have such a strong tradition of singing, and why St Gregory had been picked for the church name. John Talbot obviously liked music.

Next she investigated St Philip and, as she suspected, St Philip was one of Jesus' disciples. According to the website, some of the extra canonical books of the time said that Philip worked with his sister, Mariamne, and a man called Bartholomew. After healing and then converting the Pro-Consul's wife, the Pro-Consul flew into a rage and ordered that both Philip and Bartholomew were tortured and crucified upside down. But Philip pleaded for Bartholomew's life and so only he was crucified and Bartholomew was set free. Elaine shuddered when she read this story. What a selfless man who would plead for another man's life but not his own.

The website also said that St Philip was the patron saint of hatters. That made Elaine laugh as she tried to make a connection between the hatter's trade and a disciple of Jesus, or the hatter's trade and John Talbot. Failing to find a connection, unless John Talbot was a dandy who loved hats, Elaine decided that perhaps John Talbot had admired St Philip simply because he had given his life for another man. The ultimate sacrifice, as several men in this graveyard had done. But on reflection, Elaine thought that both her saints were worthy bearers of the church name, and when she ordered a plaque for her parent's bench, she would order another larger brass plaque as a door sign. She would call her house 'St Gregory and St Philip House,' so that neither the saints nor the name of the church were forgotten.

Having settled on the name of the house, Elaine started trying to see if she could find any descendants of the Farnworth family. As her initial search had drawn a blank, she turned to the Pendle Family History Society, of which she had just become a member. One of the members, Jill Pengelly, advised her that she could put the names into a website saying she was looking for anyone else that was researching this family to contact her. Soon the form was filled in and the message sent. She would just have to be patient.

Ben wanted a word with Elaine on site next day, so she got there just after 10am. Elaine was amazed at how much work was already completed. The sunroom had been built, the upper floor was in position, the divisions for the bedrooms and bathrooms were in place, and the wall between the kitchen-diner and the lounge was fixed. A large gap in the wall had been left so that extra-large doors between the kitchen-diner and lounge could be added. If there was a large party, the doors could be left open, but could still be shut off as well, when necessary. The downstairs bedroom and bathroom had also been divided off near the front entrance. It was beginning to look like the architect's drawings at long last.

'This is all amazing,' said Elaine. 'I can't believe how much work you've been able to do already, Ben.'

'We've been blessed with good weather and people turning up on time. The solar panels are coming next week, and the underfloor heating is being fitted tomorrow. Once the underfloor heating is in, we can start plastering all the walls. I need some decisions about kitchen fitments, light fittings, and bathrooms. I've got loads of catalogues for you to look at. Or you could go to Homebase in Clitheroe, or Howden's, or anywhere you want really. It doesn't matter to us. Just tell me what you want.'

'Will you be fitting them all, or do I need kitchen fitters and the like?'

'No, between Jake, Martin, and me we'll do all the fittings. Martin's coming next week to start all the plumbing before the bathrooms can go in. He's done the first fix so that the plastering can be started. Helen's really looking forward to her extra holiday in the Trough of Bowland. You'd think she was going to Tenerife.'

'Where is Jake today?'

'He'll be back later. He's gone into Clitheroe to get some supplies of plaster. Several tons of it,' Ben laughed. 'Why? Did you want him?'

'Not urgently. I've been trying to research the Farnworth family who had four sons die in the First World War. I wondered if he knew anything about them?'

'What do you want to know?'

'What happened to them after the war? Did they have more children? Did they stay in Dunsop Bridge?'

'I can tell you that. They left Dunsop Bridge and moved to Clitheroe. They had no more children, but sold the farm to my great-great grandfather, Jacob.'

'The farm? Your farm?'

'Yes. It was sad, apparently. They just lost heart when their sons died and sold the farm. Fortunately, Jacob was in a position to buy it and we've been here ever since. Five generations. Six if we count Anna.'

'Of course, it never registered that they had the same address as you, Greenbank Farm. What a coincidence.'

'Yep. Are you going to investigate all the graves in this graveyard? I know you like research, but you might bite off more than you can chew here.'

'As many as I can, yes. But some are too old to be able to investigate now or have lost their engravings. It'd be great to be able to contact any known relatives that are still surviving though. Especially as it will be the 100 years anniversary of the end of the First World War in 2018.'

'You are thinking ahead!'

'I've not much else to do at the moment. I'm sort of in limbo land.'

'Yes, you have plenty to do. Take these catalogues home and give me some pointers about final fittings. Go and get on with them now!' his stern voice belied the twinkling in his eyes, as he dumped the catalogues in her hands.

'Yes, sir. Right away, sir,' replied Elaine in a mocking voice. But Ben could hear her laughing as she left the building.

Throwing the catalogues on the table when she got in, Elaine decided that she would make a quick tea tonight, so that they could look at all the catalogues together. Gill agreed when she came in, and soon after tea they spread the catalogues out all over the kitchen table. Word must have got out, because first Anna, then Kirsty, and Liz all turned up, giving their own version of what the kitchen and bathrooms should look like. The night turned out to be hilarious, with everyone arguing as to what they thought best. In the end, Elaine put the catalogues away and said she was going into town tomorrow - on her own, she emphasised - to decide what she was having. But she acknowledged to their faces that she would take all their comments on board, and knew she'd do her own thing next day.

Starting early, Elaine had a riotous day in Clitheroe, going to every kitchen and bathroom supplier she could find, interspersed with breakfast and lunch as she went around. She even managed some homemade chocolate cake at the Chocolate Café before she went home, feeling she deserved a treat after all that work. But she ended up with even more catalogues to add to the ones Ben had given her. Exhausted, she headed off home as the shops were shutting anyway.

Liz and Gill were at the Women's Institute that night. Elaine had meant to go this month but decided she'd prefer the peace to make some decisions about her kitchen and bathrooms. She eventually settled on a stark white and black kitchen, with shiny white cupboard doors that would be easy to keep clean, rather than wood (which she'd had at her last house), and black work surfaces. The black and white theme continued in the downstairs wet room. But upstairs, she had a different colour in each bathroom. Pale grey in one, cream and fawn in another, and plain white in the third. That should suit everyone's tastes, whoever stays here, she decided. Another idea she had was to have all the bathrooms tiled from floor to ceiling, so that there wouldn't be much painting to do in the future. She supposed either Ben, Jake or Martin could do tiling as well. They seemed to be able to do everything between them, although she knew specialist firms were doing the solar panels and the underfloor heating.

Elaine wrote her final lists for Ben, and where she'd seen each item, and then put them to one side, so that she could show Gill later. Thinking about less painting in the future made her think about paint colours and soft furnishings, but she was too tired to do anything else that night. Besides, she thought, she might ask Kate for her advice. She'd done so well in the bungalow. She wouldn't ask for Kirsty's help: it would all be pink!

The next morning Elaine asked Gill about the cleaner who helped them on changeover days at the holiday cottages and yurts.

'Do you think she'd like more cleaning?'

'Why? Do you want a cleaner?'

'I certainly do. I've had a cleaner most of my adult life. It was just easier when I was working. But now I've bought a house that is bigger than I expected, I don't see why I shouldn't have help.'

'Don't blame you. Good idea. She's called Nikki. Really good cleaner, very reliable. She's a widow and has three young children, Katie, Holly and Oscar.'

'Poor woman.'

'Yes, she works two days a week from home as an accounts manager, as she's brilliant at maths, and then works for us. I don't think she works anywhere else. Do you want her number?'

'Yes, please.'

'I'll text it to you; it'll be easier.'

'Thanks.'

Next day Elaine rang Nikki and asked her if she wanted more cleaning work and told her that she needed a cleaner one day a week when the house was finished. Nikki suggested Fridays and Elaine said that was perfect. They discussed wages and then rang off. Elaine was very pleased. Good cleaners were hard to come by. She would also ask Nikki to come for a few extra days after the builders finished, if she could, so that they could get the house spotless before she moved in.

The following week Helen and Martin arrived in their camper van. It was fortunate that Helen didn't work, apart from doing Martin's business books. She'd found this more convenient when the children were small. They planned to stay for three weeks, but it was open-ended, depending on how soon the bathrooms and kitchen were fitted. Only Daniel was at home now; the other two children were both married and lived away. Daniel stayed on the farm more often since Ben had refurbished a small outhouse as a bachelor flat, as Daniel liked to call it.

Helen, Gill, and Elaine enjoyed lots of long walks together, sometimes without Gill if she was busy on the farm. They went regularly for coffee, and sometimes lunch in Puddleducks, the little café in the village.

'What are we going to do for our birthdays this year?' Gill asked Elaine when they got home from a walk one day.

'I don't know. It's not as if it's a big one. What do you want to do?'

'Not a lot. I think we've enough on at the moment. Why don't we just go for a meal in Clitheroe?' suggested Gill.

'Just the two of us?'

'Yes, why not?'

'Okay then. I'll let you choose where we go, being the eldest,' teased Elaine.

'Only by one day. You always rub that in. I was born on November 10th, only a day before you, but to hear you talk, you'd think there were years between us. Okay. Clitheroe Emporium it is.'

And so they did. They went to The Emporium, ate and drank far too much, and got a taxi home, despite the expense.

A few days later, when Elaine was on her own investigating a grave at the back of the graveyard, she saw the young boy come in again. Elaine crouched down and froze, hoping not to alarm him and see if she could talk to him. After a quick look round, the boy settled down to clear weeds from the grave, using his bare hands. Then Elaine watched as he started clearing the weeds from the old grave next door, which had only a date left on it. Whilst he was engrossed in his work, Elaine tiptoed nearer without disturbing him. When she got close by, she spoke quietly to him.

'That's a really good job you're making of that grave. Do you know whose it is?' The boy jumped up, shook his head, and ran off, despite Elaine calling him to come back, as she'd like to talk to him. It seemed really odd. She hadn't been stern or frowning, but gentle-voiced and smiling and giving him praise, and yet he'd run off as if the devil himself was after him. That evening Elaine asked Gill if she knew about the boy.

'Do you mean young Harvey?'

'I don't know his name. He runs away if I speak to him. He visits the new grave near the front wall.'

'Yes, that'll be Harvey. I know that he's not been the same since his family died.'

'I'm not surprised. It must have been awful to lose his whole family in one go.'

'He should have been with them on the holiday, but a mix-up in the dates of a school trip meant that he couldn't go. So, his grandmother went instead.

She'd never been abroad before as Fred didn't like foreign holidays. Harvey had to come and live with his grandfather, as his only other relative is a great uncle who lives in Australia on a remote sheep farm.'

'So, there's survivor guilt going on?'

'Yes, he hardly speaks now and is missing lots of time at school. He goes in most mornings, but just wanders off home again during the day.'

'Is he getting counselling?'

'Not initially; his grandfather wasn't keen. I know more about him as I sometimes do supply teaching at Ribblesdale School where he attends.'

'How sad. I'll try and see him again when he comes to the grave. I hope I haven't frightened him.'

'Don't expect him to talk, though. Everyone's tried.'

'I won't. I just wish I could help him.'

'Leave him be; that's the best advice. He'll come round eventually.'

'But it's been over a year since they died.'

'Yes, it was not long after John. Another shock for the community. It put my loss into perspective, though. I'd only lost one person, not a whole family. There's always someone worse off than you, whatever's happening, I reckon.' Elaine nodded wisely.

'The young family didn't live in Dunsop Bridge; they lived in Whalley,' continued Gill. 'Harvey only moved here afterwards. But Mary, his grandmother, was a real worker. She was in the WI, helped with the teas at the village hall on Sundays, and was a very popular person. We never really knew Fred. He kept himself to himself. He's a bit grumpy, to be honest.'

'Poor Harvey, losing all his family and having to live with a grumpy old man.' Gill nodded her agreement, but then remembered that she wanted to watch a film, so turned the TV on. Elaine took that as a sign that Gill had had enough talking about grief and kept silent, deciding to go to bed early as she didn't want to watch the film. But she couldn't get the boy out of her mind and lay for a long time thinking what she could do to help, if anything.

The next day Elaine went to Shackleton's Garden Centre and bought two sets of trowels and small garden forks. She also bought a small plastic box with a lid to put them in. Ordering a wooden bench, they promised to deliver it the next day. Gill made a sign on her computer and laminated it so that it wouldn't get damaged by rain. The sign said *'For use in the graveyard.'* Elaine then stuck it on the lid of the box. She'd already found an old but serviceable watering can, and when the bench was delivered, she put the box and the watering can on the bench, with one set of tools in the box.

The other set of tools she placed on Harvey's family grave with a note inside a plastic bag. She wrote:

Thank you for keeping the grave next to your family grave tidy. I'm going to try and find out who it belonged to and perhaps I can get the name re-engraved. Please use these tools for yourself. You can take them away or leave them here. My name is Elaine Barnes, and I'm moving into the church once it is finished.

Elaine didn't hold out any hope that he would contact her, but at least he wouldn't have to be digging with his bare hands anymore. She looked out for him every time she was at the church but didn't see him. He was obviously avoiding her. Perhaps she'd gone too far in leaving him a note, but it was too late now.

Next evening Elaine was surprised to get an email from a Thomas Farnworth, who was a direct descendant of 'her' soldiers. He asked if Elaine lived locally and suggested that they meet up for lunch. Elaine replied that she would be happy to meet up for lunch, and they settled on the following Saturday at the Emporium in Clitheroe. Elaine laughed to herself that she was becoming a regular there. They exchanged mobile numbers, and on Friday evening Elaine received a picture of Thomas on her phone, saying that he would be easier to recognise if she had a photo. What a good idea, thought Elaine, but didn't send one back. She wasn't into doing selfies. She looked at the picture. He looked to be around 60ish, she thought, with grey hair and a friendly smile. He looked harmless enough and at least they were meeting in public, which was better than him coming to the house. She began to look forward to the lunch with anticipation.

Chapter 11

Getting ready to go and meet Thomas, Elaine felt a frisson of excitement that she hadn't had for a while, as it had been some time since she had been out with a man, but then chided herself not to get too fanciful. It wasn't a date, just a research meeting. Besides, he could have a wife and six kids for all she knew. She recognised him straightaway as she walked into the Emporium. He stood up and shook her hand and waited for her to sit down before he sat down. He already had a glass of beer in front of him and asked Elaine what she would like to drink.

'Just a lime and soda please; I'm driving,' she replied.

'Are you sure? You could have one glass of something.'

'No, I'd rather not, but thanks anyway.' He signalled the waiter over and gave the order, and they ordered food as well.

'So how are you related to the Farnworth family? I don't remember any Barnes being in the family. Or is that your married name?'

'No, I'm not married,' replied Elaine. 'I'm not related to the Farnworth family either.'

'You're not? So why did you put the request in?'

'I'm researching some war graves near where I live.'

'In Dunsop Bridge?'

'Yes. How are you related to the men on the war grave?' Elaine asked quickly, as she didn't want to tell him where she lived just yet, even though he seemed really nice.'

'My great granddad was William Farnworth. He was the only one of the four brothers who was married. So, I'm descended from him.' Then the food arrived and they spent some time eating before it got cold. From then on, the chat was more about getting to know each other. He soon established that she wasn't attached, and he was a widower having lost his wife to cancer three years before.

'That's why I took early retirement. It makes you re-evaluate your life,' he said.

'Where did you work?'

'Ultraframe. They make conservatories. I was an engineer.'

'Where they a good company to work for?'

'Very good. We all got shares in the firm before the owners, the Lancasters, put it on the stock market. We didn't think much about it until the first news came that they'd made a fortune overnight, and we could sell our shares at a great profit: £20,000 for each person. Yes, they were very good employers. They've left the firm now. They did the old Grand Cinema up as a venue for concerts and things like that. It's a good place. All paid for by the Lancasters. Very philanthropic couple, they are. Where do you work?'

'I've just taken early retirement this year. I worked at Manchester University.'

'What was your job?'

'I taught history.'

'And let me guess, your speciality was the First World War?' Elaine laughed. 'No, actually it was the medieval period, especially monasteries.'

Thomas laughed too, and Elaine felt comfortable with him.

'I'm planning on visiting the grave next week. Perhaps we could meet up again? I could bring you what photographs I have of my great granddad. I didn't think about that today.'

'Ah, yes, I suppose we could. Shall we meet in Puddleducks café if you're bringing photos? We can look at the photos before you go to the grave.'

'That'd be great. I love that café. My granddad Sam used to take me there when I was little. He always bought me an ice cream and also food to feed the ducks. He'd been brought up on the farm as a young child and liked to go and see the village and have a walk near the farm, as well as looking at the graves. It'll be quite like old times for me.'

'Well, I'd better be off now,' said Elaine. 'So, what time next week? Shall we say twelve o'clock again?'

'Yes, that'd be great, then I can get home for the football results.'

'Oh, I wouldn't want to keep a man from his football results,' laughed Elaine. She got her purse out to pay her share but he gently pushed her purse back into her handbag.

'This one is on me,' he said. 'I've really enjoyed talking to you today.'

'So have I. Thanks for paying for lunch. Next week's on me.'

'I'll hold you to that.' Thomas formally shook her hand and Elaine walked away without looking back. Getting into the car, she thought about all they'd talked about and felt a warm feeling inside - one that she hadn't had for quite some time. And then she remembered that it would be another Saturday when she couldn't take the girls to the café. Oh, well, they'd have to get used to it if this relationship developed. Get a grip, Elaine reminded herself. You've only met once. It's not the romance of the century. But it might be, she thought fondly. Only time would tell.

The following Saturday she made the mistake of telling the girls that she couldn't take them out as she usually did, as she was meeting someone. The girls nagged Elaine until she admitted that it was a man she was meeting. Within ten minutes of Elaine getting home, Gill came in.
'What's all this about a date? Why haven't you told me? You're a dark horse, Elaine.'
'It's not a date as such. It's the Farnworth man. I did tell you I was meeting him last week. He wants to visit the grave so we're meeting in Puddleducks. I didn't tell him about the house; I don't know why.'
'What did you think about him? Was he nice?'
'Very nice. Widower. Retired. Probably early sixties.'
'Has he got a family?'
'Just one son who lives in London and sounds quite a high flyer – a banker. Never comes to see his dad anymore. Got two grandchildren as well.'
'Mmm, well, let me know. You know you always tell me everything.'
'Well, not *everything*,' Elaine laughed.
Getting ready the following Saturday, Elaine took extra care with her hair and makeup, and put on a smarter dress than she would normally wear just to go for the usual lunch at Puddleducks. She got there first, then Thomas arrived, but before they could order anything, in trooped Kate, Anna, and Kirsty. They sat at a table opposite, grinning and smirking at Elaine.
'Since you wouldn't bring us today, we thought we'd come ourselves,' said Kirsty.
Elaine turned to Thomas. 'These are my friend's three granddaughters, whom I usually bring every Saturday for their lunch. Come on Thomas, we'll go to the other side of the café so that we can get some peace.'
They ate their lunch and then Thomas got out the old photos of his great granddad William. Elaine could see the family likeness, especially round the

nose and mouth. But her favourite photo was one of all four brothers taken together, obviously just after they had enlisted. There was also one of Thomas' great grandmother Betsy, with her husband William and their son Sam - Thomas' granddad - as a small boy. It was obviously taken at the same studio before William went to war. It gave Elaine an idea that she would try to have photos of as many people in the graveyard as she could, to make a feature of them, perhaps at the 100 years anniversary. Thomas promised to let her have a copy of the photos, but she didn't tell him her full plans.

When they were almost ready to go, Thomas looked at Elaine for quite a time without speaking.

'What?' asked Elaine. 'Have I got gravy on my chin or something?'

'No, I was just thinking how much I've looked forward to seeing you again. Instead of meeting in cafés, could we go out for a proper meal next week? What about Friday night?'

'Yes, Friday night will be fine. At least I won't miss bringing the girls here on Saturday,' she replied, laughing a little nervously.

'That's true. But Burnley are playing at home next Saturday, so I couldn't have made it on Saturday. So it works well for both of us.'

'Football again?'

'It's an important part of my life. I'm a season ticket holder for Burnley home games.'

'Where would you like to go on Friday?'

'The Spread Eagle at Sawley?'

'Great, I love it there. What time?'

'I'll book a table for 7.30. Is that okay? Not too early?'

'7.30 will be fine. Do you want to meet there?'

'Can do. What's best for you?'

'Probably easier if I meet you there, as I can go on the back roads through Waddington.'

'Great,' replied Thomas, and then told her an amusing tale about one of his neighbours.

Eventually they got up and, as promised, Elaine paid for their meal. The girls had long gone, but Elaine thought that they'd probably be lurking round the graveyard to snoop. But she was wrong. There was no sign of them at the graveyard. Must have gone home to tell Gill, she decided. Thomas stopped as they got to the church and looked shocked.

'What's happened to the church?' he asked.

'It's being renovated into a house,' Elaine replied cautiously. 'It's been for sale many years.'

'Must be someone who has more money than sense.'

'What makes you say that?' bristled Elaine.

'Well, who'd want to live in an old barn like that? A proper money pit. It's probably haunted anyway.'

'I think it would make a lovely home.'

'But it's right next to a graveyard. I couldn't do with that. Creepy.'

'Quiet neighbours, though,' quipped Elaine, trying to lighten the conversation.

'Well, I wouldn't like it. Worst place I could ever think of living.'

Just at the wrong moment, Jake came out of the house shouting, 'Hi, Elaine. Are you okay? Do you want anything?'

'No, I'm fine thanks, Jake. Er, this is Thomas Farnworth, a relative of the four soldier brothers from the war grave.' The two men nodded at each other, and then Jake took the hint and went back inside.

Thomas waited for Elaine to speak, looking at her strangely, but she kept silent. Eventually Thomas spoke.

'So, you know the builder of this renovation?' Elaine nodded.

'And do you know the owner of the building?' Elaine nodded again.

'It's you, isn't it? I'm sorry, I shouldn't have said what I did,' Thomas mumbled.

'It doesn't matter,' Elaine replied. 'I came here for a holiday to visit my friend and saw the church and fell in love with it.'

'So why did you ask for contacts about my family then?'

'I also own the graveyard, but not the individual graves,' she added hurriedly. 'I wanted to see if I could contact any of the descendants of the graves to encourage them to visit and care for their graves.'

'Let's go and look at the grave, then,' said Thomas sharply, striding off. Elaine hurried after him, struggling to keep up with his quick walk, but eventually got to the grave.

'It was so sad that all four sons died in the war. I believe they didn't have any other children?'

'No, that's right,' replied Thomas. 'My granddad Samuel and his mum came to live here all through the war, but after my great granddad died, she went back home to Clitheroe - much to my granddad's disgust. He'd loved living on the farm and always wanted to go back. I never thought, I should have brought flowers for the grave.'

'It doesn't matter. I can get some for you, if you like?'

'Would you? That makes me feel better. Thanks. Would you mind if I go and look at the farm now? I always do when I visit Dunsop Bridge?'

'Not at all. I'll walk with you.'

Thomas and Elaine set off together, but conversation was more subdued than it had been before he found out about the house. Elaine wondered if he was regretting asking her out, but didn't quite know how to say anything to that effect. On arriving at the farm, Thomas commented on all the changes that had been made, with the holiday cottages and yurts, and Elaine agreed that farmers had to diversify nowadays. But she was surprised at his next comment.

'This should all have been mine,' he said quietly.

'I beg your pardon?' Elaine asked, thinking she had misheard him.

'This farm. My granddad Sam said that his grandparents should never have sold it, but kept it until my granddad was old enough to run it, instead of being forced to sell out for a pittance of what it was worth.'

'I think it went for the market value at the time,' Elaine quietly replied.

'How would you know? My granddad said it wasn't fair. And I agree. If they'd saved it for him, I'd be the owner now as I'm the only male descendant from my granddad. Well, the only descendant from my granddad, as it happens.'

'Did you and your granddad always want to be farmers?'

'No, not particularly; it's just the principle of the matter.'

'It's no easy life, farming nowadays.'

'No, to hear farmers talk they have a hard time, but they're never short of a bob or two, as far as I can see.' Elaine didn't like where the conversation was going, so she invented the fact that she wanted to go back to the café to get an ice cream.

'Ice cream? In November?'

'Yes, why not? Ice cream is for all seasons, not just for hot summer days.'

'Good idea,' Thomas laughed, seeming to recover his good spirits. 'Let's go and have an ice cream. That will remind me of my childhood visits too.' And laughing, they returned to Puddleducks to deliberate over which flavour to have. The earlier difficulty seemed to have gone and, as Thomas was leaving, he said, '7.30 next Friday then?'

'Yes, I'll see you there,' replied Elaine, and he was off, leaving Elaine pondering about the way the conversation had changed. Well, time would tell, she decided, but told no one about what had happened.

The meal at the Spread Eagle was a success, with none of the former difficulties about the house. Elaine got to know more about Thomas and she told him more about herself. The house was not mentioned. It was the first of several dinner engagements at the Spread Eagle every Friday. He seemed to have quite a rigid routine in his life. Monday was washing day. Tuesday was darts night up at the Swan. Thursday was quiz night at the Brown Cow. Friday was shopping day. Saturday was football, either Burnley or Clitheroe United. He lived near the Clitheroe ground, so was a regular when Burnley weren't playing at home. Sunday he spent with his elderly mother, Agnes. She had recently moved into sheltered accommodation, so Thomas spent every Sunday with her, often taking her out for meals or taking treats for her into the home.

Elaine was quite content with how the relationship was going. Not too fast, no flashing lights and massive mood swings, no pressure to have sex, just a gentle friendship developing. Perhaps this was middle-aged love, Elaine reflected. It was enough to be going on with, and it was good to get dressed up on a Friday night. But Saturday lunches with the girls were hard work as they were constantly asking questions about him. At least when she took Daniel instead of the girls, he wasn't interested in her love life, and was more interested in what the cows or sheep were doing.

By the end of November, virtually all the work on the old church was finished. Ben, Martin, and Jake had excelled themselves. Even when Elaine had decided to have three wood burners in the lounge, sunroom and dining-kitchen installed, Ben was gracious and followed her instructions with as much patience as possible. Elaine had realised that perhaps if there was a power cut, she would be left with no heat, hot water, or lights, so it was a sensible addition in retrospect. The house looked good and exactly as she wanted it, but forlorn with no furniture. Elaine had been to Sowerbutts furniture shop in Clitheroe to get a long table and chairs to go in the sunroom, plus a smaller matching table and chairs for the dining-kitchen. She was sure she would need both for the Christmas dinner, which, now the house was nearly finished, looked like a distinct possibility.

The final tradesman to visit was the stained-glass window specialist. With Ben's suggestion, she'd gone to Pendle Stained Glass, and although it cost a lot of money, they said that the windows would last another hundred years with the work they had done. Elaine was relieved, and laughingly said, 'It'll see me out then?' to the workmen.

Kate and Elaine did the final shopping for the soft furnishings and carpets, blending the colour schemes of the bedrooms with the colours of the bathrooms. Elaine was delighted. As the plaster was new, she just had the downstairs walls colour-washed in neutral shades. Decorating could come at a later date, if ever, as Elaine liked it as it was. The carpet fitter arrived, and she was practically ready to move in.

Eventually a removal van arrived with all her furniture on the same day as the Internet provider arrived to fix the land line, but the two sets of workmen managed to keep out of each other's way, and complete their own jobs. Elaine had already got her winter clothes when the weather turned colder. It was a delight to see all her possessions that had been in storage for six months. The three double beds that she had in her old house were soon set up in the upstairs bedrooms, and made with the new bedding, and the blinds hung. Gill asked Elaine which bedroom she was going to use, and Elaine said that she hadn't decided yet, but needed a new bed for the downstairs bedroom, so it would definitely be an upstairs bedroom for now.

The three-piece suite looked perfect in her new large lounge. It had always looked a little cramped in her old house, but here she put one chair up in the pulpit, along with her computer desk. She couldn't wait to put all her books on the bookshelves, but that was a job for another day. Finding kitchen utensils was more important than putting books away. However, she did check the Internet. It would be such bliss not having to rely on Gill's Internet in future.

By December 15th, Elaine was ready to move in. She did a massive online shop, laughing to Gill that it would be good for the driver to find her house for all her future deliveries. Putting the food away in the cupboards, Elaine said that she would sleep there that night. Gill looked a little tearful, but said that it was a good idea.

'You've a Christmas dinner to plan, so you'll be better on your own. But I'm going to miss you. It's been lovely having you in my house for so long.'

'Yes, to say I only arranged to come for two weeks, it's been a long visit. But I'm not exactly far away from you. Near enough for you to pop in every day. And besides, you've got a houseful of people next door to you.'

'That's true. I'm very fortunate.' Gill rooted in her handbag and passed Elaine a little parcel. 'I saw this in Dawson's, so bought it for you as a housewarming present.'

Elaine opened it and found a small-heart shaped sign saying, 'Elaine's Kitchen'.

'Oh, thank you. That's perfect,' Elaine said, as she hung the sign up on the cupboard door handle. 'I'll put it up properly tomorrow. Now I'd better come back to your house and collect the rest of my stuff.' The two friends walked to the bungalow and eventually Elaine was ready. She piled her stuff in the car and, hugging Gill, she made a quick exit before any tears started.

After she had put all her stuff in her new house, Elaine locked the door and looked round. Home at last - and then it happened again. The deep feeling of peace washed over her, making her feel serenely happy and somehow cherished, as if the house were loving her. Laughing at her foolishness, Elaine put the kettle on and made herself a good cup of tea. Always the answer to any feelings she had. But she couldn't deny it. She knew she had come home.

Chapter 12

Waking early next morning, Elaine wondered for a moment where she was and then remembered. She was home. How good that felt! In the end she'd chosen the grey bedroom, which was the first one on the upstairs corridor. The staircase came up from the front porch and the corridor went along the back of the house, so that all the bedrooms had a south-facing aspect. During the build she'd thought of them as bedroom one, two and three, but now she preferred to call them by their chosen colour scheme. She would sleep in the grey bedroom for a couple of weeks, then try the fawn bedroom, then the white bedroom. Elaine wanted to see which one she was more comfortable in and which had the best view. They all looked out onto the main road, but there seemed to be a different vista with each room.

Elaine went downstairs and put the kettle on, going to the front door to see if the milkman had been. Greenbank Farm didn't deliver milk, but a neighbour of theirs did, and Elaine had arranged to have her milk delivered, wanting to reduce her plastic use and keep local people in jobs. She picked up the bottle and was going inside when she noticed a plant by the wall of the porch. It was a small pot of hyacinths. She picked it up and took it inside, trying to think where it was best to place the pot, but also wondering where they had come from. Probably Gill or Liz, she suspected. Last night Elaine had ordered a flower arrangement online to be delivered to Gill as a thank you for having stayed so long. It was to be delivered today. It was going to be a Christmas arrangement, which she hoped would last throughout the whole of the festive season.

Her first task was to set the kitchen to rights, and then she started making lists of anything extra that she would need for the Christmas dinner. It was soon lunchtime and, after a quick sandwich, Elaine carried on with her jobs. There was a knock at the door mid-afternoon, but before Elaine got there, Gill was walking in. She ran up to Elaine and hugged her.

'Thank you for the flowers. They're beautiful, but you shouldn't have sent them.'

'Why not? You deserve them.'

'But it's such an expensive time of year for flowers.'

'You're worth it. No good sending them in February when I want to thank you today. By the way, thanks for the hyacinths. They were from you, weren't they?'

'Hyacinths? Not from me.'

'Perhaps they were from Liz.'

'No. She's sent you a cake. Oh, no! I've left it in the car. I'll just go and get it,' and off she ran outside again.

'That's strange,' said Elaine, when Gill returned, putting the cake on the central island. 'I wonder who they are from then? I was sure it was you.'

'Perhaps they're from Thomas?'

'No, he wouldn't have just left them there. He doesn't seem to want to come here yet anyway.'

'Perhaps you've got a secret admirer,' laughed Gill.

'Chance would be a fine thing. I've been so busy this last month I wouldn't recognise a secret admirer if I tripped up over him.'

'Well, you'll probably find out later. I'm on my way to Clitheroe; do you want anything?'

'No, despite the massive online shop I had delivered yesterday, I've done another one today for delivery on the 23rd December, for all the other things I'll need but can't get until the last minute. It's a good job that I bought a long table and loads of chairs, isn't it - making that rash promise to have Christmas dinner here!'

'We can do it at the farmhouse if it's going to be too much,' offered Gill.

'No, I want to do it here. Are we going to be eight, with Liz's mum? Or has Tim deigned to come?'

'Oh, I knew I'd something to tell you. Yes, Tim's coming and he's bringing a significant other! So, we'll be ten now.'

'Significant other? Who is it? Do you know?'

'Someone from work, that's all he would tell me.'

'Male or female?'

'You know Tim; he didn't say.'

'Curiouser and curiouser. Just wondering what type of table present to give them. Have to be a unisex one then,' laughed Elaine. Christmas dinner table presents had been something that Kath and Tom had always done for Elaine, and ever since she'd visited Gill's for Christmas, she'd done the same and it had become quite a tradition now.

The two friends speculated for a while as to whom it could be. Tim had been badly hurt when he was a young man by a girl that he was desperately in love with, and had never seemed interested in girls after that. He had never mentioned a partner of any kind before; he always said he was too busy at work.

'All will be revealed on Christmas Day. We'll just have to be patient,' said Elaine, mentally thinking if she had a present that would suit either sex.

'That's true. They're hoping to arrive about 12 noon. Will that be okay?'

'That's good. I plan to have the starters at half one, so that's perfect.'

'Tim said "thank you," by the way.'

'What for?'

'For asking, and not minding that he's bringing someone.'

'The daft thing. We're just so glad to have him come, aren't we? He's missed so many Christmases before. Always going skiing instead.'

'I don't think he liked being around happy families.'

'His loss, then.'

'True. And is Thomas adamant he isn't coming?'

'Yes, he always spends Christmas with his mother, which is very commendable, especially as she is in sheltered accommodation now.'

'But didn't you say she could come here?'

'Of course, but he said she wouldn't want that. Not on Boxing Day either; I suggested that too. But he is coming to the housewarming party on New Year's Day.'

'Good. I can't believe I'm the only one who hasn't seen him yet and I'm your best friend!'

'I'm going to visit his mother with him on Christmas Eve, though.'

'Ooh, going to meet the mother! Is that the next step?'

'Don't be daft, Gill. She wanted to meet me.'

'Mmm, probably wondering who this floozie is who's going out with her precious son.'

'I don't think so. Just curious. I've bought her a food hamper. I wasn't sure what to get her but wanted something that wouldn't be over the top but would be useful.'

'Sounds good to me. Well, I'd better get going or there'll be nowhere to park in Clitheroe, especially at this time of year. I'll see you later.'

Elaine ran upstairs to her white bedroom, where she had all the presents ready-wrapped in a wardrobe, but where she also kept all the things that she bought throughout the year, just in case. She selected a box of pink candles - always a safe bet for ladies - and a men's toiletries set, and wrapped them up for the significant other that Tim was bringing, leaving blank labels on them so that she could quickly add a name on Christmas Day.

In the evening, Elaine sat in her pulpit, making lists of what she had to do, and in what order, for the Christmas meal. She'd not closed any of her blinds preferring to let the light stream out. Suddenly, she noticed a flash of light outside. Putting her list down, she went into the sunroom to see if she could see anyone. The light was in the graveyard. Putting her coat and boots on and grabbing a torch, Elaine ran over to the graveyard, but there was no one there. Whoever it was had gone, probably when they heard Elaine opening the big front door. Elaine suspected that it was Harvey who'd been there but couldn't be sure. But what she did notice, by the light of her torch, was that both the family grave and the next-door grave had hyacinths planted in the graves. Perhaps the secret hyacinth-giver was Harvey after all. Elaine returned slowly to the house, reflecting that perhaps Harvey had made an effort to reach out to her because of her gifts of gardening tools. She really hoped so, but wouldn't hold her breath.

Next morning, Elaine was surprised by a delivery man arriving at her door. He commented on what a good job Elaine had made at the church, which pleased her. He asked Elaine to sign for a large box that puzzled her as she hadn't ordered anything. Once she got the box inside and opened it, she realised what it was. It was a case of 12 bottles of wine. Six red and six white. They would be from her ex-husband Peter's vineyard. He sent them every Christmas without fail. Must be his guilt complex, Elaine had decided long ago, but she was surprised she'd got them this year as she hadn't let him know her change of address. But obviously someone had known it. It was probably his parents, whom she still kept in touch with. At least she wouldn't run out of wine this year, as she now had plenty.

Christmas Eve came round too quickly for Elaine. At lunchtime, she went into Clitheroe to meet with Thomas and his mother. It amused Elaine that

Thomas seemed quite nervous about it all. But Agnes was a delight and she and Elaine hit it off straightaway. Agnes loved the hamper and gave Elaine a small parcel as well. They spent a couple of hours together, but then Elaine said that she would have to go as she had a lot of preparing to do. Wishing her a 'Happy Christmas', she left the house, Thomas following her and giving her a small parcel as well.

'Not to be opened until tomorrow,' he said, as he pecked her on the cheek. Elaine handed over her present for Thomas. It was a signed copy of a new book about Burnley Football Club, which Elaine had been delighted to find online. Although she was tired by teatime, she still made time to go to Midnight Mass at St Hubert's RC church further up the village. It was a tradition that many of the local farmers did, even if they never darkened the door at any other time of year apart from Harvest Thanksgiving, of course. The Robinsons were all going and they walked up together. It was the first time that Elaine had ever been in the church, and she secretly thought that it wasn't as grand as 'her' church had been. Before 1861, the Catholics had no church in Dunsop Bridge, and had worshipped in the private family chapel in Thorneyholme Hall, at the other end of the village.

The Towneley family of Towneley Hall in Burnley, who also owned Thorneyholme Hall in Dunsop Bridge, had built the church for the village, as well as the village school where all Gill's children had gone and where Kirsty had left last summer. The money for the church and school buildings had come from a spectacular win at the Epsom Derby by the horse Kettlewell, which was owned by the Towneley family.

Although not used to the Catholic tradition, having been brought up as a Methodist in her childhood, Elaine was over-awed by the service. The ancient carols, the choir singing, and the timeless message of the baby Jesus being born and laid in a manger because there was no room at the inn, moved her as they had never moved her before. When she got home, she looked at her stained-glass windows and thought about Jesus' mother, who had borne the child in a stable, but then had to see him die on a cross, even though he was innocent. Jesus' eyes seemed to pierce right through her, asking her for an answer, but she wasn't sure what the question was. Elaine turned away, leaving the matter unsettled, as she knew that she had to be up early to make the dinner. Just in case, she put the turkey in and set the timer on the oven, and then went to bed to sleep fitfully.

Next morning, Elaine was up early and opened her presents from Thomas and Agnes. They'd obviously colluded, as Thomas' present was a lovely silver necklace with an intricate pendant, and Agnes' present was a bracelet to match with a smaller pendant. Elaine put them on instantly, admiring them in the mirror before hurrying back to the kitchen. Gill arrived soon after ten. Elaine had already set the table and prepared all the vegetables, so Gill whipped the cream for the sherry trifle, then prepared the cheese board and biscuits, putting them all in the large utility room, which in its previous life had been the vicar's vestry. All the other puddings were defrosting, mostly in the large fridge that was in there, apart from the Christmas pudding which was in the microwave, ready to be warmed up and set alight at the appropriate moment. The fridge also contained the prawn cocktail starters, which Elaine had made first thing that morning.

The mulled wine and the two soups were in the pans ready to be warmed up, and croutons were in small bowls on the table. Elaine had cheated with the croutons, buying them ready-made to save time. In fact, she'd done many things to save time, as moving a few days before Christmas had been stressful enough without having to make her first Christmas dinner in many years. By half-past 11 all was ready, so Gill and Elaine had a glass of mulled wine and sat in the lounge resting before the onslaught. Gill's phone pinged and she read the text, which was from Liz.

'*Female called Lindsay, we're setting off now.*'

Gill read it to Elaine, who ran through to the sunroom, found the female present, wrote Lindsay on it, and ran upstairs with the male present. Giggling to themselves, they were sitting down in the lounge when everyone arrived.

Drawing Liz's mum Jennifer into the lounge, Gill gave her a glass of mulled wine, bringing a tray round for everyone. Lindsay was introduced and shyly thanked Elaine for asking her. She presented her with a poinsettia plant as a thank you. Elaine was very touched. Lindsay stood close to Tim, Elaine noticed, as if she was frightened to be away from him. But to be introduced to a whole new family on Christmas Day was daunting to even the bravest person.

In her planning, Elaine had envisaged gentle chats before starting the meal, but Tim and Ben were having none of it. Tim wanted to be taken all over the house, which he remembered had been a derelict wreck the last time he saw it. So there had to be a grand tour for everyone, as they all wanted to have their say about their part in the refurbishment. Tim and Ben kept up a steady banter, with Tim criticising the finish or a window fitting, and Ben rising to the bait and asking when was the last time that Tim had done any DIY? Lindsay stared at Ben and Tim making fun of each other, as if she were seeing a new side of Tim, which she probably was. No longer the uptight lawyer when he was back at home with his brother.

Eventually about half-past one, Elaine managed to get them all to sit down at the table to open their presents, and was going over to get the prawn cocktails, when Tim said he'd like to say something first. Everybody looked at Tim, but were shocked when he got down on one knee next to Lindsay and proposed to her. There was silence all round the room; Elaine wasn't sure who was the more shocked, between Gill and Ben. Lindsay blushed and whispered 'Yes', and then there was a riot of cheering going on.

Tim got his work satchel out. Elaine had seriously thought he was going to do some work whilst at the Christmas dinner table when he arrived, but now he drew out a small ring box and a bottle of champagne. The ring was a perfect cluster of diamonds and it fitted perfectly on her finger. Gill went and got clean glasses to make a toast. Lindsay was looking adoringly at Tim and he leaned over and whispered, 'Now you know why I said you had to wait for your Christmas present.'

'Could I go and ring my Mum and Dad?' she asked Tim. 'Would they all mind?' but Ben overheard her.

'Of course, we won't mind. The prawn cocktails won't go cold. Go and tell them the news.' Lindsay smiled her thanks to Ben and slipped out of the front door with her phone. She was soon back.

'They knew, Tim! How long had you been planning this?' Lindsay asked.

'Well, I had to ask your Dad first before I asked you.'

'Get you, Tim,' Ben laughed. 'I didn't ask Liz's Dad. I just hoped he'd say yes if Liz did,'

'Lindsay's Dad is my business partner. I have to keep him sweet.'

'Oh yes?' teased Ben, 'Marrying the boss' daughter are you? Very nice.'

'Lindsay is a partner in the business as well,' Tim replied in defence. Gill saved the day by handing out the champagne glasses and a toast was made to the happy couple, even Kirsty being allowed some champagne.

Straight after the prawn cocktails were eaten, the soup followed; a choice of Elaine's famous white onion soup and Liz's carrot and coriander. Most people had both! Then they had a breather whilst the first two courses went down, and Elaine managed to thank Tim for all his conveyancing work. Liz had taken Lindsay over to the lounge and was chatting to the girls.

'Do you think it'll be long before you get married?' Elaine asked Tim.

'No, it'll be a very quick wedding. Lindsay was left at the altar when she was 22. She had a nervous breakdown and took years to get over it. I've had to be very gentle in my wooing. So, I don't want her wondering if it's going to happen again. Pity this church isn't still consecrated. We could have done it here today. No need for a reception because you've provided the meal.

'Don't be such a cheapskate,' laughed Elaine. 'Besides, her parents aren't here.'

'Oh, yes, that would have been a problem. No, we'll probably have a quiet wedding quite soon, although her mum might have other ideas. But whatever we do, your invitation will be in the post soon. Can't get married without my godmother there,' Tim said, as he hugged her close.

'Thanks Tim. That means a lot to me. And now I'd better see to the next course,' said Elaine, before she filled up in public and made a fool of herself.

The turkey and roast dinner were done to perfection, and the banter round the table was even better. Kate, Anna, and Kirsty were all vying to be bridesmaids, until Liz had to tell them off. She suggested that Lindsay might have loads of sisters or cousins or nieces, and the three girls would be well down on the list. But Lindsay said that she would be delighted if they were all bridesmaids, as she was an only daughter with only boy cousins. Her best friend Victoria would be her dame of honour, but she would definitely need bridesmaids. The three girls were delighted, Kirsty hoping that she could wear pink.

After the main course was eaten, Ben and Tim went to do the milking, Anna saying she'd painted her nails so couldn't help today. Tim said he didn't think he'd lost his touch, so he'd help. Lindsay went too, to see what living on a farm was like. Elaine lent her a pair of Wellingtons, rather than get her lovely posh shoes dirty. Everyone else lazed around, Liz's mum falling asleep briefly. Elaine was envious. She could do with a quick nap herself, but not when she was the host. She'd certainly sleep tonight and was glad that she hadn't had a large family, as the thought of preparing this amount of food every day would have killed her. During this brief respite, she went and rang Thomas to wish him and Agnes a Happy Christmas and thank them for their presents, which she was wearing already. Thomas thanked her for the book, which was obviously a success, to hear him enthuse about it.

By half-past six, everyone was back, and so they had the dessert course. The flaming pudding was brought in and everyone had a tiny slice smothered with brandy sauce. After that it were the other puddings; a choice of trifle, sticky toffee pudding, Eton Mess, and hazelnut roulade. Even though everyone said they couldn't eat another thing, when Elaine brought the cheese and biscuits tray out, they all drifted to the table, helping themselves and nibbling on the grapes.

By nine o'clock Tim said that they had to be going, as they weren't staying overnight. Fortunately, apart from the champagne toast, Tim hadn't had anything else to drink, so was able to drive home. Nobody else in the room would have been capable of driving, Elaine thought to herself. Lindsay wanted to get back to her parents, as they were having a family party for Boxing Day. Elaine got their coats, and Lindsay thanked her for such a lovely day and commented on what a nice family they were. Elaine agreed. She thought that they were the best family in the world, she added to Lindsay.

The rest of the family stayed until nearly midnight, but then all walked home together, as Liz's mum was staying at the farm that night. Elaine quickly tided up and set the dishwasher on. She'd sort the rest of the room out tomorrow, she yawned, as she went up to bed and was asleep as soon as her head hit the pillow.

Boxing Day dawned and Elaine went over to Gill's around lunchtime. They always had a tradition of a Jacob's Join on Boxing Day, a sort of 'eat up what was left from the day before' sort of meal, but always with a big dish of chips instead of roast potatoes.

Daniel, Martin, and Helen came over in the camper van for Boxing Day. They'd been down to Cheshire to their eldest daughter's for their Christmas meal, but stayed overnight in the camper van in Elaine's back garden, despite

Elaine offering them all beds for the night. Although people said at first that they couldn't eat a thing, the food soon started disappearing, and there was much laughter between going out to see to the animals.

The days between Christmas and New Year passed quickly and on New Year's Eve, there was a party at the village hall, where games and challenges and a karaoke took place until midnight. Then the traditional countdown to midnight occurred followed by everyone singing 'Auld Lang Syne'. After much kissing and well wishing, everyone slowly drifted back to their own homes, Elaine reflecting how happy she was to be living in this village near her friend. She also wondered what this New Year would bring in her life in her new home, and how things would develop with Thomas.

Chapter 13

Elaine couldn't have much of a lie-in despite the late night, as she'd got a housewarming party to organise. Even though she thought she'd never need any more food again, after all the shopping she'd done before Christmas, another pile of food had been delivered the day before. She was just providing a buffet for the party, but Elaine thought that it was probably harder work than making a Christmas dinner. Liz and Gill were bringing homemade savoury and fruit pies, but Elaine seemed to spend hours putting things in dishes or trays, defrosting savouries and sweet dishes alike, and making endless sandwiches with different breads and fillings.

On reflection, perhaps New Year's Day was a daft idea for a party as a lot of people would be hung over, but she wanted to start the New Year showing off her new home, and thanking people who had been involved in her decision. She'd invited five of her work colleagues and their families, all Gill's family, Tim, Lindsay, and Lindsay's parents, the ladies from the WI with their partners and children, the staff from Puddleducks, Dot, Angie and Mags and their partners from her old tennis club, and Helen, Martin and Daniel. Both her goddaughters came as well, Katie bringing her daughter, Libby, with her, and Charlotte bringing her parents. Also, Dawn Stuttard and her husband had been invited, as Elaine had promised when she signed for the house. She'd even left an invitation on the grave for Harvey and his granddad, but hadn't received a reply, not surprisingly.

Thomas was the first to arrive and so Elaine was able to take him round the house to show him how it had been converted. He seemed suitably impressed, but said little. The house always seemed a stumbling block between them. He'd never asked to come and see the house when she first moved in and Elaine didn't really understand his reticence. But never mind, she reflected, he's here today.

Gill, Liz, and the girls arrived next, bringing baskets full of food, immediately starting to set things out on the tables, after being introduced to Thomas. Elaine gave Thomas the job of sorting out the drinks table and getting the glasses ready. Suddenly, everybody seemed to arrive at once. The doors from the kitchen into the lounge had been propped open and the doors into the sunroom were also open. It made the whole area enormous and people were milling around in small groups, finding out how they knew their host. Elaine lost count of how many guided tours of the house she had done, everybody proclaiming what a marvellous house it was, and admiring the stained-glass windows and the pulpit.

Kirsty made herself Thomas' assistant and, although checked up on occasionally by Gill, she behaved herself perfectly, whisking away empty glasses and washing them up, which amazed both Elaine, Gill, and Liz. Washing up was a chore Kirsty avoided if at all possible. Despite the vast amounts of drink that Elaine had bought, much of it was left, as many guests were either slightly hungover from last night or were driving. Only her friends from the old tennis club were staying; everyone else was driving. She was glad she'd ordered lots of different non-alcoholic drinks, as they proved very popular.

Elaine noticed that Thomas and Gill seemed to have hit it off, as they spent quite a lot of time talking together, for which Elaine was grateful. She was glad that her oldest friend and her newest friend were getting on. It would make life easier in the future, she decided, feeling slightly mawkish through a haze of pinot grigio.

Eventually, by seven o'clock, people started drifting away, saying that they were working next day or had other commitments. Elaine thanked each person for coming and also thanked them for the plethora of gifts that she had received. There were beautiful flower arrangements and plant pots, and Elaine was amazed how people could have managed to get them on New Year's Day. There were also gift vouchers, garden vouchers, chocolates, photo frames, and even pictures. Elaine was totally overwhelmed by the number of gifts she received. All she wanted was to have all her old and new friends together to celebrate her house. When they'd all gone, including Thomas, who had accepted an invitation to go and visit the farm with Gill, it just left the tennis gang. Elaine put the kettle on, finding that everyone wanted a cup of tea or coffee.

When they were all sat down in the lounge, Dot asked Elaine why she hadn't joined a tennis club, and the others all nodded.

'I've just haven't got round to it. I know that sounds trivial, but life has been so busy.'

'But you loved your tennis,' said Mags.

'I know, but I was living with Gill until just before Christmas, when I moved in here, and she hates tennis. I did get the name of the tennis club in Whalley when I went to visit Whalley Abbey.'

'Oh, you've got the name of it,' laughed John, Angie's husband. 'That's a start I suppose. And how long is it since you got the name of it?'

Elaine blushed. 'Er, must have been last summer. But then I went on holiday and then Gill moved into the bungalow and then I'd to plan . . .'

'Enough,' interrupted Angie. 'All excuses. Now, my girl, I want you to make a New Year's Resolution that you will join the tennis club without fail before Easter.'

'I will, I promise. I'll have more time now I've moved in here.'

'Mmm, a likely story,' said Dot.

'I've got an idea,' said Mags. 'You have to promise to text us a picture of your membership card by Easter or pay a forfeit.'

'What forfeit?' asked Elaine.

'Well, we'll think about that when you don't send it, but it'll cost you,' warned Bill, Mags' husband.

'Okay, I promise I'll join. That's my New Year's resolution,' replied Elaine.

'Who owns those fields at the back of the house?' Bill asked. 'I noticed them when we were parking the car.'

'I do,' said Elaine. 'Not just a house and a graveyard; I own two big fields as well. And I'm not allowed to sell them because of a covenant. But that's good because I won't be pestered by property developers. That would really ruin my home.'

'And do you think you might run a B & B?' asked Dot.

'I might, but I've not given it serious thought yet.'

'Well,' said Dot, 'you could build a tennis court on one of the fields and then advertise B & B for tennis enthusiasts.'

'Brilliant idea. I'd love a holiday with a tennis court built in,' said Mags.

Elaine groaned. 'You've got my whole life planned out. I haven't decided to do B & B yet.'

'But we'd all come and pay to visit you. Wouldn't we?' Dot asked the others, who all nodded their agreement.

'I could put in a stable and a swimming pool as well,' Elaine suggested sarcastically.

'Even better,' said Bill. 'That'd really bring the punters in. Now, if you don't mind, I'm off to bed. Where are we sleeping, Elaine?'

'You and Mags are in the grey bedroom, Dot and Tommy in the fawn bedroom, and Angie and John in the white bedroom. You'll find all your suitcases in the relevant rooms.'

'Where are you sleeping then?' asked Mags.

'In the downstairs bedroom. I'll say goodnight to you all.' They all chorused goodnight and went upstairs. Tidying away the drinks, Elaine thought about how much she'd missed their company, and hoped they would visit again whether it was to a B & B or not. And actually, the tennis court would be a good idea. She went into her downstairs bedroom and, as she went to bed, she was wondering how much a tennis court would cost, and if there was a local man who might supply one.

Next morning, after a hearty full English breakfast, her guests all left by midday. Perhaps B & B wasn't a bad idea after all, because people would go again the morning after, leaving the rest of the day to herself. She would have to think about it carefully. It wasn't as if she needed the money, but it would be something to do which she could pick up and put down as her life dictated.

A few days later, Gill came round for a coffee and a discussion about the housewarming party. Both agreed it had been a resounding success.

'You seemed to be getting on well with Thomas?'

'Yes,' replied Gill. 'He's really nice. He's coming round for tea next Thursday.'

'For tea? On a Thursday? What about his quiz night?'

'I don't know anything about a quiz night; he just said he could come.'

'What's he coming for?' Elaine couldn't help asking.

'He just said that he loved the farm and would like to come again. I felt the least I could do was ask him for his tea. Do you want to come too?'

'No, that's all right. I was just wondering, that's all.'

'Oh, come, it'll help the talking. I might not know what to talk about.'

'You? Not know what to talk about? That'll be a first!'

'Cheeky! But do come, I'd feel happier about that.'

'Okay, I'll come,' agreed Elaine, although slightly perturbed that Thomas hadn't mentioned that he was going. Come to think about it, he hadn't texted or phoned for a few days. She wasn't sure what to make of that but decided that she wouldn't say anything to Thomas about his invitation and see what happened on Thursday.

Elaine arrived after Thomas on the Thursday teatime, partly because she'd been waiting for a delivery to come. When she got in Gill's bungalow, Thomas was sitting comfortably by the fire in the lounge, with a cup of tea in his hand, looking very much at home. He was visibly shaken when Elaine entered.

'Hi, Thomas, how are you? Not heard from you for a few days,' Elaine said brightly.

'Hello, Elaine. Sorry I haven't been in touch. I've been sorting things out at home.'

'Oh? What things? So much that you couldn't text me?'

'I've been sorting out the spare bedroom and painting it,' he said lamely.

'Are you expecting a visitor?'

'Not really. It just needed doing.'

'No quiz tonight?'

'Didn't want to go tonight.'

'I've never known you miss before.'

'I don't have to go,' Thomas replied petulantly. But then Gill came in the room and announced that tea was ready if they wanted to come into the kitchen-diner.

After that Thomas seemed to totally ignore Elaine and talked constantly to Gill, asking her lots of questions about the farm, the difficulties facing farming, and the need to diversify. Elaine didn't know why Gill had asked her to come as she never got a word in edgeways, with Thomas domineering the conversation. Eventually Elaine had had enough and got up, saying that she had things to do tonight and was going. Gill jumped up and asked her not to go, but she noticed that Thomas didn't ask her to stay, which made her even more determined to go. Even when she left the room, Thomas just said 'goodbye'. No offer to walk her home or that he'd be in touch.

Elaine walked home with a heavy heart. What was Thomas playing at? He'd seemed so much happier when he came to the housewarming party, and she thought that it had started a new phase in their relationship. Now that he'd been to the house, she thought perhaps he might consider staying over occasionally. So, what had gone wrong? And why was he surprised that she was at Gill's tonight? Did he think that she and Gill never spoke about anything? Did he not want her to know he was going to Gill's? And why had Gill invited him really? Was she thinking of a relationship with Thomas? And what was Thomas' sudden interest in farming all about? Would she and Thomas be going to the Spread Eagle tomorrow as usual? They'd booked a table just before the New Year. Sleep was a long time coming that night as Elaine tossed and turned in her bed, going over and over again what had happened, and taking a long look at her relationship with Thomas.

One question was answered the next morning when she got a text from Thomas saying that he felt he didn't want to go to the Spread Eagle that night, and would like to take a break whilst he thought about their relationship. Elaine was furious. What a cheek! She typed five texts, but deleted them all without sending them. Instead, she waited all day before answering. Let him sweat about having to cancel the booking, she thought. In the end she sent the text about 6.30pm.

That's fine by me. Cancel the dinner. In fact, I'll help you. Don't spend time thinking about our relationship. Let's just call it a day. Goodbye.

Then she deleted his number out of her phone, got herself a large glass of wine, and took herself to bed early to read and distract her mind from what had just happened.

Having spent a fitful night tossing and turning, Elaine got up early and went for a long walk past the water workers' cottages. It was a crisp morning with a slight breeze and it helped clear her thoughts. In a strange way, she was glad that she'd ended it with Thomas. On reflection, she realised that they had been going nowhere. There was just something missing in their relationship. She wasn't heartbroken, but what really hurt was that he seemed to be moving in on Gill whilst he was still going out with her. What was he playing at? And what was Gill playing at? Was there a spark between them? Could she see her best friend falling in love with her ex-boyfriend? They'd never fallen out over a man before, reflected Elaine, and she didn't really want to fall out with her now. That decided her, so she called in at the bungalow before she went home, but Gill was out. She would have to wait. What made it worse was that Thomas hadn't even bothered to reply. 'Good riddance', she shouted to the air as she dug furiously into where her vegetable bed was going to be, and kept herself busy digging all day. But Gill hadn't rung either, which upset her.

On Sunday, Elaine had promised to go to Liz and Ben's for tea, but she knew she had to talk to Gill first, so she went early to the bungalow.

'Hi, only me,' Elaine shouted as she went through the door, but Gill was just finishing a phone conversation.

'Hi, Elaine. How are you?' Gill asked nervously.

'I'm fine. Shouldn't I be?'

'I just wondered.'

'Were you on the phone to Thomas?' Just looking at Gill's guilt-ridden face, Elaine knew that she had been. 'Oh, don't worry about me. I don't mind. Thomas and I are history.'

'I'm sorry Elaine. I didn't intend anything to happen. He just seemed to pester me about the farm and wanted to come again.'

'Yes, he was very shocked when I turned up to your house for tea. I don't know what his game is, but you're welcome to him. I've thought long and hard about it overnight and he made it easy in the end. He said he wanted to think about our relationship,'

'What did you say?'

'That I'd thought about it and it was ended.'

'What did he say?'

'Oh, he hasn't deigned to answer me. You are welcome to him. I just hope he treats you better than he did me.'

'I'm not going out with him.'

'No, not yet perhaps, but he's ringing you. Was that just to thank you for the tea?'

'No, not really.'

'Well, what for then?' But Gill seemed reluctant to answer.

'He wants me to go to his house to advise him about his garden,' she said eventually.

'His house? My, he's working fast with you. I was never invited to his house. Is advising on his garden the same as viewing his etchings? And when did you become a gardening expert?'

'Please, Elaine, don't be angry with me.'

'I'm not. I'm just angry that I wasted all this time with him before I found out what he's really like. Be careful, Gill. I don't want you to get hurt.'

'And I don't want to fall out with you. You are more important to me than he is. I can't lose our friendship. You're what's sustained me since John died.'

'Oh, Gill, even if you have a full relationship and even marry him, you won't lose my friendship. Just be careful.'

'I will, I promise.' They both hugged each other but were interrupted by a hammering on the door.

'Mum says if you don't come soon we're starting tea without you,' yelled Anna. 'Come on, I'm starving!' The two friends laughed and, closeness restored, walked across to the farmhouse, where Liz had prepared an excellent tea as usual.

A few weeks later, Gill came running round to the house with a letter for Elaine and was bubbling with excitement.

'It's an invite, but it's very secret.'

'What's a secret?' For one awful moment, Elaine thought that perhaps Gill and Thomas might be getting engaged or married. He seemed to be a regular visitor to the bungalow now, but Elaine always avoided going when he was around. And he was taking Gill to the Spread Eagle for dinner. On a Friday evening, of course!

'The wedding's a secret.' Oh, no, thought Elaine, she's going to marry him. Why am I so worried for her?

'Whose wedding?' she managed to ask.

'Tim and Lindsay's. Who else would it be?'

'Why is it a secret then? Don't we all know they're going to get married?'

'It's a secret because there are two dates.'

'Two dates? Why?' replied Elaine, even more confused.

'Well, because of how she was let down last time, Tim knew that she'd hate a big wedding and a long wait. So, he's pretending that they're getting married the first Saturday in July, but he's secretly booked a castle in Northumberland for the May Bank Holiday weekend. We're all going to be there, but only Lindsay will not know about the two dates. She'll think it's the July date, and the May holiday is just for them and her parents. But everything will be ready at the castle. They have a church in the grounds, so can get married there and have the reception in the castle. And the banns will have been read up there. Her mum will ensure that the wedding dress and all the hairdressers and make-up people come with them to the castle. Isn't it exciting? Can you believe that our Tim could be so romantic or so thoughtful?'

'That's amazing! What made him do it like this?'

'Last time, when she was jilted at the altar, it was a big society wedding in Manchester Cathedral. Most of the great and good of Manchester were there. So it made it even more humiliating for her.'

'Poor girl. I can't imagine how hard it was for her.'

'That's why Tim doesn't want her to have to go through that worry again. By the time she finds out about it, the wedding will be taking place and only the family and close friends will be there, which is what she wants. Even the pretend July wedding was going to be very small compared with her last wedding attempt. So, when are we going to get our wedding outfits?'

'Gracious, Gill. Give me a minute to take it all in. So, how do we answer the invitation?'

'You answer as if you're saying "yes" to the July event so that Lindsay won't suspect, but you know what's really happening and when the real date is.'

'Right. Got it. How long are we expected to be there?'

'The wedding is on the Saturday, but not until four pm, so we can travel up that day and stay over. Then we'll all go home after breakfast next day, and Lindsay and Tim will stay there for the week as a mini-moon. They've booked the real honeymoon for July so that Lindsay doesn't suspect. Great, isn't it?'

'He's really thought of everything, hasn't he?'

'Yes, so when are we going to Maureen Cookson's in Whalley? And Beryl's of course, for the matching shoes and handbags.'

'Let's not go until nearer the time as her spring collection might not have come in yet,' said Elaine.

'I bet it has, but we'll go and have a look soon anyway.'

'Good. We can go to Whalley Abbey at the same time. We'll probably need lunch after all that shopping.'

'Definitely. Must dash. Going to put my reply in the post straightaway. Do you want me to post yours?'

'Yes, you can do. Let me just do the reply. I assume they'll want cash for presents?'

'That's what they all seem to do now. Mind you, it's better than the three toasters and six clocks that John and I got, despite having a wedding list.' Gill grabbed the envelope from Elaine and rushed out of the door. 'Bye,' Gill shouted over her shoulder. Elaine replied, then laughed to herself at Gill's retreating back.

It was a relief to start getting into a new routine for Elaine, as she'd moved in so close to Christmas that life had been hectic. She was itching to make a start in the garden making her vegetable plot, but the ground was too hard, and it was snowing anyway. So, she satisfied herself with making plans for the vegetable beds and what she would grow, spending hours on the Internet and making lists of what she would need. She was practical enough to know that the hard digging was beyond her and she might need to get help, so she Googled to see if any gardeners were living in Dunsop Bridge, but didn't come up with any names. She would have to ask around at the farm or in the café. She'd already asked Frank if he was interested in doing any extra work, but all she got was a short reply.

'Don't do digging, only cutting grass,' he said in his terse voice. Quite a long sentence for Frank, Elaine considered after he'd gone.

One night she'd just made herself a cup of cocoa when she saw the familiar flashlight in the graveyard next door. Elaine didn't go out at first, but watched Harvey through the window. In the end, knowing he'd be frozen working in the snowy grave, Elaine made another cup of cocoa and took it outside to Harvey.

'I've brought you some cocoa,' she said quietly, proffering him the cup.

Harvey froze, obviously debating whether to run or stay. Slowly he looked at Elaine, nodded at her and took the cup. Without speaking, he sipped the cocoa. Eventually Elaine asked him to come inside to drink it and she turned away towards the house. Surprisingly, Harvey followed her into the house and sat right on the end of a chair as if poised to flee if she came near him. Elaine remained in silence letting him look round the kitchen-diner.

'Do you like how I've done the house?' Elaine eventually asked. Harvey nodded, but then drained his cup and hurried out of the house.

'Come anytime for a drink,' Elaine called after him, but he was gone.

Elaine sat back on her chair, thinking about Harvey. That had been a real breakthrough tonight. He still hadn't spoken, but he had come in the house. Probably either too cold or just plain nosy, Elaine decided, but felt secretly pleased that there had been a slight shift in their relationship.

For the next few visits Elaine would make him a drink, but Harvey would not speak beyond nodding or shaking his head in answer to her occasional questions. Elaine learnt to ask closed questions which only required a nod or shake of head for him to answer. He seemed to enjoy being in her home without being pestered to make conversation.

One day, when Elaine was making her lunch, there was a massive hammering on the front door. Thinking it could only be a major emergency, Elaine rushed to open the door. A wild looking man stood on the doorstep.

'What do you think your game is with my grandson?' he screamed.

'I'm sorry, I don't know you. What grandson?' asked a bewildered and somewhat frightened Elaine, grasping her phone tightly in her hand, trying to decide whether to ring the police.

'Don't come the innocent with me; I've heard about people like you. Making up to children to lure them into your house for evil purposes.' He was getting increasingly exasperated and frothing at the mouth, waving his hands about erratically. Elaine was getting more frightened by the minute.

'I'm going to ring the police,' Elaine said as calmly as she could, despite her heart pounding so loud she was sure he could hear it. But as she said those words, the man collapsed against the wall gasping for breath.

'Are you all right? Can I get you a drink of water?' The man shook his head.

'Please come and sit down for a moment?' Elaine asked, wondering whether this was wise with such an angry man, or someone who was totally unbalanced, but it seemed as if all the shouting had taken the stuffing out of him. 'I assure you I have no designs on any young man whatever you might say.' That seemed to make the man look up at her and stare into her eyes, making her feel uncomfortable. But then he spoke.

'Why are you giving Harvey drinks then?' Light dawned on Elaine. This must be Harvey's grumpy granddad.

'Because he keeps coming to the grave and it's cold. No other reason, as you hinted at,' replied Elaine, with a direct glance into his angry face.

'I'm sorry. I have to be careful. The lad hasn't been right and I don't want him taken advantage of. Fred Baxter by the way,'

'Elaine Barnes. I assure you, I'll never take advantage of him. I'm just grateful that he has a drink of something hot these cold nights. And I'm pleased at the way he's been looking after other graves in the graveyard'

'Has he? I thought he just looked after ours.'

'No, he's planted bulbs in the next grave, which is very old - so old that the names have worn off so we don't know whose grave it is.'

'That's alright then, if he's only coming here to get warm. I'll be off then. Bye.' And to Elaine's amazement, the man walked off, as calm as anything.

Elaine went back into the dining-kitchen and put the kettle on. Even if he hadn't wanted a drink, she certainly needed one now. What a strange experience! Was he hinting at her being a paedophile? How ridiculous. The man must be slightly mad to think that. Poor Harvey, she reflected, having to live with him. She picked up her phone to ring Gill, but decided not to. She would tell her eventually, but for now she wanted to think about how to handle this herself.

Not expecting Harvey to come that night after his granddad's débâcle, Elaine locked up early but at the usual time she saw the flashlight crossing the graveyard, so made him a drink and went across to call him in. Harvey complied and sat in his usual silence, holding the cup of cocoa.

Just as Elaine was checking a text on her phone, she heard a noise.

'He blames me.'

'Pardon?' asked a shocked Elaine when she realised that Harvey had spoken.

'Granddad blames me. Should've been me that died.'

Elaine's heart contracted in her chest. What an awful thing for a grieving young man to live with. 'Is that what he says to you?'

Harvey shook his head. 'No, it's in his eyes.' But then he jumped up and ran out into the night. Elaine ran after him and told him that he could come here anytime to talk, but he'd disappeared by the time she got outside.

Elaine came back into the house and sat down, thinking about what Harvey had said, and wondering how she could help him. She already knew that she couldn't rush him with anything, but would have to move slowly. However, she wanted to do whatever she could to help him get over this tragedy and not feel the blame for his grandmother's death.

Harvey didn't come for the next three nights and Elaine was worried that she'd said too much. But on the fourth night he came again, and sat in silence as he had previously, only saying 'thank you' as he left. But at least he had come again, thought Elaine gratefully. This pattern continued for several weeks. A few nights without a visit, then a silent visit again. Spring was coming and the nights were getting lighter. Eventually the clocks went forward and the nights were even lighter, although Harvey was still hardly speaking,

Elaine started telling him that she wanted to make some vegetable beds, but she couldn't find a gardener to help her and asked if he knew anyone. Harvey looked solemnly at her, and then quietly said, 'I'll help you.' Elaine's heart soared, and she thanked him and showed him all her plans for the garden. Slowly, progress was made, both with her vegetable patch and her relationship with Harvey. He had started going to school more regularly and, whilst Elaine didn't claim that she had been the reason for it, she felt that he was making progress through the slow path of grieving. Certainly, gardening seemed to help him and ease his troubles. He had even started coming to Elaine's for tea on a Wednesday before starting his evening gardening. She'd asked Fred to come too, but he'd declined; more importantly, he was happy to let Harvey come. He was probably glad to get Harvey out from under his feet, thought Elaine. Only time would tell. And time was what she had plenty of, for Harvey.

At long last Elaine joined the Whalley Tennis club. She was welcomed by the members and soon settled into playing on a regular basis. Although much out of practice at first, she soon got her rhythm back and thought again about having a tennis court in the back field. But in the meantime, she'd photocopy her receipt and text it to her old tennis pals before they came up with some ridiculous fine or forfeit. She knew their zany ideas of old and wasn't going to risk anything.

Chapter 14

Soon the great day came when Gill, Elaine, and Liz all went to Maureen Cookson's dress shop in Whalley. The three girls had already been for their bridesmaid's dresses in Manchester and were all delighted with them. Kirsty got her pale pink dress, in fact they all were wearing pale pink, a sort of dusky pink. Kirsty's was a more girlish style and Anna and Kate had a more off the shoulder adult style, but all in the same material. Kirsty had already worked out that Anna's dress would do for her own prom dress in four years' time, as she would be the same size by then, which caused a lot of hilarity.

Gill, Elaine, and Liz were at the shop by 9.30 having had a good breakfast at Elaine's to give them all stamina for the long day ahead. They found an assistant and explained that they all wanted an outfit for the same wedding.

'Whose wedding?' asked the assistant.

'My son's,' replied Gill.

'So, you want a "Mother of the Groom" outfit?'

'That's right. This is his sister-in-law, her husband is best man, and she's his godmother,' explained Gill, pointing to each of them in turn.

'Right. Let's start with Mother first then. What month is the wedding?'

'May,' said Gill, 'but don't tell the bride,' and burst into giggles, so they had to explain about the mystery of the two dates.

'Do you know what the "Mother of the Bride's" colour scheme is?' asked the assistant, still laughing at the story.

'Yes,' said Gill. 'It makes it easy really. She's wearing a multi-coloured, layered dress, with cream jacket and cream accessories. So, no particular colour to avoid. Oh, and the bridesmaids are wearing pale pink.'

'Good. Let's start then. Would you other ladies like a coffee whilst you wait and watch?'

'Yes, please,' Liz and Elaine chorused, and another assistant hurried off to provide drinks, which were brought to a small table near the middle of the shop in sight of the changing rooms.

Gill tried the first outfit on and then paraded round the shop for them to see. It was a lilac dress and jacket with deeper purple trim, and a purple hat.

'Don't say anything,' Gill shouted. 'Just look and see what you think, then tell me afterwards.' Next was a long gold lamé dress, and then there was a cerise two-piece, and a red and black dress with bolero, then a grey two-piece with pink trim, all with hats to match, apart from the gold dress.

'Right. What do you think?' Gill asked.

'No, tell us what you think first,' replied Elaine.

'I'm not keen on the gold dress even though it was beautiful, but I felt like it was a ball gown rather than for a wedding.'

'That's what I thought,' said Liz, and Elaine nodded.

'Then I've discounted the pale grey as I thought with my hair being grey it blended in too much.'

'True, although it was a lovely style and really suited you,' said Elaine.

'We do have that one in pale blue with navy trim if you like the style. It's just come in this morning, so isn't out on display yet,' said the assistant.

'Yes, please,' said Gill, looking excited. The dress was brought and tried on and both Liz and Elaine nodded.

'That's the best yet,' Elaine said.

'I agree. Is there a hat to match, like with the grey one?' asked Liz.

'I'll get it for you now,' replied the assistant. Together with the hat, the outfit was perfect.

'This is what I want,' said Gill, looking pleased.

'Well, that was easy,' said the assistant. 'You've no idea how long we spend with some customers. I must agree with your choice. It is the best one you've tried on.'

'What colour of shoes would you wear with that?' asked Liz.

'If I couldn't get the exact shade of pale blue, I think I'd go for white or navy. I'm not sure. I'll decide when I get to Beryl's,' replied Gill. 'Now it's your turn, Liz.'

'Let's go to the more ordinary outfits. I don't want one that's too dressy or that I can't wear again afterwards.'

'Good idea,' said Gill. 'They'll be a lot cheaper too,' she laughed.

'Precisely,' said Liz.

'I'll look in the same place as well,' said Elaine, and they looked together, whilst Gill helped herself to a coffee. Eventually they were both set up with outfits. They had chosen smart dresses and jackets; in case the day was cold. Liz' dress was a soft swirly fabric in beiges and browns, with a fawn jacket, and Elaine chose a fitted red and white dress, with white bolero. By then it was 1.30pm. The assistant thanked them all profusely for their custom and helped them to the shop door.

'Bet she's worn out as well,' quipped Gill, as they waved to the assistant.

'If she's on commission she won't mind being tired 'cos we've spent a fortune,' laughed Elaine. The ladies staggered back to the car with their parcels and drove round to Whalley Abbey to the Autisan café.

At first, they'd decided that they'd leave Beryl's shoe shop for another day, but on second thoughts, after getting their wind back over lunch, they decided that there was no time like the present, so drove to Clitheroe.

Another hilarious time was had in Beryl's as they tried on virtually every shoe on display, matching colour schemes with their outfits. But eventually they were all fixed up with co-ordinated shoes, handbags and fascinators for Liz and Elaine, who didn't want big hats like Gill had chosen. Exhausted, they all arrived home and went to Liz' house, as she had driven. All the girls were at home, so a fashion show had to be staged, showing off their purchases to the delight of the girls, who thoroughly approved of everything that had been bought. Anna especially liked Elaine's red, white, and navy shoes, with handbag to match, which she hadn't been able to resist, despite the price, but which set the red and white dress off perfectly.

Elaine was the first to leave. 'I'm off home; I'm ready for bed now,' she yawned.

'I know what you mean,' Gill yawned back, which set Liz off yawning, then the girls, and then it started round again, so Elaine ran out of the house before another round of yawns came. Elaine had a snack and then did have an early night and slept soundly.

Just before Easter, Gill came round with a large box for Elaine, saying she wanted to talk to her.

'Hi Elaine. I found this in the spare bedroom last night. It's yours from the vestry, isn't it? We only looked at the one box, with all the church leaflets in. What was in this box?'

'I've no idea.'

'Before we start looking at the box, I need to talk to you.'

'Yes, you said. Can't we talk whilst we're looking in the box? Shall I put the kettle on?' asked Elaine.

'Glass of wine would be better probably.'

'Oh dear, sounds serious.'

'It is,' said Gill, as she waited for Elaine to bring back two large glasses of wine. 'I've finished seeing Thomas.'

'You have?' said Elaine quietly, hiding the elation she was feeling inside.

Gill nodded. 'Yes, he was going increasingly strange. He first started saying that the farm should have been his and that his granddad had been cheated of his inheritance.'

'Oh, he said something like that to me the first time he came to the farm. But then he just laughed it off and it was never mentioned again.'

'I wish you'd told me.'

'It never crossed my mind until you mentioned it. So, what happened next?'

'Well, he started saying things like we should get married and then he'd share the farm. But then he said that he would get back at least half of the house if he were married to me and it would rightfully belong to the Farnworths again. That's when I started getting worried.'

'And would you have married him?'

'I don't know. I was getting used to having him around. He wasn't a patch on John, of course, but he was so overpowering at first. Bowled me over for a while.'

'Yes, I noticed even at my housewarming party he was coming on strong to you.'

'It's quite powerful when it happens like that. You do get swept into it, even though I was feeling guilty that he was your friend first.'

'So, what finally made you finish things?'

'I told him about the arrangement I'd made with Ben and Tim after John died. I gave the farm to Ben and it's all in his name now and gave a cash settlement to Tim to help towards buying his partnership. Tim insisted he wanted no part in the farm's future and was happy for it to go to Ben.'

'So, what did Thomas say to that?'

'He said it was a very irresponsible thing to do and could it be altered back? When I said, definitely not, he got angry. And then I realised. He didn't want me. He wanted ownership of the farm. He'd lived with his granddad's bitterness all these years, and when he heard I was a widow and lived at the farm, I think he saw it as his way of making it better for his granddad's memory.'

'Warped.'

'Definitely.'

'You've had a close escape there. Thank goodness you'd already signed the farm over to Ben, or else he'd have probably married you just to get his hands on the farm.'

'Exactly. Well, it has taught me a lesson. I'll just stay a merry widow now!'

'Good idea.' Elaine reached over and hugged Gill. Then she refilled the glasses of wine and made a toast: 'Here's to singleness and down with men.'

'I'll drink to that,' said Gill, and they both took a long drink.

'Let's have a look now,' replied Elaine, lifting the lid of the box. Inside were two books: one very old and one much newer. She picked up the older book and looked inside. On the first page was a large square divided into four smaller squares, marked A, B, C, and D. She turned over the page and on the next page was one of the squares marked A, divided up into 40 tiny squares, each numbered. On the next page was a title 'Plot 1, Square A'.

'Oh, it's a map of the graveyard!' said Elaine excitedly, quickly turning the page. 'Look, plot one is the first grave nearest the communal wall, the one with just a weather-beaten wooden cross. It says who the grave belongs to, what date they were interred, how much was paid for the grave plot, and who the officiating minister was. How interesting! That'll really help me in finding out who everyone is. I can put a name on that old cross now.'

'Whose grave was that?' asked Gill.

'There are two entries. One on March 18 1779, name of Martha Ann Webb, died aged 80 years. And the second entry is her husband, late of the above in "grave speak," Joshua Arkwright Webb, aged 88 years, died on March 25 1779.'

'That's only a week after each other,' said Gill.

'Yes, so it is. Wonder what happened?'

'Probably died of a broken heart,' guessed the ever-romantic Gill.

'More likely the same dose of flu or cholera or something equally gruesome in those days.'

'They were a good age for the 18th century: 80 and 88 years.'

'That's true. Let's see who's on the next page,' said Elaine. 'Oh, this is the Ashton family, with several entries. Plot 2 Square A. There's no grave next to the cross, just a mound. That's sad. Perhaps they couldn't afford a stone or even a cross. It was a Barnabas Ashton who died young, only 29, then three young children and then Susannah Ashton, aged 81 years, relict of the above.'

'Relict?' asked Gill. 'What sort of description is that?'

'It's an old-fashioned name for wife or widow,' explained Elaine.

'Relict is a widow? So, I'm a relict, you're saying? Doesn't sound very nice,' giggled Gill.

'I'm not surprised it went out of fashion. But she lived to a good age for those times too.'

'Must be the water in Dunsop Bridge,' decided Gill.

'Must have been hard trying to bring up three children as a widow though.'

'But the children didn't last much longer than the father.'

'Poor woman. Life was hard.'

The pages for the next three plots were empty, but as Elaine kept looking, it was amazing to see all the different names in the book. Turning to the second book, she saw it was set out like the first book, but they were more recent graves that were listed. Elaine decided that she would do a spread sheet to combine both books to show where graves were occupied and empty.

'If I combine both books, we'll be able to see where there are gaps in the graveyard.'

'That'll be very useful,' said Gill. 'You'll be able to pick the best available plot for yourself and make sure you keep it.'

'All right don't be so sarcastic. But you're right, I might do that. I've always wanted to be cremated, but now I think about it, seeing I own the graveyard, I might as well have my ashes in here.'

'You've got me thinking too; perhaps I could have John's ashes interred here? Then I could come and visit him anytime I wanted to.'

'Have you not already done that?'

'No, never got round to it. They're still in his shed in the garden.'

'Poor John. Left in the garden shed,' Elaine teased.

'But he loved that shed. It was Anna's idea to put him there. I think she goes in and talks to him sometimes. It'd be nice to have a proper focus to visit rather than sitting in a scruffy old shed.'

'There's a retired vicar in Whalley, Alan Reid. He used to be a guide at

Whalley Abbey, but he can't walk too far now. I bet he'd come and do a service for you.'

'Would he? That'd be good. We could have a little private family service.'

'And you can come back here for afternoon tea afterwards.'

'That would be lovely, thank you so much. You make such a lovely afternoon tea. Are you sure you don't mind?'

'That's what friends are for. I'd be delighted. When do you think?'

'What about the end of May?'

'So soon after the wedding?'

'I was thinking that it will be the second anniversary of John's death. And besides, the bride and groom are only staying for a week's holiday, so they'll have been back a couple of weeks before.'

'Great. Do you want me to ask Alan? He's a lovely man. Proper comedian. Always got a kind word for everyone and a joke, of course. Sometimes they're pretty corny, but he's delightful.'

'Yes, ask him. It'll be a Saturday on the 27th May, so it'll be easier on the farm and for others who come.'

'Who are you going to ask?'

'Just the immediate family, a couple of local farmers, and his two best friends and their wives. I think that's enough. I was so glad that you came and stayed with me that first week. I don't think I'd have got through without your help.'

'It's just lucky it was Bank Holiday week, so classes had finished and I was able to do my marking at your house.'

'You'd better pick a plot then.'

'Oh, yes, I'll go for Square B, plot 10.'

'That's right up against the far wall near the road.'

'Yes, it's nearest to Greenbank Farm.'

'Great idea.'

'Where will you pick?'

'I've no idea. I'm hoping I've plenty of time to choose yet. And let's face it, I've plenty of choice. There seem to be lots of empty plots. Who else can pick their own plot in their own graveyard?'

'Not many,' Gill giggled, the effects of the wine getting to her.

'Now what shall we have for the afternoon tea?'

'Oh, I'll leave that to you. Whatever you make will be lovely. Well, I must be going.'

'Okay. I'll ring Alan tomorrow.'

'Thanks. Let me know what he says. Bye.'

'Bye,' echoed Elaine, then turned inside and decided she would ring Alan immediately to make sure she didn't forget. As she knew he would be, Alan said he'd be delighted to perform the committal and arrangements were made. He was happy that there was to be an afternoon tea, too.

Chapter 15

On the first Saturday in May, the rain was pouring down and Elaine and the family were disappointed. They piled into two cars and after a big breakfast, set off to Northumberland for the wedding, leaving the farm in the capable hands of Daniel and his mum and dad. Fortunately, as they got further north, the weather improved and by the time they got to the castle there was glorious sunshine.

The bride-to-be was a little puzzled when they all turned up, and even more surprised when two cars full of cousins and families arrived as well, followed by three cars full of business partners and office staff. Then Tim announced that it was their wedding day. Lindsay said, 'Don't be silly, that's in July,' to which Tim replied, 'No it isn't, it's today.' The discussion was disrupted then by another car arriving. It was Lindsay's hair and make-up people and they were carrying her wedding dress in a large box.

'Now do you believe it's today?' asked Tim, laughing, to which the bride burst into tears. Tim cuddled her, and the family and others decided that it was time to go upstairs and find their rooms, leaving Tim to explain.

When Elaine and Gill, who were sharing a room, arrived back downstairs, Tim was sat with a large glass of fruit juice in his hand and there was no sign of Lindsay.

'Is Lindsay okay?' asked Gill.

'Yes, she's gone to have her hair and makeup done. It was just a shock for her, that's all, but she's really glad I've done it. Even though we'd only invited a small number of people this time, she was naturally getting worried again as the wedding drew nearer.'

'Have I ever told you that you're a lovely son, Tim.'

'Oh, give over, Mum. You'll have me blushing,' he laughed. Gradually other people drifted down, except for the bridesmaids, who were helping Lindsay get ready and getting their own hair and makeup done too. Conversation flowed between the groups of wedding guests as they all got to know who each person was, and how they fitted into the family, friends, or business category.

Gill said that she was going to get changed, and everyone else seemed to decide the same, and the lounge emptied. Soon everybody congregated back in the lounge wearing their best outfits and admiring each other's clothes, waiting for the service to start.

Eventually Tim gave the signal that it was time to walk over to the church in the grounds, so everybody set off and sat in the ancient pews, on the correct side of the church according to whom they belonged. An organist was playing gentle music and people were quietly chatting, when there was a sudden cessation of the music. Talking stopped, and then the familiar strains of Lohengrin's 'Wedding March' by Wagner filled the church. Eyes turned to the back of the church and young Kirsty was the first down the aisle carrying cream roses and looking very important. Behind her were Anna and Kate, followed by Victoria, Lindsay's best friend. Then finally, Lindsay slowly walked down the aisle, her arm on her father's, beaming shyly to all as she passed them. Her dress was beautiful. It had a basic satin under-dress with a high-necked lace over-dress, not unlike Kate Middleton when she had married Prince William. However, Lindsay's sleeves were shorter and the lace came down to a very low V at the back, almost to her waist. The veil was only short.

'Probably to show off the back of her dress,' whispered Gill to Elaine, who agreed. Her bouquet was quite old-fashioned in style and was made of several shades of pink roses.

The service followed the usual format; vows were taken, rings were exchanged, the groom kissed the bride. Then the main bridal party went to the side of the church to the small vestry to sign the register, whilst the organist played several short pieces, until the main family arrived back. Then with a triumphal burst from the organ, the happy couple walked back down the aisle arm in arm and went outside the church. Confetti was showered everywhere and hundreds of photos were taken by the official photographer, but also on everybody's mobile phones. Chaos reigned for a little while, but eventually all photos had been taken from every angle and with every computation of bridal party, family, friends, and business partners.

As soon as they arrived back at the castle, young people carrying trays of canapés were circulating, whilst others were offering glasses of Bucks Fizz or fresh orange juice. Being only a small gathering by a lot of wedding's standards, everybody soon knew who everybody was, and were mingling together and talking about how they knew either Lindsay or Ben. There was a lot of laughter and more photos.

Eventually the meal was served, followed by speeches, all accompanied by wine and champagne for the toasts. Afterwards Lindsay announced that she was going to toss her bouquet and Kate caught it, with a lot of speculation going on about whether she would be the next bride. Lindsay's mum explained that the bouquet was an exact replica of her own bouquet when she had married Lindsay's father. *That explained why it was old-fashioned*, Gill and Elaine said to each other, without words. And then the dancing started. Tim wasn't a natural dancer, and neither was Ben. They took after their dad for that. Two left feet, Gill had always said of John. But Gill knew Tim had been having dancing lessons so that he didn't let his bride down and they danced beautifully together. After the first dance everybody else, (well almost everybody - Ben couldn't be persuaded) took to the dance floor and, loosened by alcohol, the dancing got more outrageous as the evening went on. Kirsty and Anna were enjoying dancing with all Lindsay's male cousins and were having a ball. Then a conga started up and snaked its way round the ballroom, dragging almost everybody into it.

At midnight, Tim announced that he and Lindsay were going to bed, which provoked a round of ribald comments, but unabashed, they left the party, which seemed to have an effect on everyone else. People started drifting upstairs and soon the wedding was over, leaving a lot of tidying up for the catering staff.

'Perfect day,' said Gill, as she fell onto the bed fully clothed.

'Won't be perfect if you don't get out of your posh outfit,' laughed Elaine, and, trying to lift her up, they both collapsed with laughter onto the bed. Eventually, Gill got up and changed into her pyjamas and got into bed, Elaine followed quickly after, and they were both soon snoring.

Next morning breakfast was served and, amazingly, people were tucking into the large spread of typical English breakfast, although one or two had bad headaches and were preferring just black coffee. Tim commented that he hadn't envisaged having breakfast with all the wedding guests, but Ben reminded him that he would have a private honeymoon later in the year. After breakfast, the Dunsop Bridge contingent left to get back to the farm, but some guests were staying a little later. By evening however, Tim and Lindsay would be on their own in the enormous castle to begin their mini-moon and their married life alone.

Life was soon back to normal in Dunsop Bridge after the excitement of the wedding. Elaine was starting to plan the afternoon tea she would make for after the interment of John's ashes, but also getting to grips with her vegetable plot. This was the time of year when small vegetable and salad plants could be put in the ground. Harvey was keen to help and they were pleased that there were no late frosts to kill the young plants. There was going to be an amazing show of produce hopefully, Elaine told Harvey. She knew that there would be too much food for her to eat, so had already agreed to give Harvey and the farm some of the produce, and Puddleducks café said that they would buy any surplus from her. Elaine decided that Harvey could be responsible for delivering the produce to the café, but she would let him keep the money they gave him.

Whilst they were planting out one day, Harvey suddenly said, 'Birthday tomorrow.'

'Whose? Yours?' asked Elaine. Harvey nodded.

'How old?'

'16. Freya's birthday as well.' Harvey had never mentioned any of his family before, let alone his sister.

'She was your twin?' Again Harvey nodded. Poor lad, thought Elaine. That must be even harder for twins to bear separation. No wonder he rarely talked.

'Then we must have a party tomorrow. And tell that granddad of yours that he has to come. No excuses.' Harvey nodded, but then he also grinned. It was the first genuine look of happiness that Elaine had ever seen on his face.

'What's your favourite meal?'

'Lasagne.'

'Pudding?'

'Crumble.'

'Custard, cream, or ice cream?'

'Ice cream.'

'Does your granddad like lasagne and crumble?'

'Yes.'

'Right, be here for five o'clock then, with granddad. Okay?' Harvey nodded, and then in his usual way he suddenly darted off home, probably going to badger his granddad into coming tomorrow, Elaine thought. She mentally scanned her food cupboard to check she had everything she needed, but then decided that she'd nip into Clitheroe and buy him a birthday cake rather than make one and try to ice it. The lasagne and crumble would be easy to make, but she'd cheat and buy some garlic bread. Quite pleased with finding out what his favourite foods were, she went inside and decided to make a batch of scones and a Victoria sponge for them to take home.

When she was in town next day, she managed to get him a birthday card with a number 16 on and bought him a mobile phone. He was the only young person she knew that wasn't permanently attached to a phone. She hoped his granddad wouldn't disapprove. On impulse, she bought a few balloons with 16 on, some small and one large helium one, from the Party Shop on Moor Lane. Elaine knew that this was what his mother would probably have done if she'd still been alive, and was equally sure that his granddad wouldn't be doing anything special for him. But his granddad had to attend first and that could be a problem. But Elaine was pleasantly surprised when at a quarter to five both Harvey and granddad turned up, wearing their smartest clothes by the look of it.

'Happy Birthday,' beamed Elaine, 'you'll be glad I'm not going to sing to you. I'm a rubbish singer. Come into the kitchen.' Harvey's face lit up when he saw the balloons and the small pile of presents on the table.

'I'm so glad you've come,' Elaine said to Fred.

'Yes,' was his only reply. Oh dear, thought Elaine, this is going to be hard work.

'Do you want to show your granddad round the vegetable garden whilst I finish making tea?'

Harvey nodded and the two of them went out into the back garden. Elaine popped the garlic bread in and checked on the lasagne and crumble in the oven. The table was already set and she'd put jugs of squash and water on the table. There was also a bottle of wine if Fred wanted any. After about ten minutes the two came back in again.

'Perfect timing,' breezed Elaine, 'Now come and sit down at the table.' As soon as they were sat down, she brought out the lasagne and garlic bread with dishes of salad and coleslaw. They soon tucked into the food and Elaine could see that they were enjoying it, even though there was not much said.

After they both refused second helpings, Elaine brought out the crumble with ice cream, as requested. They were obviously a family who ate first and talked later, or not at all with these two. Remembering how irate Fred's shouting had been when he came to see her previously, she couldn't believe how quiet he was today.

As soon as they had finished their puddings, Fred stood up as if about to go.

'Sit back down, Fred,' she commanded. 'This is a birthday party and no party is complete without a birthday cake.' She produced the cake, complete with lit candles in the shape of a number one and a number six.

'Happy birthday, Harvey.' Harvey grinned. 'Shall we say Happy Birthday to Freya, too?' Elaine asked tentatively. Harvey nodded and didn't seem bothered that Elaine had mentioned Freya.

'Happy birthday, Freya,' Harvey whispered, then blew out the candles. Elaine had to bite her lip to stop from crying and busied herself with cutting the cake. After they'd all eaten a generous slice, Elaine decided it was time for the present giving.

'Now the presents, Harvey. Happy Birthday,' said Elaine, as she passed the pile of presents over to him. Besides the phone, there was a book about vegetable gardening, some toiletries, a box of chocolates and some funny socks. Harvey opened them all, but came to the mobile phone last. Elaine had put her own number in the phone in case he needed to contact her, but doubted that he'd ever ring.

'Thank you, Elaine,' he said quietly, then turned to show his granddad his phone. He quickly turned it on and started messing with it. His granddad looked disapprovingly at Elaine and the phone, but Elaine justified herself, and said that Harvey had helped her a lot in the garden and this was his wages. That seemed to satisfy Fred, and he muttered about not wanting to be beholden to anyone. Elaine tried not to laugh. She didn't think she'd heard the word 'beholden' in many years.

Eventually the two of them were getting ready to go home. Elaine didn't press them to stay, as she was so pleased that they'd turned up. She encouraged them to take all the lasagne, garlic bread, crumble, and birthday cake home with them, along with the scones and Victoria sandwich. Harvey looked delighted. There was enough food to last them another meal tomorrow and the cakes would last longer. Fred asked if he might use the facilities, which amused Elaine. She directed him to the ground floor wet room and then got a big plastic reusable shopping bag to put everything in. As she turned round, Harvey gave her a quick hug then ran out of the room. When Fred returned he thanked Elaine for the tea, cakes, and Harvey's presents, and then asked where he was.

'Think he's set off or gone outside,' Elaine answered, and Fred nodded a thank you, then left the house shouting for Harvey. Elaine watched through the window as both Fred and Harvey walked slowly up the road together balloons bobbing along behind them. Her heart was breaking for these two lonely men who lived together, but didn't seem to be able to communicate with each other. Wanting to keep herself busy, Elaine shoved all the pots and plates into the dishwasher. She'd soon cleared the table of everything else and the room was back to normal. To distract herself she decided that she'd go up into her pulpit and read, as there was nothing much on TV that she wanted to watch that night. She got a large glass of wine and settled down to read her book.

About an hour later, her phone pinged with a message. She checked her phone and her heart nearly stopped when she saw the text was from Harvey.

Thx Elaine 4 everything. Nobody lets me talk about Freya anymore and I miss her so much. I miss my Mum and Dad and Gran too, but Freya specially.

Elaine stared at the message. She couldn't believe how much anguish there was in it, but also that he'd managed to text such a long message. She replied quickly.

Glad u liked everything. U can talk about Freya 2 me anytime.

Quickly, another message came back.

Thx x

Elaine couldn't believe it. He'd put a kiss at the end of his text. That was enough to make her finally burst into tears and she sobbed for a long time, wishing she could make things better for Harvey and his granddad. But at least, she consoled herself, she had got Harvey talking through his mobile phone. It had been worth every penny, and she'd also paid for a contract for him so that his granddad didn't have to pay for it. Now perhaps Harvey could move on a little in his grief. He needed to talk about his sister and Elaine vowed she would do everything she could to help him. And then she realised just how much she had come to love Harvey. She couldn't imagine her own life without him now. Such a strange relationship, but he had eaten his way into her heart and wasn't going to leave. Perhaps this new kind of love, a sort of mother love, was going to be what filled her life from now on.

It was as if the phone had unlocked something in Harvey. Although he didn't talk a lot to Elaine, he poured out his heart in his texts, usually late in the evening, probably after he'd gone to his bedroom and was away from his granddad.

It was soon time for the interment of John's ashes and Elaine got Harvey to help her fill planters to put in front of the house. She'd arranged for the gravedigger from St Hubert's to come and prepare the grave for the service, and to attend afterwards to fill in the soil. Rev Alan Reid arrived, along with his lovely wife Muriel, and Elaine welcomed them into her home to await the arrival of the family. Alan had already been to the farm and talked with Gill and Ben and had rung Tim, so that he had an idea of the family and what they wanted.

The procession arrived, Anna carrying the urn. The family had all walked down from the farm together, including Tim, Lindsay, and her parents. There were also farmer neighbours and close friends following behind. They all gathered around the plot and Alan gave a lovely, simple, but meaningful service, injecting a little gentle humour about John into his homily. Anna read a poem called 'My Granddad', which she had read at the original funeral which brought a tear to everyone's eyes. Gill thanked Alan and then invited everyone into the house for afternoon tea. The rest of the day was a blur, as Elaine was rushing round, keeping teapots topped up and filling wine glasses, and adding more sandwiches, savouries, scones and cakes. Eventually everyone left except Gill who'd stayed behind to pay the minister and grave digger.

They both sat with a cup of tea cradled in their hands in the sunroom and were silent for some time. Gill broke the silence.

'That was a lovely fitting tribute to John and a lovely meal. Thank you for everything you've done. You've made it really special. How much do I owe you? This must have cost a lot of money.'

'My treat. It's the least I could do after all that you've done for me.'

'Me? I've done nothing.'

'Yes, you have. You let me stay with you until my house was ready. You let Ben build my house even when he should have been on the farm working. And you've been my friend forever through thick and thin, so how can you say you've done nothing?'

'Well, thank you anyway,' said Gill and reached over and held Elaine's hand and there they sat, until it was dark. Suddenly Gill got up and said it was time for her to go home.

'Will you be okay in the dark? Why don't I drive you home? I've only had one glass of wine and that was hours ago.'

'If you don't mind.'

'I wouldn't have offered if I minded,' teased Elaine. So, Elaine got the car out and drove Gill up to the farm. As she was getting out, Gill hugged Elaine very tightly and said, 'Thank you for being such a good friend,' and got out of the car.

'Takes one to know one,' Elaine shouted after her, and Gill raised her hand in greeting as she went into the bungalow.

Chapter 16

Next Sunday, when Elaine was at Liz and Ben's for Sunday tea, Elaine asked Ben if he was busy with building work.
'Oh no, what have you got planned now?' asked Gill.
'I was just thinking . . .'
'Yes, that's what I'm worried about; you're always just thinking,' laughed Gill.
'Leave her alone, Mum. What is it you want now, Aunty Elaine?' said Ben.
'I was just wondering about having a tennis court built in the back field.'
'What on earth for?' asked Gill.
'To play tennis on, of course,' replied Elaine, with a glare at Gill.
'Oh, yes, could I come and play on it?' asked an excited Kirsty.
'You?' smirked Anna, 'since when have you played tennis?'
'We play at school sometimes, but I don't have a racquet and there's nowhere in Dunsop Bridge to practise. I watched Wimbledon last July when I was off school with a chest infection and loved it. I'd really like to learn. Can I have a racquet for my birthday, Mum? Can I? Can I?'
'Oh, Kirsty, it was a skateboard last week and a new bike the week before. Ask me again when it's nearer your birthday,' laughed Liz.
'So what do you think, Ben, seeing it was you I was asking, not the rest of the family,' Elaine asked at last.
'Depends on what you want. Grass or macadam or polymer surfacing? I wouldn't be able to put the surface in, that's specialist stuff, but I could do all the groundwork and drainage. Would you want fencing round? And lights?'
'I wouldn't want grass. Too much maintenance. I'm used to playing on polymer or macadam surfaces. I'd have to look into which is best value.'
'Fencing? Lights?' Ben prompted.
'Yes, to both. Wouldn't want balls crashing onto my vegetable patch or smashing my windows,' Elaine laughed.
'Yes, I can do most of the work. When shall I start?' Ben teased, 'tomorrow?'
'No, next week will be fine,' joked Elaine.
'I'll find out who could supply polymer or macadam surfaces locally and cost it all and let you know.'

'Thanks Ben. And could you extend the drive right up to the field?'
'Anything you want, Aunty Elaine.'
'What's made you think about this?' asked a bemused Gill.
'It's something we talked about with the Manchester tennis club friends at the housewarming.'
'But who would use it besides you?' asked Gill.
'Anyone who wanted to. I might even get you interested in tennis, Gill.'
'No chance.'
'But would you let the public use it?' asked Liz.
'If I knew them. If they were from the village or the Whalley Tennis club. The Manchester gang suggested that I could do B & B and offer tennis as well. They said it'd go down well, and they said they would all come and pay to stay.'
'You've not given up on the B & B idea then?'
'Not really, but then I've not done anything about it either.'
'It'd be useful to us when we're fully booked,' suggested Liz. 'Then we can keep the booking people happy if we can offer an alternative in the village for the same dates.'
'That's a thought,' replied Elaine.
'If you're short of something to do, why don't you come to work with me at Browsholme Hall on Wednesday?' asked Liz.
'Why? Are you short staffed?'
'I didn't mean to work, I meant to have a look round the grounds and visit the house. You've kept saying you'll come and visit.'
'That's an idea,' added Gill. 'I could come with you as well. It's ages since I went round Browsholme Hall.'
'That's even better if you come, 'cos then Elaine wouldn't have to wait until I'd finished work to come home.'
'Right. We'll go on Wednesday,' said Elaine. 'Shall I pick you up, Gill? We can have lunch first before we go round the house?'
'Yes, why make lunch at home when we can have it made for us?' answered Gill.

Elaine picked up Gill on Wednesday, the late morning promising to be a scorching hot day. They had the windows wide open to let air in, preferring that to the cold blast of the air conditioning. As they drove the few miles up the valley to Browsholme Hall, Elaine asked how long Liz had worked there.

'Off and on most of her life. She was brought up at Home Farm on the estate, so was going in and helping with various jobs as soon as she was a teenager. But now she runs the tearooms, with the help of Adele, who is the housekeeper for the Hall, and Tora in the kitchen. You should talk to Tora if you're serious about doing B & B. Besides working as the cook at the tearooms, she runs a B & B herself.'

'I will do if we get the chance. Liz has been the perfect wife for Ben hasn't she, Gill? Already a farmer's daughter and used to farming ways.'

'She has. A good wife and a lovely mum. And such an excellent cook!'

'You're not bad yourself at cooking.'

'No, neither are you.'

'Where did they meet? I've forgotten over the years.'

'Federation of Young Farmer's Club in Clitheroe. Same as me and John. Best dating agency ever!'

'Well, at least they understand farming life before they let themselves in for a lifetime commitment.'

'Absolutely. Oh, here we are,' and Elaine turned into the gateway. Parking at the Tithe Barn where the tearooms were, Gill and Elaine went inside, finding the barn nice and cool away from the heat outside.

'Shall we eat first?' asked Gill, after they had said hello to Liz.

'I would,' said Liz. 'We've got a small coach party coming in for a tour and afternoon tea at two o'clock, so it's the quiet before the storm.'

'Good,' said Gill, reaching for the menu, 'I'm hungry anyway. What's the soup today, Liz?'

'Tomato and basil or carrot and coriander. The quiche of the day is salmon and broccoli.'

'Tomato and basil for me, with a ham sandwich on brown please,' said Elaine.

'And I'll have the same,' added Gill. 'We're easy to please, aren't we Liz?'

'You certainly are. Tea for two?'

'Yes please,' the two friends chorused together.

The tea arrived swiftly and, whilst they were waiting for their food, Elaine asked Gill about the weddings.

'Is this where the weddings take place?'

'Yes, the ceremony takes place in the lower floor there and then the meal can take place either in the same space or here, depending on the size of the wedding. Oh, look, the door into the wedding area is opening. We can perhaps have a quick peep.' The two ladies jumped up and stepped down to the lower area. It was already set up for a wedding. A central aisle was between the two sets of chairs, which were covered in white satin with lilac bows on the back. Lights twinkled all over the ceiling from lacy material draped across the roof all going up to a central point.

'Why, it's magical,' said Elaine quietly. A lady came out of the door and turned on a light switch and all the walls of the room were filled with swirling colours, mainly lilac and purple.

'It's a lilac-themed wedding tomorrow,' the lady said.

'Rebecca, can I introduce my friend Elaine. She's just bought a house in Dunsop Bridge.' Gill turned to Elaine. 'Rebecca set the wedding business up from nothing. Nowadays she has to have an assistant because there's too much work for one person.'

'Are you the lady who has bought the old church?' asked Rebecca.

'I am,' said Elaine. 'This is an amazing venue. Do you have a lot of weddings?'

'Between 70 and 80 a year.'

'So many? No wonder you needed help.'

'Precisely. Look, I think your food's arriving.'

Gill and Elaine turned to see Adele bringing their food. Sitting down, the two friends ate the food, chatting about the ambience of the place. The food was delicious, and afterwards Liz asked if they wanted anything else.

'No thanks,' said Elaine. 'I'm full already, but perhaps after the tour and a walk round the gardens, we'll be ready for some cake and a coffee.'

'Same here,' added Gill.

'The next tour of the house is at one o'clock. Shall I book you on it?' asked Liz.

'Yes please,' said Gill, and she paid for the tour and their food, even though Elaine objected and said she would pay. Gill said you brought the car, so I'm paying. Then Elaine insisted she'd pay for the coffee and cake.

'Now stop arguing, you two,' said Liz. 'You're worse than my girls. Your tour guide today is Irena. She's our longest-serving guide. I've got to be careful how I say that now. I once said she was our oldest guide, meaning longest-serving, and she said she wasn't that old,' laughed Liz. 'Oh, she's here now. Just talking about you, Irena.'

A small, smartly dressed, grey-haired lady came up to where Gill and Elaine were standing.

'Hello Liz. Hope it was nothing bad you were saying. How many for the one o'clock tour?'

'You've got 12, which includes these two: my mother-in-law Gill and her friend Elaine.'

'Hello. Have you been before?' Irena asked.

'Yes,' said Gill

'No,' said Elaine.

'But it's years ago when I came, so I've probably forgotten it all,' explained Gill.

'We might as well walk up to the house together then,' said Irena. 'Come this way.' Gill and Elaine said 'bye' to Liz and followed Irena. They walked through the old stable yard where the old stables and barns had been converted into private houses. Then they passed through the gateway and followed the path round until they came to the house. Elaine stopped and stared. It was a large three-storey house nestled in front of trees, with rose trees growing all the way up part of the wall.

'Is it a Tudor house? Is it listed?' asked Elaine.

'Yes, but hang on until everybody arrives and then I can tell the story. I'll just count up the people waiting, looks like most people are here already.'

'How long is the tour?' asked one lady who was waiting.

'Between 50 minutes and an hour, depending on how long I talk or how many questions you ask,' at which all the waiting people laughed. Irena did a head count, collected the tickets, and began the tour.

'The house was built in 1507, so it's a Tudor house and is roughly H-shaped. The Parker family, who still live here, first arrived in about 1381,' started Irena. Elaine was riveted from the first word and listened carefully to all that Irena was saying. After the initial introduction, they were all taken inside, and Elaine was amazed at how cold the house was inside compared to the outside temperature. The first room, which was the original Great Hall, was set up to look as it would have been in 1507, with an array of artefacts from all round the world and from every century, including original furniture and lots of weaponry. They were taken from room to room: a library, drawing room, dining room. Irena regaled them with stories of both the furniture and artefacts and also tales about the diverse family members through the centuries.

On the way upstairs they paused to look at a stained-glass window comprised of fragments of windows from several local medieval monasteries, probably including Whalley Abbey, Irena said. This made Elaine prick her ears up. After a visit to two upstairs bedrooms, they were taken to the family sitting room. A large modern TV was a laughing point, as everyone commented on its modernity compared with the rest of the house.

'But it's a family home not a museum. This room is used daily,' replied Irena. 'Just look out of the windows and you'll know why.' The people turned and saw the long vista across the gardens, after the manner of Capability Brown, which drew their eyes to a gatehouse at the end of the drive.

On the way back down the staircase, Gill commented to Irena that Elaine had stained-glass windows in her house.

'Are they as old as this one?' asked Irena.

'No, they were installed around 1770. My house was originally a church, but there was a covenant that said the windows couldn't be removed.'

'How did you feel about that?' asked Irena.

'Delighted! I love the windows. The central window depicts Christ, with St Gregory and St Philip on either side. The name of the church was St Gregory's and St Philip's,' replied Elaine.

'Sounds very interesting,' said Irena.

'So was your tour. I've really enjoyed it. How long have you been a tour guide?'

'Oh, about thirteen years, I can't really remember when I started, but it was shortly after I retired. Are you going back to the Tithe Barn? I need to get back there or else I won't have time to eat before my next tour at three pm.'

'Yes, we'll go back with you,' said Elaine.

'Thought we were going to do a tour of the grounds first?' asked Gill.

'Can we do that later? I want to ask Irena some more questions if she doesn't mind.'

'No, I don't mind,' replied Irena, and they headed back down to the Tithe

Barn.

'You're back early,' commented Liz, as they arrived.

'I know,' said Gill. 'Elaine wants to talk to Irena, so we're walking the grounds later.'

'So, what do you all want to eat?' asked Liz. 'Is it your usual, Irena?'

'Yes please.'

'I'll have some of Tora's Bakewell Tart and a cappuccino, please,' said Gill.

'I'm torn between a scone and carrot cake,' said Elaine. 'Which would you recommend, Liz?' Irena answered.

'Both! They're both gorgeous. Best carrot cake I've ever eaten. But the scones come piled high with cream and jam. Difficult choice.'

'I'll have the carrot cake and a cappuccino then, please,' said Elaine.

'That's good timing because Leslie, one of our other guides, has just set off with the two pm tour with the coach trip as well. She's got 24 people and then 20 of them are having afternoon tea so it would have been a bit busy later. Right, let me get these orders into the kitchen.'

The cakes and drinks soon arrived. Irena was right. The carrot cake was the best Elaine had ever tasted.

'All the food is locally sourced and homemade,' said Irena.

'Tastes gorgeous,' said Elaine, with a mouthful of cake. And then she started asking Irena lots of questions about the house and the people and how she had come to be a tour guide.

'Don't mind Elaine,' said Gill when she could get a word in. 'She's a tour guide at Whalley Abbey.'

'Are you?' asked Irena.

'Only just. I've only done my first guided tour last week. It was just a small group of the Mothers' Union from Read and Simonstone, St John's and St Peter's church. They were a delightful bunch.'

'That sounds a mouthful for a church title,' said Irena.

'Yes, it's two neighbouring villages who have separate churches but have now combined. Mind you, it's only like my house with two saints in the title.'

'How often do you do tours at Whalley Abbey?' asked Irena.

'Just as and when anyone orders it. Not like here, where you are open on set days. How often do each of you do tours here?'

'We can do as many or as little as we please. The rota comes out in April and we all choose which we want to do.'

'Is it just Wednesdays?'

'No, we do private tours as well, which are very often history groups, Women's Institutes, gardening clubs, or church groups. And we open about four Sundays a year. What made you become a tour guide at Whalley Abbey?' So, Elaine told her of her childhood visits and her subsequent career, and that she had retired last summer and moved to the Ribble Valley.

'You'd make an ideal guide here then as well. A lot of us are retired teachers or people who've worked with the public.'

'Do you think so?' asked Elaine. 'What do you think Gill?'

'Why not? You're used to speaking to groups of people and are very knowledgeable about a lot of history - far more than me.'

'Come on, Gill, you're a history teacher. You know a lot as well. So why haven't you become a guide then?' Elaine asked Gill.

'Because I'm not retired and I work on a farm.'

'So does Liz.'

'Yes, but Liz loves it here, with having been brought up on the estate farm. Anyway, she says that her wages are her spending money for holidays, Christmas presents, and going to the hairdressers every week.'

'I don't blame her,' said Elaine. 'It must be difficult to feel that any money is your own, when you run businesses with your family.'

'Precisely. She works mainly in the summer months when the tearooms are open, but increasingly, she's helping out at weddings. And Kate is too, when they need her.'

'How many guides do you have?' Elaine asked Irena.

'About ten of us. Although two of them, Sue and John, still work so can't do as many as the others. Leslie even does tours in French if necessary.'

'That's impressive. How come?'

'She lived in France for many years. She recently did a tour for Adele's family who are French. Adele is the housekeeper for the Parkers. She originally came as a nanny for the children, but ended up staying when the children went to boarding school. She's a Jill of all trades really. She helps out in the tearooms as well when it's busy.'

'So if I wanted to be a guide, what would I do? Would I need to write to Mr Parker?'

'Not really. Just talk to Catherine first.'

'Who's Catherine?'

'Catherine is the secretary that organises everything and everyone and is based in the house up in the attics, and Nicola helps her on the finance side. Talking of which, here's Catherine now.'

A slim blond lady with very high heels walked quickly towards Irena.

'Hello, Irena, sorry to interrupt your chat, ladies, but can I ask a favour of you? Are you free on Bank Holiday Monday in August? I've not managed to fill that slot yet.'

'No, sorry, I'm away.'

'Oh, never mind, I think everyone is away that week. I'll have to get Robert to do it then.'

'Can I introduce Gill and Elaine? Gill is Liz' mother-in-law, and Elaine is Gill's friend,' said Irena.

'Hello, I think I've met you before, Gill, haven't I?' said Catherine.

'Yes, at Liz' 30th birthday party, wasn't it?'

'That's right,'

'My friend Elaine is a tour guide at Whalley Abbey, and Irena's just been trying to persuade her to become a tour guide here,' said Gill. Catherine's head swivelled round and she beamed at Elaine.

'Really?' Catherine said.

'Only thinking,' said Elaine.

'She was a lecturer in history and retired last year,' added Irena.

'Perfect. I'll tell Robert.'

'Who's Robert?' asked Elaine.

'Robert Parker, the owner,' said Catherine. 'He'll love your historical background and the fact that you've been a lecturer.'

'Why don't you come again next week and go round with another two guides and see what you think?' suggested Irena. 'That's how we all learned the job first. We went round with a few different guides and then did our own tours. We all do it slightly differently, depending on our own interests.'

'How do you remember it all?'

'It comes easy after you've done a few tours and then you hardly use the notes. Just keep them as a reference tool,' replied Irena.

'Yes, why don't you come again next week and then make up your mind?'

asked Catherine.

'If you don't mind I'd love that,' said Elaine, whilst Gill just sat with a big grin on her face.

'Best go, I need to catch the organiser of the coach trip to get some money from her,' smiled Catherine, and she was off to the lower part of the Tithe Barn where the coach party were just arriving for their afternoon tea.

'I must go, too,' said Irena. 'My next tour starts any minute. Bye for now. Nice to have met you.'

'Thanks Irena. You've really inspired me today.'

'A pleasure. Bye.' And Irena was off, hurrying back to the house for another tour.

'Well, my girl, you've really got involved here, haven't you? You won't get much time to have a tennis court built now, or even play tennis at this rate,' smirked Gill.

'I haven't committed to anything,' said Elaine.

'No, but you will. I saw your eyes sparkling. And I know you. Hey, Liz, come here,' she shouted to her daughter-in-law. Liz joined them. 'She's only just gone and said she'll be a tour guide. What's she like?'

'Good for you, Elaine; you'll be a good one too. When do you start?'

'Don't listen to Gill. I'm coming again next week to go round the house with two other guides and, then if I like it, I may become a guide.'

'Good. I'll have a look on the rota and see who's on next week. It's Jean at 12 and two pm, and then Barbara at one and three pm. They're both really good, but do it differently.'

'Yes, that's what Irena said.'

'Come on, Elaine, let's get you home before you enrol to help in the tea rooms as well,' laughed Gill.

'That's what happened to Gail,' said Liz. 'She lives in the gatehouse at the end of the drive, and when she retired, she was bored, so she became a tour guide, but has ended up working in the tea rooms as well.'

'No, I don't think I fancy doing the tea rooms unless they were really desperate. I'll see what happens next week; that's all I'm saying,' insisted Elaine. 'Bye Liz, see you later,' she added. Gill said her goodbyes too, and the pair of them left to return home. Elaine was quiet on the way home and Gill left it that way, as she knew her friend would be thinking about all the facts she had heard that day and turning them over in her mind.

The next day Elaine was working in the garden with Harvey, when she asked him what he planned to do when he finished school in July.
　'Myerscough,' he said.
　What's Myerscough?'
　'College near Preston.'
　'To do 'A' levels?' Harvey shook his head.
　'Gardening course.'
　'A gardening course? And then what? Don't you want to go to sixth form or college?' Another shake of the head.
　'And what after the gardening course?' This time Elaine got a different response. Harvey shrugged his shoulders.
　'What does your granddad think about this?'
　'Doesn't know.'
　'Don't you think he ought to know what you want to do?' Another shrug of the shoulders.
　'Honestly, Harvey. It's about time that you and your granddad started talking to each other. Where did you find out about this course?'
　'School.'
　'Your careers teacher?'
　'No, Carl.'
　'Your counsellor?' Another nod.
　'Said I should do the work I want to.'
　'It's a great idea, but I still think your granddad ought to know.'
　'Tell him tonight.'
　'Make sure you do.' They continued weeding the vegetable patch and talked little after that. After he had gone home, Elaine looked on the Internet to see the courses available for gardening at Myerscough. She found several courses available for 16 year olds, which lead to different awards. Eventually they could progress onto a degree course in Horticulture. As she was getting her supper ready, she got a text from Harvey.

Told him. Said it's OK if I want to do it.

Elaine wasn't having such a short reply and rang him up.
'What did he say, Harvey?'
'Told you. Said okay.'
'Give him the phone, please.' Elaine waited until Harvey went downstairs and she could hear Fred muttering under his breath. 'Fred, what do you think about this course Harvey wants to do?'
'If he wants it, I'm happy. There'll always be a need for gardeners.'
'Well, that's true. But how will he get there? Or will he live in?'
'They have a minibus to take students. Or they can live in.'
'Would you want him to live in?' There was a pause and then Fred answered in a low voice.
'No. Got used to him now.'
'Well, tell him so,' replied Elaine, in an exasperated voice. Then she rang off, wishing she could get them to talk more. She didn't hear from Harvey again that night, but two nights later he started talking via text. Elaine suggested that he write down everything he was thinking as it could be helpful.

Already doing that.

You are? Since when?

Since Carl gave me a book and told me to write everything down.

And has it helped?

Yes.

Good. Keep writing.

But then the texts stopped coming that night, so Elaine just thanked God that Carl had appeared in Harvey's life, as this seemed to be a real breakthrough for him.

Chapter 17

The following week Elaine returned alone to Browsholme Hall. She met Jean and Barbara, who did quite different tours but still gave the same information. Elaine was beginning to see what Irena meant about everyone having their own style. When she got back from the first tour with Jean, a plated salad and a cup of tea appeared for Jean, delivered by Gail, who was working in the tearooms that day.

'I believe you're thinking of becoming a tour guide?' Gail asked.

'Yes, I think so,' Elaine admitted. 'Everyone seems very friendly.'

'Yes, they are. Are you a relative of Liz?'

'Almost. Liz' mother-in-law is my closest friend so I've seen the family grow up over the years and I'm godmother to both of Gill's sons.'

'That's great. What would you like to eat?'

'Just a piece of cake please or rather a scone. I had the carrot cake last week and had dithered between a scone and carrot cake.'

'And to drink?'

'Cup of tea please.'

The scone soon arrived and Elaine was amazed at the size of it, accompanied with a dish each of jam and cream. It was as delicious as the carrot cake she had the week before.

As they were finishing their food, Catherine popped in and asked Elaine if she could call up to the office in the attics before she left. Elaine agreed. After doing a tour with Barbara, Elaine went upstairs to Catherine's office. Slightly out of breath after climbing all the stairs, Elaine sat herself down in a seat in Catherine's office. Nicola, was also working at another desk by the window and said hello..

'Thanks for calling in,' said Catherine. 'Robert wants a word with you. I'll just buzz him.'

Seconds later, Robert Parker arrived in the office, a man similar in age to herself, Elaine thought as he introduced himself. They had a chat about being a tour guide and he asked if she was interested. Elaine said yes, she was.

'Great,' was Robert's reply, 'we need to have more guides as we're getting so many tours booked nowadays. Have you met some of the guides?'

'Yes, I've done a tour with Irena, Jean and Barbara, and I've also met Gail and Leslie.'

'That's good. Why don't you do a tour with someone else next week, then have a go yourself for the second tour. Could you manage that?'

'Yes, I think so.'

'Great. I'll leave you to sort out the details with Catherine. Nice to meet you, and thanks for coming on board,' and off he whirled.

'Let me look at the rota,' said Catherine. 'What about coming next Wednesday and working with Janine and then you can meet Lynn as well?'

'Yes, I can do that.'

'Just give me your details and I'll get Nicola to print off a set of notes for you to study and use in your tours.' Elaine gave her address and phone numbers to Catherine then, grasping her tour notes, she left the house. This time she walked to the bottom of the drive, and realised what people meant by the best view of the house being from the gatehouse. The house looked far more majestic from that viewpoint than viewed coming from the Tithe Barn. There were trees surrounding the house which was set on a hill, which she hadn't realised before. It gave a totally different perspective. Wandering round the lake and the gardens, Elaine eventually arrived back at the tea rooms.

'Thought we were going to have to send out a search party for you,' teased Liz.

'I got lost in the grounds.'

'Lost? How could you get lost? They're pretty straight forward,' said Liz.

'No,' Elaine laughed, 'I don't mean I lost my way, just lost in enjoying them.'

'That's all right then. Are you going home now?'

'Yes, but I'm coming back next week.'

'As a guide?'

'Yes.'

'Good for you. I'll see you later then.'

'Yes, I'll go home now and start learning my script for next week,' laughed Elaine, as she waved goodbye to everyone. It was only on returning home that she realised that she still hadn't spoken to Tora about her B & B. Oh, well, thought Elaine. There's always next week. I'll concentrate on being a tour guide before I plan my B & B.

A couple of weeks later Elaine and Harvey were working in the vegetable plot. As he was leaving he rooted in his bag and gave Elaine a book then did his customary running off. Elaine shouted after him, but he was gone.

After her tea Elaine took the book into the pulpit with a cup of tea and started reading it. It was as she guessed. It was the book that Carl had given Harvey to write in, and Elaine felt very privileged that Harvey had let her look at it.

On the first page it was obvious that Carl had written the following:

This is your book, Harvey, to write down what thoughts you have. You don't ever have to show anyone this book. If you can bring something that you've written to our meetings, that will help us both. Enjoy writing. It will help. Trust me.

Elaine turned to the next page. Not very much was written there.

Stupid book. Stupid idea. How can writing help?

I wonder if Carl has seen this entry? thought Elaine. She turned the page over.

How do you think I feel? I'm angry. Hurt. Fed up. In pain. Lonely. Nobody to talk to. Nobody understands. Nobody cares.

Elaine's heart lurched as she read this. Poor lad. Such a lot of anger, she thought as she turned over the next page. She thought that perhaps Carl had asked him what he missed when she read the next page.

I miss my Sister. And my Mum and Dad and Gran. If only I hadn't gone on the school trip. Gran would still be here for Granddad. I miss my mates at Whalley and the church youth club. I miss my bike. I miss having a mobile phone. I miss my Mum's Sunday lunches. I miss my Dad's jokes. I miss my old belongings. I don't know where they went when Granddad sold our house. I don't know where anything went. I've got no photos. I'm afraid I'm going to forget what they looked like.

At least she had already bought him a mobile phone and Sunday lunches would be easy to sort out from now on. And she could badger Fred in to buying him a bike. But the next page was a bit embarrassing for Elaine as she read it.

I like visiting our grave. I go alone 'cos Granddad can't hack it. But an old woman has bought the church now and owns the graveyard. I'm frightened of her. I'm frightened she'll stop me going to the grave now. I can't stop going. It's the only time I feel happy, when I'm working in the graveyard.

What a cheek! thought Elaine. Old woman indeed! But on reflection, she supposed that to a teenage boy she was old. It explained his abject fear and mistrust of her in the beginning. The pages continued, with Harvey pouring out his anguish; but slowly there was more mention of Elaine and the work that they were doing together. The cups of cocoa were mentioned and the tools that Elaine bought for him. His writing sounded more positive. But the entry just before his birthday brought tears to Elaine's eyes.

I can't face another birthday without Freya. I miss her so much, even though she was a pain at times and drove me mad.

And then on the next page it was like a different person was writing.

Elaine made me a birthday party with a cake and candles, and she even made Granddad come too. And we sang Happy Birthday to Freya, too. Granddad wouldn't have let me do that, but he couldn't say anything with her there. And she bought me a mobile phone and loads of other stuff. It's so good that I've got a phone again. And she's paid for a contract for me. How good is that? But I've lost my best mate's phone numbers 'cos they were in my old phone that got lost on the school holiday. And Ethan's moved abroad. I do miss them. I'll have to try on face book to see if I can find them.

The start of tears that had gathered in Elaine's eyes now became a torrent and she wept for some time. The party had been such a small thing and yet it had meant so much for Harvey. She looked up at the stained-glass window and noticed that the sharp questioning piercing eyes of Jesus were gone. Instead, he seemed to be looking at her with compassion and love. I must be going daft, thought Elaine to herself, imagining the stained-glass can change. She deliberately looked away. But she vowed that she would look out for Harvey until he didn't need her any more. She felt like he was her responsibility now, perhaps to be the mother he was missing. And she started planning little things that she would do for him.

The first thing she did was to ask Harvey and his granddad to Sunday lunch that weekend. Gill would understand if she didn't go to the farm when she explained why. Eventually perhaps, she could ask Gill to come to her house with Harvey and his granddad, but not just yet. That would take even more time.

Expecting difficulties, Elaine was surprised when Fred agreed to come to Sunday lunch, and she sent a text to Harvey to find out what their favourite meat was. *Roast pork with apple sauce for Harvey and roast beef with Yorkshire pudding for Granddad,* came back the reply. Elaine decided to do the beef for the first time, probably to keep granddad sweet, she reflected, but would do the pork the week after if they agreed to come again.

The following evening, when Harvey came to garden, Elaine gave him the book back and thanked him for trusting her to read it. Harvey seemed embarrassed and didn't want to talk about it. Elaine changed the subject and told him about the large book which she had, which would be able to identify the grave next to his family which Harvey had always cared for. She went to get the large book and found the plot page. It was Square A Plot nine, so Elaine looked in the older of the two books.

'Here you are, Harvey. It's the grave of Joshua Walker, his wife Jane and their children James, Henry and Janey.'

'They lost three children?' Harvey asked.

'Yes, but there was virtually no medicine available in those days, especially for poor people because you had to pay for a doctor and for medicine. That's why many children died.'

'Sad that no one survived. Like our family.'

'But some might have survived. They had much bigger families in those days. Do you want to help see if we can find them?' Harvey nodded. 'Although it might be difficult,' continued Elaine, 'because 1813 is before the first Census, so registrations of births and deaths were a bit unreliable. But the last death was Joshua's in December 1841, so we might be able to find some direct descendants.' She reached for the computer and typed all the information in for Joshua's death and found an address in Dunsop Bridge, where he'd died. Then she checked the 1841 census there was an entry for Joshua, listing him as head of household. No wife was listed, but three generations were living at the house. There was a son Ralph, aged 40 years, his wife Winifred, aged 38 years, and four of their children: Hetty, Matthew, Jane, and Joshua. Harvey was watching intently as all the information came up.

'Could I do that with my family?'

'Yes, do you want to do it now?' asked Elaine.

Harvey shook his head. 'Don't know names. I'll ask Granddad.'

'Well, we'll leave it for now and see what else we can find about the rest of the family. So, I'll see you on Sunday?' Harvey nodded, then said 'thanks' in a quiet voice.

Sunday lunch was a success. Fred really seemed to appreciate the meal, as well as Harvey. There wasn't much more conversation this time, but Fred and Harvey both seemed more relaxed than before. Elaine decided to bite the bullet.

'What happened to Harvey's bike, Fred? He was saying he missed having a bike.'

'Probably still in storage. Probably too small for him now.'

'Are the family photos still in storage?' But Fred's face changed and Elaine knew she had pushed him too far.

'Think it's time we were going now, come on Harvey. Thanks for the meal. Goodbye.'

'Wait, Fred, take this cake home with you.'

He stopped, grabbed the cake, muttered thank you, and left without another word. Harvey gave her a rueful glance but then followed his granddad out of the door. Elaine didn't know what to do for the best. She knew she'd gone too far, but didn't know how to mend it. She loaded the dishwasher and then rang Gill, asking her what to do. Gill advised her to leave well alone and see what happened. But Elaine worried all evening, desperately searching for the peace which her house usually gave her; but tonight it was missing. She went to bed early but spent a fitful night, tossing and turning, and reliving the conversation.

Harvey didn't come the next day, or the day after, and Elaine's anxiety increased, but on the Wednesday he arrived on a brand-new bike.

'Nice wheels,' Elaine said.

'Granddad took me to the Green Jersey in Clitheroe and bought it for me. Thanks.'

'Was he very cross with me?'

'Yes.'

'When did you get the bike?'

'Today, after school.'

'Job done, then?' Elaine asked. Harvey nodded, but there was just the slightest sign of a smile coming on his face.

'Is he still coming this Sunday for lunch?' Harvey nodded.

'Good. Right, let's get on with the weeding and planting out. Our crops are doing very nicely.'

Whilst they were gardening, Elaine told him about her plans for a tennis court, but he didn't react very much.

'Do you play tennis?'

'Sometimes.'

'Do you like it?'

'Not really, don't like the PE teacher.' And that's all she managed to get out of him. They worked companionably together for another hour and then Harvey went home.

The next day Ben and Jake started work on preparing the grounds for the tennis court. Elaine was very excited. Jake was teasing her that she was having it done for show, but when she told him that she loved playing tennis, and he could come and use the court if he wanted to, he changed his tune a bit. And both men loved it that Elaine fed them whilst they were working. Within a couple of weeks, the base was prepared ready for the polymer court floor, and the foundations for the fence and electric lighting was all ready. The base was delivered on a sunny day, for which Elaine heaved a sigh of relief. It would have been so much worse in bad weather. As soon as the firm had finished laying the court and it was safe to walk on, Ben and Jake came back to put up the protective fence and connect the lights. They tested the floodlights just as it was going dusk. It looked amazing, and Ben had to admit that it would be an asset for Elaine.

As soon as it was finished Elaine rang her new friend Barbara at the tennis club, and invited her round for a game the next night. Elaine had already brought a selection of racquets with her, but decided to treat herself to a new one. Barbara had brought her own racquet and they had a fast and furious game, dropping exhausted in the sunroom with cups of tea.

'It's a lovely house you've got here, Elaine. So unique. So peaceful. I love the stained-glass window. A church, wasn't it?'

'Yes, and the windows and the pulpit were both in a covenant and had to stay.'

'Well you've made a really good job of incorporating them into the lounge. I could sit here all night.'

'No you couldn't. You've to get up for work in the morning.'

Barbara pulled a face. 'Don't remind me. Just 'cos you took early retirement.'

'Best career move ever,' Elaine laughed. 'And anyway, you love your job. You'll keep going 'til you drop.'

'You're probably right. But it gets harder to get up in a morning when you're past 50, doesn't it?'

'Certainly does. Why don't you go part-time?'

'It's difficult when you're a partner. You work full-time, then sell your partnership when you retire, and that becomes your pension pot.'

'Yes, my godson's a solicitor.'

'Locally?'

'No, in Manchester.'

'What's his speciality?'

'Conveyancing. And you?'

'Family law.'

'Bet that can be gruelling at times.'

'Yes, there's nothing like a scorned wife for revenge!' Barbara laughed. 'It's the children I feel sorry for.' Elaine nodded.

'Well, I'd best be going. Thanks for tonight. I've really enjoyed it.'
'We'll ask Philip and Alison, or Jan and Nick next time and have a doubles match.'
'That'd be great, thanks. See you on Monday at the club?'
'Yes, I'll be there. Are you going to the history club on Thursday as well?'
'No, I can't go this week and I'm annoyed 'cos it's Brian Jeffreys again. He's a really good local historian. Are you going?'
'Yes, I'll probably see Lesley there, who works as a tour guide at Browsholme Hall, so I'll sit with her.'
'Well, make sure you take notes. I'll want to know what he says. Night and thanks again.'
'You're welcome. Night,' and Elaine watched until Barbara had got into her car before she turned the lights off.
The next evening, she asked Kirsty to come over and have a game with her. On arrival, Kirsty said that she didn't have her own racquet cos her mum was mean and wouldn't buy her one. Elaine pulled a wrapped parcel out of the cupboard and gave it to Kirsty.
'What's this?' she asked.
'Open it and see,' replied Elaine. 'It's an early birthday present.'
'Oh, Aunty Elaine, thanks!' Giving her a hug, Kirsty said 'I'll look after it, I promise,' as she threw the wrappings from the tennis racquet on the floor. 'Can we play now?'
'That was the general idea.'
The pair of them went out to the tennis court and Elaine tried to teach the rudiments of the game to Kirsty. There was a lot of hilarity and not much hitting of the ball, but Kirsty was loving every minute of it.
'Can I come again tomorrow?'
'Yes, if you want to. Come any time after homework.' That wiped the smile off Kirsty's face because she knew how much importance her Aunty Elaine gave to education. As they were going back into the house to get a cool drink Elaine noticed Harvey stood by the hedge, but he hurried away back to the garden as soon as they saw him. After Kirsty had gone, Harvey came in for a drink.
'How did you think Kirsty did?' Elaine asked.
'Not very good.'

'Oh, clever clogs! Can you do better?' All she got was a shrug. 'Come on then let's see what you can do.' She got a racquet out of the press and gave it to him. He was better than Kirsty, but not brilliant. But his face seemed to relax when he was concentrating on the game. Perhaps this was another way he could get rid of his angst, Elaine wondered.

The following week Kirsty came again and, only a few minutes into the game, Elaine went over on her ankle. It wasn't too painful, but she said she wasn't playing again that night, so Kirsty pulled a face.

'Harvey. Come and play a game with Kirsty for me. I've hurt my ankle.'

Reluctantly, Harvey came over and picked up Elaine's racquet and went to the other side of the court from Kirsty. They were both a little jerky at first, but soon managed to get a decent volley between them. When he won a point Harvey actually laughed out loud. It was the first time Elaine had heard him laugh. It took all her time not to cry. The match went on with greater enthusiasm from both Harvey and Kirsty and then an argument broke out. Kirsty said the ball was in the lines and Harvey said it was out. Elaine came over to referee and realised that Harvey was right. Kirsty was counting from the doubles lines not the singles. She gave an explanation, but Kirsty had a strop and decided that she'd had enough for that night. She announced that she was going home, and off she went.

Harvey looked at Elaine and grinned. Elaine didn't speak, but waited for Harvey.

'She's not happy,' he said.

'You could say that again.'

'Is she usually like that?'

'Not really. Just occasionally.'

'I enjoyed playing with her.'

'Good. You can do it again. By the way, I was thinking about something you wrote in your book.' Harvey froze, his smile disappearing. 'You said that you miss the youth club. Would you like me to take you this week?'

'Don't even know if it's still on. Not been since . . .' There was a distinct pause.

'How could you find out? Have you got your mate's phone numbers?'

'No, they're in my old phone that I lost.'

'Do you want to go to church on Sunday? I could take you. Then you'd be able to see your mates and find out.' Harvey thought about it for a while and then nodded.

'Yes, please.'

'Okay, we'll go this Sunday. Would your granddad want to go?'

'No,' said Harvey very quickly.

'What time does it start?'

'Half ten.'

'Right, we'll set off at ten then.' Another nod, then Harvey said he had to be going and left quickly. Elaine wasn't sure whether he was happy or sad about going, but she'd find out on Sunday. She just hoped she hadn't pushed him too far, too early. He seemed to be making so much progress now that sometimes she forgot how far he had already come.

On Sunday morning it poured with rain, and Elaine was concerned that it was ten o'clock and there was no sign of Harvey. She paced around a little, but didn't really want to go outside to see if he was coming and get drenched. Perhaps he'd had second thoughts. Perhaps she'd pushed him too much again. Elaine bit her lip nervously, wondering what to do. She tried his phone, but he didn't answer. Then she heard Fred's old Volvo estate arriving.

'Sorry, Elaine, Granddad's car wouldn't start. Wouldn't let me walk in rain.'

'Never mind we might just make it.' They both got in the car and set off. The rain got even worse and Elaine had to drive slowly through the lanes to Whalley. Then when they got to Whalley there was nowhere to park, so they had to leave the car up a side street near Maureen Cookson's shop and hurry across to the church, Elaine shaking the rain off her umbrella as they got in. The service had already started, but a lady welcomed them and grinned when she recognised Harvey.

'So good to see you Harvey,' she said. 'The service has just started.'

They hurried into the church and slid into seats near the back. The people were all singing. It was a lively tune that Elaine didn't know, but they were all singing with great gusto and Elaine soon picked up the tune. Harvey didn't sing, but then neither did some of the other young people who were there. Elaine noticed that people were aware of them coming in and heads were turning round to smile at Harvey. As soon as the service was over, Harvey dashed off to see his friends, telling Elaine that coffee was in the back hall. Elaine remained in her seat for a while, watching Harvey with his friends. The friends were chatting animatedly and Harvey seemed to be answering them. They were all using their phones, so perhaps Harvey was getting their numbers, Elaine hoped. A voice at her side startled her. It was the lady who'd welcomed them at the door.

'Hello, I'm Jennifer Lockwood. Has he abandoned you?'

'Yes,' Elaine laughed, 'but I don't mind. It's so good to see him talking with his friends. I'm Elaine Barnes.'

'Are you a relative?'

'No, just a neighbour but he wanted to see his friends so I offered to bring him. He helps me with the gardening at my house.'

'We were so sorry about the accident. We never saw Harvey again, as he went to live with his granddad and we never heard from them again either. Come on through and we'll get a coffee.'

Elaine followed Jennifer into the back room and they both got a coffee and biscuit and stood talking. Jennifer introduced her to several of the other church members and they all commented on how good it was to see Harvey. Elaine got the impression that the whole church had grieved for the Tattersall family, but had not been able to resolve that grief, feeling helpless at having lost contact with Harvey.

Eventually people started leaving and Elaine went over to where Harvey was talking.

'Are these your friends, Harvey?'

'Yes, this is Tom Dillon, and that is Oliver Targett. And this is Lily, Tom's sister, and Kate, Oliver's sister.'

'Hello, good to meet you all. I'm Elaine, a neighbour of Harvey's.' They all chorused 'hello' back, and then Tom and Lily's mum came to take them home, so there were more introductions. Kate and Oliver's dad came to collect them, making more introductions. Eventually they were leaving and Harvey sat in the car with a big grin on his face and hardly spoke all the way home.

'You might as well stay here for lunch rather than go home. You can peel some potatoes,' suggested Elaine, but saw the look on Harvey's face and laughed.

'Don't worry, I've done them already. I prepared everything this morning and I left the meat in the oven cooking whilst we were out. Ring your granddad and tell him to come up when he's ready.'

'Okay.'

'Did you find out if there's still a youth club?'

'Yes, Fridays at seven.'

'And would you like to go?'

'Yes.'

'And would you like me to take you?' Elaine said, thinking that it was like drawing teeth getting anything out of him.

'I could go on my bike.'

'It's a bit far. I can take you.'

'What would you do?'

'I've friends in Whalley now. But I could go and sit in the pub to wait for you.'

'You don't mind?'

'No. Not if it makes you happy.'

'Thanks, Elaine. You've changed my life.'

'Oh, go on with you,' replied Elaine. 'You've changed your own life.'

After Harvey and his granddad had gone home, Elaine decided to watch the latest episode of a costume drama on TV, so settled herself on the settee in the lounge. After it had finished Elaine lay staring at the picture of Christ in her window. She remembered the talk from church this morning. It had been about the disciple Peter denying knowing who Jesus was three times before Jesus' trial and crucifixion. After Jesus had risen from the dead Peter had met Jesus again by the lakeside. Three times Jesus asked Peter if he loved him and Peter replied three times in the affirmative, one for each of his denials. Suddenly Elaine realised that was the question Jesus was asking of her too. Did she love him? Did she love Jesus? She supposed she'd always loved him since she was a child in Sunday school, but felt he was asking her now as an adult. Elaine looked at Jesus and whispered, 'Yes, I love you,' and was filled with peace throughout her whole body. Looking up at Jesus, she was sure he was smiling at her, but knew she was probably imagining it. Elaine had the best night's sleep she'd had for a long time and woke totally refreshed and at peace. She felt ready for anything life could throw at her.

The following Friday Elaine didn't need to sit in the pub on her own as during the week she got a message from Debby via Harvey saying that she could go round to her house whilst the youngsters were at youth club.

Taking a bottle of wine as a thank you, Elaine took Harvey to Debby's next Friday. The youngsters were soon away to the club and Debby got two wine glasses out.

'You can come round here any time,' Debby said, 'especially if you bring a bottle of wine.' They both laughed. 'No, seriously, you can come round without the bottle of wine. It's good to have some adult company.'

'Did you know Harvey's parents well?'

'Yes, we used to have barbecues in each other's gardens, with Oliver and Kate's parents too. Well, not in our garden, as I'm no good with a barbecue, but I used to take my signature chocolate cake for afters.'

'Sounds good. I hope you don't mind me asking, did you take any photos of Harvey's family?'

'Loads, why?'

'He hasn't got any.'

'No photos? I wonder where they went. Jason was forever snapping his camera or phone. He was quite well known locally as an amateur photographer. He used to win competitions.'

'Really? I wonder what happened to them.'

'Doesn't Harvey's granddad have any?'

'Not that he's telling us about. Harvey is frightened that he'll forget what his parents look like. And he wants to be able to have pictures in his bedroom.'

Debby rooted in her pocket and brought out her phone.

'Here, I'll show you.' Scrolling down her phone, she found lots of pictures and showed them to Elaine. 'Here, that's Jason, and that's Amanda, and the young girl is Freya.' The photos were all very carefree and casual, but the thing that struck Elaine most was the happy expressions on their faces. Elaine felt very emotional. Poor Harvey, being denied access to these lovely memories.

'Give me a minute and I'll print some off for you.' Debby disappeared into another room and after about fifteen minutes came back with a sheaf of photos. 'I've printed some copies of some of the rest of us too, so he can remember some of the fun times we've had.' Elaine looked at the photos with tears in her eyes.

'Thanks,' she managed to mumble. 'Harvey will love these.'

'I'll probably be able to find some more if I search hard enough.'

'Who's this boy? I don't recognise him.'

'Oh that's Ethan, Harvey's best mate. They lived next door to Harvey.'

'He's not mentioned Ethan, but then Harvey's only just started talking again.'

'Really? You couldn't shut him up before.'

'He didn't speak to me for months. But he's having counselling and he's started talking again, but not much. Mind you, his granddad doesn't have much to say, so I don't suppose there has been much communication between them. So where's Ethan now?'

'They moved to France, about two years ago, quite suddenly. Ethan's dad got a promotion to the head office in France and they sold up very quickly and left. It was, er, let me see; it was the October of the same year of the accident. It must have been hard for Harvey because the two of them were inseparable. They both went to Ribblesdale together, whereas the other children in the gang went to St Christopher's and the Grammar School.'

'So not only did he lose all his family, but his best mate as well?'

'Yes.'

'No wonder he didn't speak and wouldn't go to school.'

'Didn't go to school?'

'Oh, he's going now, but he kept missing or leaving school early when I first knew him. Debby, there's something that's been puzzling me.'

'What's that, Elaine?'

'Didn't Jason have any family? Couldn't they look after Harvey?'

'Jason was a Barnado Boy and very proud of it. He was left in a telephone box just after birth. His mother left a letter saying she loved him dearly but couldn't keep him. So he was brought up in children's homes.'

'That's terrible. Poor Jason. Did he ever try to find out anything about his birth mother?'

'Yes. He had a DNA test just before they went on holiday, but I don't know what will have happened to that.'

'It's important to find out now before his birth mother isn't here anymore. I wonder if Harvey will be able to find anything out?''

'I suppose that he . . .' but Elaine wasn't to find out what Debby thought, as the door flew open and all the children ran in, Tom and Lily talking away and Harvey laughing.

'Good time, Harvey?' asked Elaine.

'Yes, thanks.'

'Good. Well, thanks for having me, Debby. We'll get going now.'

'Come any Friday; you're very welcome.'

Elaine and Harvey got into the car and went back to Elaine's house.

'Come inside before you go home. I've got something for you.' Harvey nodded and followed her inside. 'Hot chocolate?' she asked.

'Yes, please.'

When they were both sat comfortably, nursing their hot chocolates, Elaine reached in to her handbag and pulled out the sheaf of photos, passing them to Harvey without saying a word. Harvey just kept turning them over and over in his hands, then looked up at Elaine, obviously trying to stop the tears in his eyes from spilling over.

'Where did you get these from?' he eventually asked.

'From Debby's phone. She printed them off for you.'

He finished his chocolate and then jumped up and said he had to go.

'Wait,' said Elaine. 'I've got something upstairs for you.' She hurried upstairs to the white bedroom where she kept all her spare presents and rooted out a photo frame which she'd won at a raffle and didn't need. She went downstairs again, half expecting Harvey to have gone, but he stood in the doorway waiting for her.

'Here's a frame. I thought you could put that photo of all four of you in it, for your bedroom.'

Harvey grabbed the frame, said thanks and ran out of the door clutching the photos in his hands. Elaine stood watching long after he'd gone out of sight, then slowly turned back inside, hoping that she'd done the right thing. Just as she was going to bed Elaine got a text with a picture. It was a picture of Harvey's bedside cabinet, complete with frame on top with the family photo inside. The caption just said '*thanks*'. Elaine was happy. She knew she'd done the right thing.

Chapter 18

Gill and Elaine were having coffee together in Gill's bungalow and the conversation turned to holidays.

'Are you going away this year?' asked Gill.

'Not a big holiday. I'm at Browsholme Hall on August Bank Holiday, so can't go away that week.

'You're really enjoying being a tour guide, aren't you?'

'I am. The first tour on my own was a bit nerve racking, but it gets easier every time. You meet really nice people too. What about you? Have you booked a holiday?'

'Nothing planned.'

'I've been so busy and not thought about it. And the Manchester tennis lot are coming soon. First week of July, just before the school holidays start.'

'How long for?'

'Just a week. Going to try out my court for themselves. They were very impressed when I wrote and invited them.'

'I'm not surprised. Tennis lovers' heaven, I should think.'

'Something like that.'

'Do you fancy a city break?'

'When? Where to?'

'I thought Spain. I'd love to do all the Cathedrals and the historic parts that you don't see on holiday usually.'

'When were you thinking? In the summer?'

Gill pulled a face. 'No, it'll be too hot for me in the summer. I thought later in the year.'

'Why don't we go for our birthdays?'

'That's a good idea. Yes, let's.'

'You Google it all and let me know how much I have to pay you when you've booked.'

'Let's have a look now,' said Gill, as she got her laptop out. After a few minutes of searching she asked, 'Madrid or Barcelona?'

'Not bothered really. Barcelona?'

'There's a five-day special offer going from the ninth of November. Historic Barcelona, it's called.'

'Sounds good to me. Book it.'

'Book it?'

'Why not? We've nobody to bother about apart from ourselves. Will they mind on the farm?'

'No, they'll be glad I've got something booked even if it's only a short holiday. They keep nagging me to go away. But next year we really need to plan something a bit more spectacular for our 60th birthday. What do you fancy doing?'

'Well, on my birthday, I've got my commemorative service for Remembrance Day, with it being the 100 years anniversary of the end of the First World War.'

'Yes, I know about that. But that's only one day. What shall we do after?'

'We've plenty of time to think of something spectacular before then,' Elaine laughed. 'It's well over a year. A lot can happen in a year.'

'True. Right, that's booked then. You owe me for the deposit. I've used my credit card.'

'Okay. By the way, are there any city breaks to Paris in the summer?'

'I don't fancy Paris. What makes you want to go there? Thought you didn't want to go to France again?'

'I've got an idea, that's all. Besides, I wasn't asking you to go,' Elaine teased.

'Oh, yes? Have you got another fella on the go?'

'Wouldn't you like to know,' Elaine replied.

'You don't have to tell me everything,' Gill said, a bit huffily.

'No, I don't, but I will.' And she told Gill about the photos and that Harvey's best friend had moved to Paris just after the accident. 'I thought I'd take Harvey, and his granddad if he'll come, to visit Ethan.'

'That poor boy really had a bad time, didn't he?'

'Yes, to come back from holiday to find all his family had died, and then to find his best friend had gone to live abroad must have been the final straw.'

'No wonder he didn't talk for ages,' said Gill sadly. 'Mind you, living with Fred Baxter must be hard at the best of times. What does Harvey think about going to Paris?'

'I haven't told him yet. I've only just got Ethan's dad's contact details. I'm going to email him tonight.'

'You've really got involved with Harvey, haven't you?'

'Yes. It's been so lovely to see him slowly coming back to life again. His counsellor has been amazing, and the gardening's really helped.'

'Look, there are some city breaks in France. See what you think. Some are very touristy, with lots of trips and visits.'

'No, I wouldn't want trips, as Harvey needs to spend as much time as he can with Ethan. I could just wander round on my own if the boys were doing something together.'

'True. You've always been able to amuse yourself.'

'Comes of living alone for most of my adult life,' laughed Elaine.

That night Elaine emailed Ethan's dad and received a reply almost immediately. Yes, they would love to see Harvey and they could stay at their apartment. After a few more emails, it was decided that Harvey would stay with the family, but Elaine would stay in an apartment nearby, and she'd got a phone number to ring and book. Good job I can still speak fluent French, thought Elaine. But first she had to ring Harvey. When he didn't answer, she sent a text instead.

Have you got an up-to-date passport?

Yes, why?

You're going to Paris to stay with Ethan.

What?????

What I said.

When?

When you've finished your GCSE exams.

Does Granddad know?

No, not yet. Do you want me to tell him? Or rather, I'd better ask him first.

No, I'm at home. I'll ask him.

Ask him if he wants to go as well.

He won't!

I know that but ask him all the same.

But they were both wrong. Fred did want to go. Not to Paris, but to the old battlefields. His father's twin brother had been killed in the Second World War, and just before the accident, he'd been planning to go on a special trip to the battlefields and then visit his uncle's grave. Eventually, with lots of emails to-ing and fro-ing, it was decided that Fred would stay with Harvey at Ethan's, whilst Elaine stayed at a bed and breakfast place. Then after the weekend they would all drive down to the battlefields so that Harvey could visit his great-great uncle's grave as well.

First though, Harvey had to do his GCSEs. Elaine was pleased to see that he was studying for them, whereas a year ago he had no interest in schoolwork, but now he had to make the grades so that he could go on the course at Myerscough. That was enough to get him studying.

At long last, the final exam was done and the following weekend the three of them set off. Elaine had decided to take the car, as it would be easier to get from Paris to the battlefields at their own leisure. From the ferry she drove to Paris and they arrived in the middle of Friday afternoon. Dropping Harvey and Fred off at Ethan's, Elaine went to get herself a meal before settling into her bed and breakfast place. It was a large, homely room, with ensuite, drink-making facilities, and a TV, so Elaine was pleased with it.

She spent a glorious weekend doing all the touristy things. But on the Sunday evening she'd been invited to go to Ethan's home for a meal. The apartment was very large and impressive and overlooked a quiet courtyard. The meal that Ethan's mum made was excellent, as was the wine that flowed all night. Even Fred became more talkative! Elaine was glad she'd only to walk to her lodgings that night.

The next morning they said their goodbyes, and Elaine offered to host a visit for Ethan later in the summer if they wished to. Both Ethan and Harvey looked happy about that, and Ethan's dad said that they intended visiting family in late August, so could include a visit to Dunsop Bridge. Soon they were on the road and motored down to the war graveyard where Fred's uncle was buried. It was very moving to see all the white graves. Row after row after row, all representing a loved one who had been missed and mourned. It really brought home the scale of loss that occurred during both World Wars and all three of them had a tear in their eyes when Fred laid a wreath on his uncle's grave. Fred and Harvey later went on a conducted tour of the battlefields, whilst Elaine stayed in the town where they were staying that night, to let them have some time alone together. She spent the day wandering round the town shopping, and having coffee.

The next day, they were back on the road to the ferry and then driving back to Dunsop Bridge. They took it slowly, stopping off to have regular meals. When they got back, Elaine drove round to their house and, as she was leaving, Fred came and thrust something into her hands.

'No arguments,' he said brusquely. 'You've paid for everything. I won't be beholden to you.'

Elaine looked in her hands. There was a bundle of £20 notes. She tried to protest.

'No, Fred, it was my treat. I wanted to take you and Harvey. Besides, it was easier for me to pay as I'm used to French currency and the language.'

'I've said, I'll not be beholden to you. Take it, or Harvey never comes to your house again. Or me.' The look in his eyes scared Elaine a little, so she accepted gratefully, thinking that she would put the money into her graveyard fund to help her get some stones put back again. She couldn't risk Harvey not coming to her house again. That would be too painful. He had buried himself too deeply into her heart now.

'Okay Fred, I accept the money, thank you very much,' she said quietly and got in her car quickly and set off home before she burst into tears in front of them.

It was only a week before the Manchester tennis friends were coming, and Elaine was glad as it gave her something to do. It was such a good reunion. They talked and played tennis all week, although the six of them went out on trips locally on their own, whilst Elaine got on with her own life, but they all went out for a meal together on the Wednesday night. On the Thursday evening a few friends from the Whalley tennis club came over and lots of games of doubles were played. Both Manchester and Whalley tried to win the most games, but it ended in a draw, amid much hilarity.

Dot said after the tournament that they should make it a regular event every year. And John suggested that they have a cup made to present annually. Elaine was just thrilled to watch all her old and new friends getting on together and thought an annual tournament was a great idea and she offered to be the host. By Saturday morning the six friends were all packed up ready to go, and Elaine hugged them all in turn.

As soon as they had gone, she went upstairs to strip all the beds to get the washing done. Nikki was coming in later to give all the bedrooms a thorough clean, not that they really needed it. Each couple had stripped their beds and neatly folded the bedding and the towels. In the grey bedroom there was also an envelope. Inside was a thank you card containing money. The card said they appreciated their holiday and were unhappy that Elaine wouldn't let them pay, so here was a donation to her graveyard fund, which she'd told them about. It was £300. That was so naughty, thought Elaine. She hadn't wanted money, just their company. But it was a reminder that she really needed to get on with sorting the graves out where she could. Her graveyard fund was growing, as she still got paid every time there was a funeral in the graveyard.

It would be too expensive to buy new headstones for all the graves, but she would start with the 1813 grave, which was next to Harvey's family grave, and three others where the names weren't clearly visible. Finding a local stonemason, she organised him to come and redo the grave's carving, but she didn't tell Harvey. She wanted it to be a surprise for him. And surprise it was. Elaine watched him as he went to his family grave for his daily visit and then glanced over at the next grave. He stood up quickly and went over to look closer at the 1813 grave which now proudly stated who was interred there. He turned round and saw Elaine watching him and gave a thumbs up sign to her. Later he came into the house and thanked her properly, as if it were his own family grave that had been improved.

'Something to tell you,' Harvey grinned.

'Oh yes, what's that?'
'Got a job.'
'A job? I thought you were going to Myerscough?'
'I am. Weekend job but might be more hours for the summer holidays.'
'That's great. Where is it?'
'Shackleton's Garden Centre.'
'When do you start?'
'This Saturday.'
'Well done! How are you going to get there?'
'Bike.'
'Fair enough. I'm so proud of you. Did you have an interview?'
Harvey nodded.
'Well, tell me more. What was it like?'
'Told them I loved gardening. Told them about your garden and graveyard.'
'Did you tell them you've got in at Myerscough?'
'Yes. Think that's what got me the job.'
'And will you be able to carry on whilst you are studying at Myerscough?'
'Yes.'
'That's great then. Bit of money for yourself too.'
'Going home now.'
'Okay. Take this cake with you. It's your granddad's favourite, lemon drizzle.'

'Thanks,' and off he went, carefully carrying the cake with him until he got to his bike, then he put it in his rucksack. Probably be in crumbs when he gets home, thought Elaine, but she didn't say anything. She just waved him off. She was so proud of him. To have gone and applied for a job when he still wasn't very fluent at times was a miracle. Perhaps it would be the making of him, as he would have to talk to customers and staff. Perhaps it was linking up with all his old friends at Whalley and with Ethan that had made the difference, but it was a very different young man that she now saw from the one she first met less than a year ago.

Two weeks later on the Saturday, Elaine persuaded Anna, Kate, and Kirsty to go to Shackleton's café for their lunch instead of Puddleducks, so that they could see Harvey at work. They didn't need much persuading, especially Kirsty. Elaine suspected that Kirsty was a little keen on Harvey, despite their spectacular fallouts when playing tennis. First, they wandered round all the shops and then the garden centre, and Elaine picked up some plants for her garden but didn't see Harvey until they were ready for giving up. He came out of the greenhouse and Anna spotted him first.

'Hi, Harvey,' she called, and, although Harvey blushed a little and looked quickly around, he came over to say hello.

'We're going to the café here instead of Puddleducks,' Kirsty added.

'Good,' said Harvey, then said he had to be going. He was supposed to be moving some stuff from the greenhouse to outside, so off he went. But Elaine watched as she saw him talk to a customer and give advice, and her heart swelled with pride as if he was her own child. But then she thought of him as her own child now, however wrong that was. Giving herself a mental shake, she gathered the girls around her, and after paying for the plants and taking them to the car, they went to the café for lunch.

The following week, the Vaughtons arrived to stay in Liz' holiday cottages together with their grandson Charlie. Charlie's school had found asbestos in the ceilings of one wing of the school, so they had closed two weeks early. As both his parents worked, Charlie had been dispatched off to stay with the grandparents, so they'd decided to take him on holiday with them. Elaine had invited them all round for lunch on the Monday. They arrived about 11.30am and she showed them round the house, but it was only when they went into the graveyard that they all seemed to get excited.

'Where's your war graves?' asked Ray.

'Over on the far wall. First World War in the middle and Second World War next to them, towards the top of the graveyard. Why? Are you interested in war graves?'

'Not all war graves, only some. First World War. Do you have a grave belonging to a Robert Carroll?'

'Yes, the middle one of the three First World War graves.'

'Have you investigated the history of the grave?'

'Not yet. I did the Farnworth grave but never got round to any others.' No wonder thought Elaine to herself, after the fiasco with Thomas, but didn't say anything.

'Well, we can let you know, can't we Charlie?' said Maureen.

'Really? That would be great. Because I'm trying to contact all the families before Remembrance Day 2018. I intend to hold a commemorative service.'

'Charlie had to do a project for his history GCSE this year and had to find out if any of his family had served in the war. You tell the story, Charlie,' said Maureen.

'I found two Great-Great Uncles of my Dad's who'd served in the army, but Granny's been researching her own family history. We found out that Robert Carroll was her Great-Great Granddad, so he's my four times Great Granddad, I think.'

'Yes,' interrupted an excited Maureen, 'we couldn't believe it when we found out he was buried in Dunsop Bridge. It seemed so strange that we met you in Italy and you'd just bought this place, but we had no idea about Robert Carroll when we met you. I've been dying to tell you but decided to wait until we were here.'

'What a coincidence,' said Elaine. 'You've made me realise that I need to get on with the other war graves if I want to contact all the relatives before next year.'

'Why don't you let Charlie help you? He's a whiz kid on the Ancestry.com website.'

'Well, if you don't mind, Charlie?'

'He'd love to. We were worried he'd be bored on holiday with us, but this would be a nice project for him.'

Elaine looked at Charlie and he did seem pleased. 'Do you play tennis at all, Charlie?'

'A bit when I can.'

'I just happen to have a tennis court out back, with plenty of spare racquets, so if you get bored with researching the family trees, you could have a game of tennis.'

'Hey, Charlie, this holiday is suddenly looking up, isn't it? Play on your computer all day and tennis when you've had enough.' said Ray. Charlie just beamed.

'A tennis court? Here?' Charlie asked.

'Yes, come on and I'll show it to you. And come and use my laptop here if you like. I won't disturb you.'

'Thanks,' said Charlie, and they all followed Elaine round to the back field and admired the tennis court.

After lunch, Charlie decided that he wanted to start researching Arthur Hacking's grave straightaway, the third of the First World War graves. Elaine got her laptop out and logged in for him and they never heard a peep from him all afternoon, so Elaine, Maureen and Ray had a good chat.

The following day the family were going to the Lake District for the day, but on Wednesday Liz was taking them to Browsholme Hall and Elaine wasn't on duty that day. She saw Charlie pull a face, so suggested that he might prefer to stay with her and do some more research. A very relieved Charlie agreed and thanked Elaine.

'Didn't fancy stately home,' he muttered.

'No, I haven't managed to take Harvey there yet. I must tell you about Harvey. You may see him about the graveyard. He keeps a lot of the graves up to scratch and helps me with my vegetable patch.'

'Is he one of Gill's grandchildren?' asked Ray.

'No, he's just one of the boys from the village. Come on and I'll show you his family grave. That's how we first met.'

They stood beside the family grave and Maureen asked in a low voice what had happened. Elaine briefly told them the story and explained that Harvey had been mentally scarred by it but was improving rapidly now. They'd gone back in the house for another drink when Harvey turned up so Elaine was glad that they'd moved away from the grave.

'Hi, Harvey. These are some friends I met on holiday in Italy. They've brought their grandson, Charlie, with them.' Both boys nodded and looked away, as teenage boys do.

'Going to weed vegetable patch,' Harvey announced.

'Okay,' replied Elaine, and he was off like a shot. That prompted the Vaughtons to go home and, after thanking Elaine for her hospitality, they left. Elaine went out to find Harvey, but he didn't seem to be in a talkative mood, so she left him to it.

By the end of the week, Charlie had a sheaf of papers for Elaine. He'd printed out his own family tree, and then the next grave which was Arthur Hacking, and the two Second World War graves, which were Nicholas Heaton and Stanley Wood. Not only had Charlie found their war records but had worked out all their family trees and last known contact with potential phone numbers. He had saved Elaine hours and hours of painstaking research. He'd even found out that Stanley Wood was something of a hero. He was known as 'back again Stan' because he took great risks by returning to help soldiers who'd been wounded. And Nicholas Heaton had been a pilot, enduring many raids over Germany before being killed. Elaine was impressed.

'What do I owe you for all this work, Charlie?' Elaine asked him quietly.

'Nothing, I've enjoyed doing it.'

'Well, you must come to the celebration service next year. Promise?'

'Try keeping me away,' he grinned.

Elaine went round to the farm next morning to wave all the Vaughtons off. She gave Charlie a large box of chocolates as a thank you, and his face lit up as he thanked her. As soon as they'd gone Elaine went on Amazon and sent him a generous gift voucher for doing all the work. He couldn't argue now he'd gone, she laughed to herself. And then she went to take Daniel out to Puddleducks for lunch, as it was his turn.

When Elaine had been talking to the stonemason, she'd mentioned about wanting to put some kind of memorials on the graves which had no stones or only had rotten wooden crosses, but explained she couldn't afford to make proper headstones for them all. He suggested that engraved plaques could be put up instead which would be much cheaper, and she could use a durable material such as cement for the base, which wouldn't rot. Elaine liked that idea and gave him a list of all the graves that had no known relatives, 27 in all. Thanks to Charlie's research and because of the two old books from the vestry, she now had a much clearer picture of the people in her graveyard. It was all part of her plan before the commemorative service. And the plan was now one stage nearer.

Chapter 19

The summer flew past. Between Browsholme Hall, tennis club, Whalley Abbey, Women's Institute and history club, life was always busy. There were always outings with Gill and the girls and Daniel, and old work colleagues came to stay. Elaine had managed to write to all the contacts that Charlie had found for her and now had a list of people who were coming to the commemorative service. Charlie was investigating the other families who weren't war graves, but only if she promised not to send him anymore vouchers. Elaine agreed reluctantly and gave him all the information from the two old books that had been found in the vestry.

One evening when Harvey was having his hot chocolate, which he liked just as much in summer as he did in winter, he asked Elaine if he could put a beehive in the back garden. He said it was really important to have lots of bees, as they were declining and were needed to keep the world going round, so Elaine agreed. Harvey insisted on paying for everything himself even though Elaine offered to pay. She only made one proviso, which was that she never had to help Harvey with the bees as she didn't want to be stung. She'd just eat the honey. 'It's a deal,' Harvey replied.

Harvey started his course at Myerscough in September, but still worked at Shackleton's Garden Centre when he could. Nowadays he would often go over to Whalley to see Oliver and Tom on his bike. Elaine was pleased that he was getting more independent but was missing him a little if she was honest. But they still came round for tea every week on a Wednesday and for a meal on Sunday, which was no longer lunch, but more usually teatime, as Harvey was often working. Carl had arranged with the pastoral care team for him to continue his counselling at Myerscough, and that seemed to be going well as far as she could get any information out of Harvey. But he seemed much more relaxed around people nowadays. Elaine reckoned that working at Shackleton's had helped him enormously, as he had to talk to people there. Things got quite heated sometimes when he was playing tennis with Kirsty, and Elaine was glad to watch them sparring together. And you couldn't stay in Kirsty's presence and not talk for long! She was just like her gran for asking questions, Elaine decided.

With Harvey working most Sundays he'd got out of the habit of going to church every week, but Elaine often went on her own and found friendship and spiritual succour from her visits. It somehow felt right to be going to church after all the years that she'd missed going.

In October, Gill and Elaine were discussing Christmas, always wanting to be organised, Gill said. They knew that Lindsay and Tim weren't coming this year as they had news that Lindsay was expecting a baby next April, so they wanted to go to her parents this year. Gill was all of a flurry with knitting patterns and wondering if she would at long last get a grandson, but she hastened to assure Elaine that she'd welcome any baby of Tim's, whatever sex, just as long as the baby and mother were okay. Elaine suggested that she would like Fred and Harvey to come this year but wasn't sure whether they would. Gill said that if you ask now, they've plenty of time to get used to it, which Elaine agreed with. So the following Sunday she asked them to come on Christmas Day. Fred, as expected, said he'd think about it.

It was soon time to go to Spain for their birthday weekend mini holiday. Gill and Elaine thoroughly immersed themselves in all the local Barcelona history and came home exhausted, having walked miles around the city, especially the Cathedral and the Gothic sector. But it did them both good and they talked idly about a big holiday for their 60th birthdays. Finally they agreed that as soon as the commemorative service was over, they would Google last minute special holiday offers and see what came up, but they would have a family party as well before they went away.

Christmas Day came round far too quickly, both Gill and Elaine agreed, but they were ready as always, despite the last-minute panics. Amazingly, Fred and Harvey came as well, and the house was full of laughter, teasing, charades and forfeits, and great hilarity, as well as good food. Although Elaine couldn't honestly say that Fred was the life and soul of the party, he did seem to enjoy himself. And Elaine noticed that Kirsty and Harvey weren't arguing for a change. Great progress, she reflected. This year, the Boxing Day party and the New Year's Eve party were at Liz and Ben's farmhouse, and it was a relief for Elaine to only do Christmas Day this year.

In the January of 2018, Elaine started seriously organising her commemorative service. First, she booked Alan Reid, the retired vicar from Whalley, to perform the service, but also asked the Priest from St Hubert's

Roman Catholic church to take part as well. Next, she wrote formal invitations to many of the local families who were represented in the graveyard, and even sent one to Thomas but wasn't sure if he would reply. Her next booking was to find someone to perform the 'Last Post' and found that Slaidburn village had a Silver Band and could send someone to perform on the day. Most of the Remembrance Day services took place in the morning, so Elaine deliberately planned hers for the afternoon. She also invited the Mayor and Mayoress of Ribble Valley to attend and they accepted. Her god-daughter Charlotte's best friend, Daisy-Belle Dumsday, was a classically trained soprano. They'd met at primary school and been friends ever since, just like Gill and Elaine. So Elaine booked Daisy-Belle to come and sing some wartime songs after the service.

As it would probably be a very cold day, Elaine decided that she would provide a hot meal. She asked Liz and Gill if they'd help bake pies so that she could serve pie and peas, followed by cake afterwards. Already about 50 people had said that they would attend, including the Vaughtons so Liz offered them a holiday cottage for the weekend, with Elaine being the backup in case they were already booked out, although winter bookings were usually quieter. Even though her house was large, Elaine realised that 50+ people wouldn't fit into her house, so she booked a large marquee which would be put next to, and open into, the sunroom so that there was plenty of room for everyone.

The spring came early that year and Elaine was glad when Browsholme Hall opened again for the season, as she loved her tour guide work. Inspired by the gardens at Browsholme Hall, she decided that it was time that she sorted out her front garden. The vegetable patch was well organised now, and she sat with Harvey one night and asked him what she should do with it.

'Got to do a project for my course work. Design a garden. I could do it.'

'Go for it,' said Elaine. 'That'll save me thinking what to do.' So they spent a good hour talking about what she would and wouldn't like.

When it was Harvey's 17th birthday, Elaine decided to really splash out for him and bought him 20 driving lessons, as she knew he wanted to learn to drive as soon as he could. Gill recommended a lady called Karina, who'd taught both Kate and Anna. But Fred Baxter's present for Harvey totally shocked Elaine. They'd been together to a second-hand car dealer and bought

Harvey a five-year-old Toyota Aygo with low mileage. Harvey was ecstatic. You'd have thought he'd got a Porsche, to see him taking care of his new wheels. Fred took him out for lots of extra lessons and he soon gained in confidence. Two months to the day after his birthday, he took his test and passed first time, so they had to have another party to celebrate.

Elaine gave him the hard word about driving carefully, but he insisted he'd be careful, as Karina had instilled in him from the first lesson, saying that he was in charge of a killing machine. But the car made life a lot easier for them. He was able to take Fred shopping or go shopping for him instead of having to rely on the old Volvo, and he drove to Myerscough and the garden centre now for work. Elaine just had to hope and pray he would be sensible.

It was a bright sunny day at the beginning of August. Elaine was upstairs when there was a thundering knock on the door. Elaine smiled to herself, knowing that only one man had a knock like that.

'Coming, Fred,' she shouted, and she wasn't wrong, but when she opened the door it was to find Fred looking very agitated again, as he had done on his first visit. Barging straight past her, Fred staggered into the dining-kitchen and sat down gasping for breath.

'Whatever's the matter, Fred, are you poorly? Can I get you a drink?' He shook his head and told Elaine to sit down. Although shocked, Elaine did as she was told.

'Dying,' he gasped.

'Who is?'

'Me. Got a year at the most.'

'But . . .' Elaine started.

'Went to see doctor. Bad chest. Sent me to hospital' Elaine's heart plummeted. How would Harvey cope with yet another loss in his young life? What would happen to him now? Where would he go? But Elaine had to stop thinking these questions and concentrate on what Fred was saying.

'In my liver and bones now.'

'Is it cancer?' Elaine asked. Fred nodded.

'And is there no treatment?'

'Too late. Can keep me going for a year probably.' And then he burst into tears. Elaine darted forward to hug him, but he stopped her and said, 'Put kettle on.' Passing the box of tissues, Elaine went over to the kettle and said she was just going upstairs for a minute, so that Fred could get himself together again. When she came down, she didn't go to him straightaway but made them both a cup of tea. She passed him the cup of tea and he took it, slurping noisily as he drank without speaking. They sat in silence for a while, and then Elaine spoke.

'Does Harvey know?'

Fred shook his head.

'Are you going to tell him?'

'Not yet.'

'When then? He needs to know.'

'Soon. Got to get my head round it first. Had to tell someone though. Felt like I was bursting on the way home.'

'Have you come straight from the hospital?'

'Yes.'

'And you went on your own?'

'Yes.'

'Why didn't you ask me to come?'

'Didn't want to be beholden,' Fred replied.

'You'll never be beholden, Fred. We're almost family now.'

'Got to go now. See you Sunday,' and he jumped up and left the house without another word, despite Elaine going after him and calling him to come back. Elaine watched the battered old Volvo as it went down the road, then returning to the house she sat on her settee and stared at the stained-glass image of Jesus. 'What do I do now?' she asked Jesus, then burst into tears herself.

'Anybody home?' Gill shouted from the door and was horrified to find Elaine weeping. 'Whatever's the matter?'

'I'm not sure I can tell you,' Elaine replied.

'Not tell me? It must be bad then.'

'It is bad. The worst case possible.'

'Tell me then; don't leave me wondering like this. What's the matter with you? Have you found a lump or something?' At that Elaine burst into fresh tears.

'Don't worry, Elaine, if they get it early enough, they can sort it nowadays.

Have you been to the doctor? What did he say? Are you going to the hospital?'

'It's not me, Gill.'

'Well, who then?' asked a puzzled Gill.

'It's not my story to tell really, but I've got to tell you, so please keep it to yourself for now.'

'You know me, Elaine, I'm not a blabbermouth.'

'It's Fred. They've given him a year to live.'

'Poor Fred. Poor Harvey. How's he taken it?'

'That's the problem; Harvey doesn't know. Fred had just got the news at the hospital and came straight round here. He's not telling Harvey yet.'

'Oh dear. What a mess. How's that poor boy going to cope with this? On top of everything else?'

'I don't know. That's why I'm so upset. It could undo all the progress he's made.'

'How old is he now?'

'He was seventeen in May.'

'And no family left?'

'No. Well, there is an uncle in Australia who keeps saying he'll come and visit, but never does. Fred was annoyed that he wouldn't take Harvey to live with him when the accident happened, but the man said he lived alone in the outback on a sheep farm miles from anywhere. Said he was selling up as soon as he got a buyer, so couldn't have Harvey.'

'Sounds a bit callous.'

'That's what I thought.'

'Well, I hope Fred lets him know what's happening now.'

'So do I.'

'I need to get going now; I'm making tea for everyone. Will you be okay?'

'I'll be fine. Thanks, Gill. What would I do without you?' Elaine asked with a wan smile.

'What would I do without you?' Gill asked in return, and the two friends hugged each other for a long time before Gill left. Elaine tried to keep herself busy for the rest of the day, but her mind kept going over the problems that lay ahead for both Fred and Harvey.

Two days later Harvey came into the house without knocking, flung himself at Elaine, and held tight to her. Elaine knew what had happened. He wept for quite some time without speaking, and Elaine just held him and comforted him as best she could. Suddenly he pulled away and asked if he could go to the toilet. Elaine nodded. When he came back, he seemed to have composed himself, so Elaine made some hot chocolate. They sat together in the sunroom and were silent for some time.

'I'm frightened, Elaine. What am I going to do? I'll have no one left.'

'Yes, you will. You've got me now. I'll look after you, and your granddad as well, if he'll let me.'

'He cried when he told me.' Elaine just nodded. 'It was awful seeing him cry. He hasn't cried since the accident.'

'Harvey, if you need me at any time, if you're worried about your granddad, even in the middle of the night, you will call me, won't you?'

'Thanks, Elaine. I feel better now. I'll go back to Granddad. He needs me.'

Elaine just nodded and Harvey straightened up and, with great resolve on his face, left Elaine alone. Poor lad, she thought. Only 17 but looks like he has the weight of the world on his shoulders. It was going to be an even harder journey than he'd already been through. She waited until she was sure he'd gone and then rang Gill and told her what had happened. Gill rang off, but arrived at the house five minutes later and held Elaine in her arms. Whilst Harvey had been there, Elaine had managed to keep her tears under control, but now, receiving sympathy undid her, and she wept for a long time in Gill's arms.

Some weeks later Fred arrived early for their tea and said that Harvey wasn't coming, as he'd gone to see his friends. He was carrying a carrier bag with him and gave it to Elaine. It was full to the brim with £20 notes.

'What's this for?' Elaine asked.

'My funeral. I don't hold with banks and like to keep money hidden in the house. So I'm giving it to you now. There's over £3000, so should pay for the funeral. You know where to put me when I'm gone.'

'I can't take this now.'

'Yes you can. It'll be hard to get money out of the bank to pay straightaway. And I wouldn't want to be beholden to the funeral director.'

'Oh, Fred, you could have ages yet. Shall I put it in the bank for you?'

'In your bank. Not mine. I've seen the solicitor as well. Left everything to

Harvey in trust 'til he's 18. That'll help him if he wants to do a degree, for his fees and that. And then when he's 21 he'll get the money from his Mum and Dad's trust.'

'That's a good idea, Fred.'

'And I've made you executor and guardian of Harvey. Reckon you care for him more than anyone else will when I've gone.'

'I will Fred. I feel like he's my family now, and you too.'

'Aye, well, you're a good lass. I know you'll watch out for him.'

'And for you, Fred. I'll watch out for you, too. Right, I'll finish making the tea, and then we can eat.' As she was setting the table, Elaine was amazed at how much Fred had organised, and was humbled that he'd made her the executor and guardian of Harvey, but she didn't say anything. He seemed utterly spent now that he'd said all that. Elaine wasn't surprised; he'd spoken more in one conversation than he'd ever done in all the time she'd known him.

As if he'd used up all his energy, Fred couldn't manage to eat much, so Elaine packed up two doggy bags for him to take home for his and Harvey's supper in case they got peckish later, along with a batch of scones and a lemon drizzle cake, Fred's favourite. Fred left almost immediately, leaving Elaine drained. She decided to have an early night.

The next day Elaine was going into Clitheroe with Gill, so she took the money to the bank and had to explain where it had come from.

'Honestly,' said Elaine, 'you'd think I was taking money out, not putting it in.'

'I know, they're like that nowadays. Frightened of money laundering,' replied Gill.

'Do I look like a drug dealer?' asked Elaine.

'Not really,' giggled Gill. 'Now where are we going first?'

'Lunch?'

'Good idea. Blueberries?'

'Yes.'

The two friends went for lunch and then went back into the town as the market wasn't on. They wandered into Season's dress shop, and Elaine found a long-sleeved dress in a soft wool that was black with poppies on.

'Look at this, Gill. This is perfect for my commemorative service. I'm going to try it on.' She picked the right size and asked the assistant if she could try it on.

'Certainly, madam. That's just come in this week, part of the new winter stock.'

Elaine tried it on and did a pirouette for Gill. 'What do you think, Gill?'

'Perfect, it really suits you, and is so suitable for what you want.'

'I did think of having one made, as a lady at the Remembrance Service on TV had a long poppy skirt on last year, but this is even better, as it's more suitable for a daytime event, and I'll get more wear out of it.' Elaine bought the dress and Gill also bought a royal blue dress - not for the commemorative service, but just because she liked it, she laughed to Elaine.

And then, of course, they had to go to Beryl's shoe shop to get the perfect shoes to go with their outfits. Elaine bought black shoes with red flowers and sequins on the front, so they would look perfect with her new dress. And then Kirsty, the shop assistant, uttered the fateful words as she was wrapping the shoes up.

'There is a handbag to match these shoes.'

'Oh no,' groaned Gill, 'she's a real sucker for matching handbags.'

Kirsty smiled and produced the handbag, and that was duly bought and wrapped up as well. Gill already had the perfect shoes to go with her new dress, but needed some flat shoes for every day. And she definitely didn't need a matching handbag to go with hers.

Next, they went to the Chocolate Café to buy Fred some chocolate-covered cinder toffee. Elaine had found out that it was his favourite chocolate last Christmas, so tried to buy him some every time she came into town. They couldn't resist buying some of the beautiful homemade chocolates for themselves either, and munched them on the way back to the car. A more mundane shopping trip to the supermarket was next, collecting essentials that both Gill, Elaine, and Liz wanted, and then the pair headed off home again, satisfied with their day's purchases.

Chapter 20

Harvey got the news in late August that he'd passed his first year at Myerscough, and could do a second year, before going on to the degree course the year after. Elaine decided to have a party in her new garden that Harvey had designed single-handedly for her, as part of his course work, for which he'd got a distinction grade. Instead of just being a large plain lawn with an odd shrub, her front garden was now a riot of colour with different areas to sit in, perfect for an afternoon tea party. Against the wall between her garden and the graveyard, there was now a row of shrubs in differing heights. There were young rhododendrons of every hue, azaleas, and lots of buddleia to attract the butterflies, Harvey told her. It was also a bee-friendly garden, he added knowledgeably.

In front of the shrubs was a patio area which Ben had helped with, and garden seats and a table. At the other side of the garden near the drive there was another quiet seating area screened with small trees. There were little paths throughout the rest of the garden with different flower beds scattered around each corner, connected by gravel paths. Wherever you looked in the garden there was a different vista, and Elaine couldn't believe the detail that had gone into the design. No wonder he'd got a distinction. The before and after pictures were quite dramatic and Elaine couldn't believe it was the same garden. Harvey had left the area near the patio in front of the sunroom without planting for now, knowing that there was going to be a marquee for the commemorative service. In the meantime, he'd put planters there to cover the bare ground that could be easily moved in November.

When Fred came and looked at the garden, he was very impressed and told Harvey that he had a future in garden design, but Harvey just laughed it off. Elaine noticed that Fred was looking a little bit thinner nowadays, but otherwise he was his usual dour self, with little to say. But he did still enjoy coming to Elaine's for Wednesday tea and a meal on Sundays. He never discussed the future again, so Elaine respected that, after insisting that he tell his brother in Australia.

One sunny Saturday afternoon, Elaine held her tea party instead of going to Puddleducks. She invited Kate, Anna, Kirsty, Liz and Ben, Gill, Daniel, and

Fred and Harvey. First, they had a conducted tour of the new garden by Harvey, which thrilled Elaine, as she saw how much his confidence had grown. He gave his talk about the importance of bees and butterflies again, and then they had a look at the beehive, all listening respectfully. Then it was party time. Elaine had bought several tiered afternoon tea stands, and each person got their own selection of savouries, soup, sandwiches, cakes, and scones. She'd even done some strawberries dipped in chocolate, which were very popular. Wine, soft drinks, and cups of tea were in plentiful supply to accompany the food. Then Elaine challenged all the youngsters to a game of tennis and there was a lot of hilarity going on. Even Ben had a game, much to Gill's surprise. It was a perfect afternoon, Gill said to Elaine when they were leaving, and she hoped it would become a regular event. Elaine told Gill that it was her turn next, as they all left to go home, laden with doggy bags of leftovers. Elaine was glad that she had arranged it, as it was another day of memories for Fred and Harvey, so it was worth all the hard work.

Whilst talking to Jean, one of the other guides at Browsholme Hall, Elaine learned that it was possible to purchase Perspex life-size soldiers for church graveyards and memorials. Jean had bought one as she owned a medieval house and opened her gardens every year to raise money for charities such as Help the Heroes and British Legion. It made Elaine think that she could also have an open garden event next year to raise money for charity, but for now she bought five Perspex soldiers, to put one soldier next to each of her war graves. Not waiting for November, Elaine put them up as soon as they arrived and was pleased. Because the war graves were on the far side wall of the graveyard, it looked like the soldiers were keeping guard on the whole graveyard and really enhanced the entire area. They'd not been cheap, but Elaine thought they were worth every penny, to show her respect for all the soldiers who made the ultimate sacrifice in laying down their lives for others. And they could stay there forever, not just for the commemorative service.

Elaine was also pleased with the pictures that she had had blown up with captions underneath, telling the stories of the soldiers who had served and died for their country. They were all mounted on pull-up banners that could be stored away easily when not in use. There was also a short history of the church and John Talbot's life, and some of the leaflets from past special services and concerts were displayed too. It would make interesting reading for the visitors, and they could be used again next summer and subsequent years, if she had Open Garden days for soldiers' charities.

When the marquee arrived on the ninth of November, Elaine began to get excited. Ben and Daniel brought down lots of chairs and tables, that Elaine had borrowed from the village hall. They set them up in the marquee ready for the meal afterwards, but if it rained on the day, they could move them around to accommodate the service. All the banners were placed around the sides of the marquee so that people could look at them.

On the Saturday it rained all day, and Elaine was worried that the service was going to be a wash-out. However, she still braved the rain to go to the farm with a funny birthday card for Gill about old-age. Elaine had also bought Gill a necklace and bracelet set, plus a massive helium balloon with a 60 on which she'd got yesterday. Gill gave Elaine an equally funny old-age birthday card, plus the full box set of 'Downton Abbey' which Elaine loved.

'I didn't get you any balloons. I thought they might look a bit tactless tomorrow,' Gill laughed.

'True. I've not told anybody that it's my birthday. We can celebrate next Saturday when we have our joint party.'

'It's going to be busy. I think half the village is coming.'

'Well, I can let my hair down once tomorrow's done. I just hope the rain clears up. It'll be disastrous if it's raining like this.'

'Better pray for fine weather, then,' laughed Gill. 'Seeing you own a church and a graveyard, you should have some influence.'

'Hope so. Are you bringing the pies tomorrow, or shall I take them now?'

'You can take them now if you like. Less to bring tomorrow.' Gill went into her fridge and brought out four large catering size tins with a selection of pies in. There were cheese and onion, meat and potato, steak and ale, and chicken and mushroom. She helped Elaine put them in the back of her car and then said goodbye, as Elaine drove home carefully with the pies. They were soon in the utility room fridge. One less thing to worry about, thought Elaine, and was glad she'd bought a large fridge just in case she did start a B & B. She'd only just got home when the flower arrangements arrived. She'd ordered 20 arrangements of artificial poppies in small containers for each of the tables in the marquee, and also some large arrangements of poppies to put around her house. There were also eight wreaths of poppies: one for each of her five war soldiers' graves, one for Harvey's family grave, one for John's grave, and one for John Talbot's grave.

Harvey arrived and helped put up all the bunting in the marquee. Having checked the weather on his phone, which said that it would be fine tomorrow, they decided to risk setting the tables ready. White paper tablecloths were laid down, making a dramatic contrast with the red poppy arrangements. Knives, forks, white serviettes with poppies on, and small salt and pepper pots were set out and the tables were complete. A larger table was set up at the side for drinks, and paper cups and plastic teaspoons were laid out in readiness, plus dishes of sugar covered with cling film. There were also large dishes with serving spoons into which would go beetroot and red cabbage tomorrow. Elaine looked round the marquee when they'd finished and was happy. She couldn't do any more tonight, so she and Harvey went inside for the usual cup of hot chocolate.

Next morning, Elaine looked outside and saw with relief that it was a fine day with no sign of clouds or rain. Indeed, it was a crisp, fine day, albeit cold. The postman brought her a large number of cards, but she put them to one side. She wanted to savour them later when everything was over. She had worked towards this event for two years and, now it was here, she became nervous that it wouldn't be the event she'd planned in her head. She had a light lunch, too nervous to eat properly, but she could eat the pie and peas with the others afterwards, she decided.

Putting her new dress and shoes on, Elaine came downstairs and looked round the room. Nikki had had given the house an extra special clean and everything looked sparkling. Nikki's grandparents were buried in the graveyard and so she was attending today but said that she would help with the teas as well, which pleased Elaine.

Suddenly, people were arriving. Gill and Liz were the first wishing her 'Happy Birthday,' and Liz giving her a pile of presents from her family. Elaine explained that she would open her cards and presents after the event, but thanked Liz for them. Kirsty was with them and she'd brought a box full of hand-made poppies, one for each person attending. Elaine fastened hers on immediately, giving one each to Nikki and Harvey who'd just arrived. Shortly after the Vaughton family arrived, as did Barbara from the tennis club. Elaine checked with Charlie that he was still happy to read one of the poems from the First World War poets and he agreed. When she'd decided to ask Charlie to do this, because of all the research he'd done, she told Harvey, who said that he would like to do that as well. Elaine couldn't believe it. Harvey was volunteering to read in public. Never in her wildest dreams did she imagine he would want to, but he had become as involved as she had with the lives represented by these old graves. Charlie and Harvey had already emailed each other to check that they weren't reading the same poem.

It seemed to Elaine as if the whole village was here. All Gill's family had arrived now, including Tim and Lindsay and her parents. Most of the WI were here, as well as many villagers who all had relatives' graves in the graveyard, not necessarily connected with the war, but they were attending out of respect for the Dunsop Bridge boys who did go to war. Elaine noticed that Fred was wearing his army service medals and commented on how smart he looked. Robert and Amanda Parker with their children Eleanor and Roland, and some of the guides from Browsholme Hall came as well. The Parker family had a long history of Colonels who had served in many wars: the Crimean, Boer, and both World Wars.

But the biggest surprise was that a very distant relative of John Talbot came up from London. Elaine lost track of how many 'greats' this granddaughter was in relation to the original John Talbot, but was thrilled anyway. Samantha Talbot was taking photos of all the information about her relative and was very pleased to be there. She promised to keep in touch with Elaine. She was so busy talking to Samantha that she didn't notice straightaway that the Mayoral car had arrived, until she saw Rev Alan Reid talking to the Mayor and his wife and leading them to Elaine. Elaine thanked them for coming and then left them with Alan whilst she checked if everyone else had arrived. She could see the bandsman and Daisy-Belle and Charlotte, so she checked her watch. It was time to begin.

Alan led the procession, followed by the Mayor and Mayoress, to the war graves at the far side of the graveyard. Alan welcomed them all to this special 100th Year Remembrance Service and opened with prayers. The priest from St Hubert's then read a Bible passage, followed by Daisy-Belle who sang an old hymn, 'For those in peril on the sea,' as Arthur Hacking had served in the navy and had died at sea. Then Charlie read the poem with the words, 'They shall not grow old' by Lawrence Binyon. Next Alan gave a homily on the Bible reading about 'Greater love has no man than to lay down his life for his brother.' Harvey was next, and he read the poem by John McRae starting, 'In Flanders field where poppies grow'. Elaine was so proud of him and fought back tears. No time for tears today I've too much to do, she told herself firmly.

It was then time to lay the wreaths. Harvey laid one on his family's grave, Ben laid one on John's grave, Samantha Talbot laid a wreath on her ancestor's grave, the Mayor laid one on Arthur Hacking's grave, Charlie laid one on Robert Carroll's grave, and a young man laid one on the Farnworth men's grave. Elaine frowned. She wasn't sure who this man was, but it didn't matter, as he had done it very respectfully, and she could find out later where Thomas was. Nicholas Heaton's grandson laid a wreath on his grave and Stanley Wood's great granddaughter laid a wreath on his grave.

As they laid the wreaths, the Last Post was played with a haunting heart-wrenching clarity. No one moved a muscle, affected by the solemnity of the whole service. Then with a final prayer by the Priest from St Hubert's, the procession led back to the marquee, and Elaine had to hurry into action.

Brewing tea and coffee in the massive teapots borrowed from the village hall, Elaine sent those in with Kate and Anna, so that everyone could have a hot drink before the food was served. Kirsty had been round each table to ask which pie each person preferred, organised by Liz, who was well used to catering for great numbers. The relevant type of pie and peas was delivered and people helped themselves to red cabbage and beetroot. There was great merriment going on in the marquee in contrast to the sad and emotional service of such a short while ago.

Elaine was circulating round the marquee, saying that she would eat later, talking to people, and asking who they were if she didn't know them. Then she spotted Agnes, Thomas Farnworth's mother, sitting with the young man who'd laid the wreath on the Farnworth war grave.

'Hello, Elaine. Thanks for inviting us. You heard about Thomas, I suppose? This is my grandson, Jonathan.'

'Hello, Agnes, Jonathan. Heard about Thomas? No, what do you mean?'

'Sorry to tell you bad news, but he died last month. Heart attack.'

'Oh, Agnes, I'm so sorry. That must have been a shock.'

'Yes, you don't expect your children to die before you. Wrong way round isn't it? But that's how it is. But my grandson promised that he would bring me today, as we knew how important his family ancestors were to Thomas, and he was looking forward to coming today.'

'He wished for his ashes to be buried in your graveyard,' Jonathan added. 'Can I give you my card and we can discuss it at a later date?'

Turning to Jonathan, Elaine said 'of course,' took the business card, thanked him for coming, and then said she would leave them to get on with their food. She made a quick exit to find Gill and tell her the news. Gill was as shocked as Elaine had been and were both sorry that Thomas hadn't made it to the service, as he would have loved it. He'd answered immediately in the affirmative when Elaine sent an invitation to the service.

But there was no time for further sad thoughts, as Daisy-Belle was now singing old war songs from both the First and Second World Wars, whilst Liz and her girls and Nikki's girls tidied up the dirty plates and put plates of cakes out. The tea and coffee pots were refilled in readiness. As Daisy-Belle came to the end of her set of songs, she said that she would like to make an announcement. She thanked Elaine on behalf of everyone present for putting together such a special afternoon, both the service and the meal. But what nobody knew, said Daisy-Belle, was that it was Elaine's 60th birthday today, and so they were going to sing. Daisy-Belle led them into singing 'Happy Birthday' to a red-faced Elaine. Then a large birthday cake was brought in with candles blazing, but not 60 of them, Elaine was pleased to see, as that might have set the marquee on fire!

Not wanting to be outdone, Elaine thanked everybody for coming and for singing to her, but then turned the tables and told everyone that her friend Gill, who was much older than her, had celebrated her 60th birthday yesterday. So Daisy-Belle and everyone present sang all over again to Gill, and there were more cheers and clapping. But Elaine would never have imagined what happened next. Fred, who'd been sitting very quietly, not saying much, stood up and said that as it was a double birthday, why didn't they have a whip round and collect money for the British Legion in honour of these two lovely ladies? His remarks were greeted with an uproar, and Liz found a large bowl, which was passed round all the tables.

As Gill was topping up the cakes on each table, she was amazed when she saw the number of £20 notes that were going into the bowl. When it had been round all the tables, Gill took it into the dining-kitchen and gave it to Elaine for safety.

'Why don't you count it and then we can tell people how much we've made?' Gill suggested.

'Good idea; I'll do it now.'

'No, I'll do it. You go and circulate. Make sure everyone has enough cake.'

Elaine laughed. 'I think we'll be eating up pie and cake for weeks to come.'

'Give them all a doggy bag then. We've loads more in the freezers just in case more came than we thought.'

'That's a good idea. I bought some polystyrene trays for take-outs for Fred and Harvey. Glad I bought them in bulk now.' Elaine got the trays out of the utility room and left them on the central island before going out to talk to people in the marquee, but noticed that some people were looking ready to leave. Gill eventually arrived with a slip of paper and Elaine gasped.

'Could I just announce before you all start going home that you have raised the amazing amount of £880 for the British Legion. Thank you all so much, and thank you for coming today. And thank you to everyone who has taken part. It has been such an amazing project for me, and I'm glad you were able to attend. I will make the amount up to £1000 before I send off the cheque to the British Legion.'

'No, you won't,' said Gill. 'I'll go halves with you. That makes it £60 each. Perfect amount for our 60th birthdays.'

'Now who wants a doggy bag to take home?' asked Elaine. Several people queued up to get one. Kirsty stood by the door as everyone left, giving them a piece of birthday cake which Liz had hurriedly cut up and wrapped in serviettes. Elaine said goodbye to everyone and gave a small vase of poppies to all the dignitaries and those who had taken part, and several of the other people who had attended, especially Agnes Farnworth. She'd keep the large arrangements in her house for future use, she'd decided.

Eventually everyone had gone home except for Gill, Liz, Harvey, and Fred, and they all sat in the sunroom. Tidying up could be done tomorrow.

'Anyone want a brew?' Elaine asked, and they all said yes. But Liz jumped up first.

'You sit down, Elaine, you've done enough today. Besides,' she said with a grin on her face, 'you're in your 60s now,' and rushed off to the kitchen-diner before Elaine could say anything.

'That reminds me,' said Elaine. 'I'd better open my cards and presents.' She got them from the downstairs bedroom where she'd put them out of the way. As she opened each card, she put them on the sunroom windowsill until that was full, and then moved round to put some in the dining-kitchen. Her presents were varied and just what she wanted. Plenty of shower gel, her favourite perfume, lots of books, a spa voucher, plants, tennis balls and tennis socks, a box of beautiful notelets, and the obvious book about how to cope with being over 60. That was from Tim and Lindsay.

'Thank you, all of you. I love all my presents.'

'Haven't you noticed that there isn't one from me and Granddad?' asked Harvey.

'I've opened a card from you,' replied Elaine.

'But no present.'

'That doesn't matter; it's enough that you came and took part.'

'It was the cake.'

'What was the cake?'

'Our present, from me and Granddad,' replied Harvey. 'It was my idea. I went to talk to Gill about it and she said to do it.'

'Thank you both very much. That was a great idea. I couldn't have had a better present. I wondered how Daisy-Belle knew it was my birthday. Now I know! But I've given most of the cake away.'

'Doesn't matter, we've ordered another cake for next Saturday,' Harvey grinned.

'Another cake? But I thought Liz was making one?'

'That's what we told you,' said Liz laughing. 'I was going to make one, but when Harvey came up with his idea, we went along with it.'

Elaine couldn't believe that Harvey had thought of this and gone to see Gill. It was such a shock. And yet she was so pleased that he'd planned it for her. And another cake for next week. She looked round at all the people in the sunroom and beamed. She was a very fortunate woman with such good friends around.

'Well, I have got good friends, haven't I?' was all she managed to say, and then asked if anyone wanted anything to eat. They all groaned and said they should be going, and within ten minutes Elaine was on her own. At least she'd sleep tonight, she thought, as she stacked the dishwasher - and sleep she did.

Next morning, Ben and Liz came round early to take the tables and chairs back to the village hall and empty the marquee before the firm came to take it down in the afternoon. Nikki came round to sort out the rest of the house and give it a once-over, as she called it, even though she'd cleaned it all thoroughly before the service. In the afternoon, the florist from Clitheroe arrived with several bouquets of flowers for Elaine. They were from many of the people who had been at the service, obviously grateful for the day they had had, but pleased to be part of her milestone birthday as well. There was even a bouquet from Jonathan and Agnes Farnworth which she didn't expect. She started arranging them in vases, and then had to go round to Gill's to borrow some more vases, but Gill was struggling just as much. She'd also received a lot of flowers by the same delivery and was struggling to find enough vases and had already used Liz' supply. So Elaine walked down to the café to see if they could help her. She managed another two vases from them, but still didn't have enough. So she rang Nikki, who lent her another two. Elaine decided she'd better put labels on all the vases, to make sure they got back to whom they belonged. But her house looked stunning. There was at least one vase of flowers plus an arrangement of poppies in every room of the house, even all the bedrooms and an extra one in the pulpit.

Elaine spent most of Tuesday writing many thank you letters to all and sundry. Deciding she'd spent enough time indoors, she took them straight to the café, which was also a post office, and posted them all.

'You've been busy writing,' said Julie.

'All my thank you letters,' replied Elaine.

'Popular woman then, there's loads there.'

'I've had so many flowers, presents and cards. It's been amazing.'

'Good, you deserve it. It was a lovely service. I think all the villagers appreciated it.'

'It's the first thing I wanted to do when I bought the church. I'm just glad it didn't rain and everything went according to plan. Well, must be off. Bye.'

Julie returned the greeting, and Elaine walked to Gill's on her way home.

'Is everything ready for Saturday?'

'Yes,' said Gill. 'Liz says we just need to turn up and not worry about a thing.'

'That's so hard to do. Liz has a lot on and I'd feel much better if I could help.'

'I know, I feel the same, but it's Liz' orders. She says Kate, Anna, and Kirsty are helping her.'

'Think I'll wear my poppy dress again.'

'I'm going to wear the dress I bought the same day. I was just thinking about our party, not your service, when I bought it,' laughed Gill.

'I didn't even think about our birthdays. I was so obsessed with the service. Right I'll be getting off.'

'Not staying for a cup of tea?'

'Oh, go on then. You'll think I'm poorly if I refuse tea. Gill put the kettle on and the two of them chatted companionably together, drinking their tea.

Chapter 21

It was soon Saturday November 17th. The joint birthday party was starting at seven pm and when Elaine arrived at half-past six, Gill dragged her into the kitchen area.

'Look who's here!' she said excitedly. It was the two lady owners from Blueberries in Clitheroe, Julie and Katharine.

'I didn't expect to see you two here,' said Elaine. 'You're very welcome, mind you,' she added quickly.

'Oh, we're not stopping,' said Julie.

'We've done the buffet,' added Katharine, seeing the puzzled look on Elaine's face.

'And I've been feeling guilty that Liz was having to do it all on her own. What a great idea!' replied Elaine.

'Liz isn't daft,' added Gill. 'I'm glad she's done that, as it would have been so much work for her.'

'Right,' said Katharine. 'We'll just get everything set out and then we'll be on our way,' and the two of them set out all the cold food on trestle tables at the back of the room.

'The jacket potatoes are keeping warm in the oven for those who want something hot, and the fillings to go with the potatoes, and the puddings are all in the fridge,' explained Julie. 'Right, we're off. You can let us have all the trays back at your leisure.' And they both left, after giving Gill and Elaine a card and a plant each for their birthdays. At that point, another delivery lady came in. It was the cakemaker who'd made the original cake for last Saturday. Elaine gasped when she saw it. It was massive and was in two halves. One half was a farm with farm animals and the other was a church with a graveyard. It was stunning. It must have taken hours to make, thought Elaine, and as if she knew what Elaine was thinking, Gill commented on the cake.

'That must have taken ages to make. It's so perfect. It's too good to eat.'

'Yes, look. It's got our names on our own half in front of the large number 60 candles,' Elaine laughed. Just at that point Harvey and Fred arrived. Harvey made sure his granddad got a good seat away from draughts and then came to look at the cake. Gill and Elaine both thanked him and told him off for spending so much on them, as the cake obviously cost a lot of money. But Harvey laughed and said he hadn't paid for it, as his granddad had insisted on paying. He said they were the two loveliest ladies in Dunsop Bridge and they deserved a nice cake. Both Gill and Elaine went over to Fred to thank him, but he brushed them away and didn't want to talk. So they took the hint and left him alone.

Gill went over to check on the drinks table to see that there was plenty for everyone. Ben was going to manage the bar with Tim and Daniel, but there was plenty of soft drinks for those who were driving or for the youngsters. Ben must have set it up earlier.

Liz, Ben, the girls, and Daniel arrived next. Helen and Martin, Daniel's parents, were coming later. Elaine teased Liz about the surprise of having Blueberries doing the catering, but Liz just laughed.

'Our girls and Nikki's girls will help serve. We just thought we could enjoy the party instead of worrying about everything being ready together and making us tired before the party even started.'

'Who did the trimmings?' asked Gill, looking round at all the banners and balloons spread all over the room.

'Ben and Daniel,' replied Liz. 'And look, Kate's made two boxes like at a wedding, in case more cards and presents arrive.' One box had a church on the top with Elaine's name, and the other had farm animals on the top with Gill's name, just like the cake.

'Thanks, Kate, they're really good. You could set up a business making these,' said Elaine. 'I don't think we'll be getting anymore presents or cards. We've already had lots last weekend, plus housefuls of flowers.' Gill nodded her agreement. They were both wrong. More cards and presents arrived and, when they looked afterwards, there were envelopes containing money for the British Legion, from people who'd heard about the collection last Sunday and wanted to contribute.

Crowds were pouring in now and suddenly the room looked full. All of Gill's and Elaine's friends arrived, some of Gill's colleagues from Ribblesdale school, and some of Gill's and John's relatives. Elaine was pleased that all her godchildren were there for the event. Katie had brought her mum Marian and her daughter Libby and Charlotte brought her parents and sister Louise. Nikki and the children were there, and the staff from

Puddleducks. Old and new tennis friends arrived, members of the WI and village friends, plus former work colleagues of Elaine's. Then the ceilidh band arrived. They were soon ready to start the fun and made everyone get up to dance - well nearly everybody. Harvey said he didn't dance and needed to sit with his granddad, but Elaine dragged him up to dance anyway, encouraging Liz' mum Jennifer to sit with Fred and keep him company. Ben had a good excuse for not dancing because he was looking after the bar, so he said.

The evening was a riot of fun, with a break for supper, which was very well received by everyone. The cake was then brought out to 'oohs' and 'aahs' from everyone; lots of people took photos of the unusual double cake. Everybody sang Happy Birthday, twice, once each for Gill and Elaine.

And then the dancing started again. Gill was exhausted by ten o'clock and sat out from the dancing. Elaine soon followed her.

'Getting a bit too old for this lark,' said Elaine.

'You can say that again. Must be because we're 60 now,' said Gill, and they both laughed.

'It's been a great party though, hasn't it?' asked Elaine.

'Best ever. And no washing up!' replied Gill. 'Tomorrow, we're on the laptop to book a holiday.'

'Definitely,' replied Elaine, then they both got up as people were starting to leave. It was hugs, thanks, and well wishes all round, and by midnight everyone had gone, complete with a slice of cake, except for Gill's family. Harvey had left much earlier, as Fred was feeling very tired.

'Let's leave all this and we'll sort it out tomorrow,' suggested Ben, and everyone agreed with him. As they'd all had far too much to drink, everybody walked home leaving their secured cars in the car park, and only taking the presents and money home.

It was 11 o'clock when Elaine surfaced next day and after a quick shower and putting on her old clothes, she walked round to the village hall. All signs of the party had gone and there were neat piles of kitchen equipment belonging to Blueberries waiting to be returned. A very large box contained all the empty bottles for recycling, bin bags full of rubbish were collected by the door, and the balloons and bunting were heaped on another table in two piles.

'Hello there. How's your head?' Ben asked, as he came back into the village hall.

'How's yours?' asked Elaine.

'Oh, I'm fine. You have to behave when you're the barman. Besides, we drew straws for this morning's milking and I lost, so I had to be up early.'

'It was a good party, though.'

'It certainly was. Never had a better party, I don't think. Right, I'll just get these bottles into the car,' and he picked up the large box of bottles.

'We drank rather a lot, didn't we?'

Ben laughed. 'This is the second box. I've already taken a bigger box out to the car.'

'If you'll bring the kitchen stuff for Blueberries round to my house, I'll take them back tomorrow.'

'Thanks.'

'Who washed them up?'

'The girls and Nikki. You now Nikki can't sit still if there's anything to be cleaned,' laughed Ben.

'That's true. A very good trait in a cleaner, though. Right, I'll be off. I came to help tidy up but I see I'm too late. Are these my half of the balloons and bunting?'

Ben nodded.

'Thanks for everything you and Liz did, Ben. I really appreciate it all.'

'You can do the same for me when I'm 40.'

'That's not for 18 months yet.'

'Just giving you plenty of notice,' Ben laughed, as he picked up yet another bag of rubbish to put in the car. Elaine also picked up a bag of rubbish and put it in Ben's car, and then, saying goodbye, walked slowly home carrying some leftover food from last night that Ben had given her, and her banners and balloons.

When she got there, Harvey was working in the garden.

'Not working today?'

'No.'

'Did your Granddad enjoy himself last night?'

'Yes, but he's worn out this morning, so having a day in bed.'

194

'Good. I take it he's not coming for Sunday lunch?'

'No, too tired.'

'I've got some leftovers from last night if you want to take some home. There's far too much for me.'

'That'd be good, thanks.'

'Do you want a hot chocolate?'

'Yes, please.' So Elaine went inside and made the drinks then sat in the sunroom watching Harvey tidying the garden up for winter, wondering what the future would hold for him.

Her reverie was disturbed by Gill arriving with Elaine's side of the cake which was left over.

'Time to book a holiday,' she laughed.

'Right, here's the laptop. You have a look and I'll just take some cake out to Harvey. And make sure it's winter sun. No fiords this time of year.'

When she got back, Gill was excited. 'Come and look at this, Elaine: 14 nights cruising the Canary Islands for just over half the usual price.'

'What's the catch?'

'It's this Friday. Starting from Southampton.'

'This Friday? That doesn't give us much time to get organised,' gasped Elaine.

'It's only passports and clothes. How much time do you need?'

'True. Why so cheap? Are they filling empty cabins up?'

'Yes, they always do at the last minute. So, are you up for it?'

'Yes, book it.'

'Done. Can you lend me your credit card? We have to pay in full, with it being so near, and I haven't got enough credit on mine.'

'I've heard that one before,' Elaine teased. 'Here let me do the card bit.' And Elaine walked to the computer to clinch the deal.

'Right, I'd better be going and tell Ben and Liz I'm going away. And start sorting through my wardrobe,' Gill laughed.

'Let me know if we need to go shopping again,' said Elaine. But Gill just raised her hand in farewell and went home.

As soon as she'd gone, Elaine rang Nikki.

'Can I ask you a massive favour, Nikki?'

'What is it?'

'I'm going on holiday on Friday for two weeks, and I'm worried how Fred will be whilst I'm away.'

'And you want me to call round every day and take him a meal?'

'Well, it doesn't matter about a meal so much as checking up on him. It's great that he's letting you clean a bit for him now.'

'I wouldn't want to be beholden to you,' replied Nikki, mimicking Fred's voice. Elaine laughed.

'He always says that, doesn't he? He's such a proud man.'

'But he lets me take food round when I go cleaning already.'

'Does he? I'm surprised. I suggested taking him food round, but he refused. He always takes food home when he's been here for a meal, but not inbetween times.'

'I've found he likes soup, so I always make a bit extra and put some in his freezer. Soup and scones he likes.'

'That's great. So you don't mind keeping an eye on him then?'

'Not at all. Enjoy your holiday. Where are you going?'

'Winter sun. Cruising the Canary Islands.'

'Lucky you. Don't think about me here in the freezing cold, traipsing up to old Fred's house with my basket of goodies like Red Riding Hood.'

'I'll try not to,' replied Elaine laughing. 'I am grateful, Nikki.'

'Well, if you are grateful, go to the duty-free shop on your way home then,' replied Nikki, grinning.

'I'll see what I can do. Have to go now, Harvey's coming in and I don't want him to know what I'm up to.'

'Okay, bye.'

Harvey came into the sunroom and said that he was going. Elaine told him about the holiday she'd booked, and then Harvey left. Elaine ran upstairs to the white bedroom, which she tended to use the most, and turned her wardrobe out, just as she suspected Gill was doing right at this minute. It felt strange getting shorts and t-shirts out at this time of year, but the cruise line assured them that the weather would always be warm. Thank goodness she had plenty of summer dresses that would do for the evenings on the cruise; no need to go out to buy more. She also rooted out scarves and shawls if the evenings got cooler. She just needed to add some undies and toiletries, a couple of pairs of walking sandals for visiting islands, and a couple of pairs of sparkly sandals for evenings and she was sorted.

Elaine remembered that she hadn't opened the envelopes with the money for the British Legion, and found that there was another £300. Getting her cheque book out, Elaine wrote a cheque for £1,500 and decided to drive into Clitheroe and order some money for the holiday and post the cheque at the same time. Calling at Blueberries whilst she was in Clitheroe, she dropped off all the tins and gave them a thank you card and a piece of birthday cake each, for all their efforts.

Satisfied that she had done as much as she could for Fred, Elaine was ready to go on their lifetime birthday cruise. They flew down to Southampton and stayed overnight before boarding the cruise ship. Surprisingly they had a good cabin with twin beds on the outside of the ship. After putting their clothes away, they took a stroll round the deck so that they would be outside when the ship sailed. Elaine had forgotten how good it felt to be on a ship, but it was a first time for Gill and she was a little apprehensive. Gill said she kept thinking about the Titanic, to which Elaine laughed, but reassured her that they'd learned lessons by now. Besides, added Elaine, there aren't any icebergs in the Canary Islands, which made Gill laugh.

They spent the day finding out about the boat and what was on offer. The first night there was a welcome dinner followed by entertainment. Gill and Elaine both got ready and went into the main dining room and found their table. There were already several people sitting at the table and introductions were made. The other guests were from all parts of the country and most had cruised many times before. Gill and Elaine felt quite the novice cruisers. The food was excellent, as was the entertainment afterwards, and both ladies fell asleep very quickly when they got back to their cabin, probably aided by the wine they'd drunk.

The holiday flew by, with visits to exotic islands interspersed with fine dining and good company. Elaine was pleased to find tennis courts on board so was able to have a few games. Gill preferred to read or people-watch. But they both enjoyed a daily swim in the pool.

'You'll be having a pool built next,' Gill teased.

'No, they're too much trouble. In our climate you'd have to have them indoors or greatly enclosed.'

'Only teasing.'

They didn't get invited to the Captain's table, but they weren't bothered about that as they liked the company on their own table. But the Captain did come round one evening to say 'hello' which pleased them both. All too soon the holiday was over, but both had a lifetime of memories to live on, not to mention all the photos. There was a special offer to book another cruise at a reduced cost, and Gill and Elaine looked at each other for a moment, but then decided not to bother. They preferred the spontaneity of going online or visiting a shop and seeing what was available, rather than booking for next year. Besides, reminded Gill, you never know what might happen, and knew that they were both thinking about Fred.

Visiting the duty-free shop, Elaine remembered to get a gift for Nikki. She ended up buying her a large bottle of expensive perfume that she knew Nikki loved but would never buy for herself. She also bought presents for Liz and Ben's girls and a large bottle of Fred's favourite whisky. For Harvey she bought a smart top that she thought he would like. He could wear it for gardening if he didn't like it!

The flight was delayed going home, but they got back to Manchester airport just an hour late. They'd managed to text Ben, who was picking them up, with the new arrival time and caught him before he set off. He was waiting for them as they came into the arrivals lounge. Taking their bags, he guided them to where his car was parked and drove home. They were both quiet on the way home and Ben said he was worried. He'd never heard them so quiet before.

'Too much partying,' replied Gill, with a grin on her face, and Elaine agreed.

'Better not ask then,' laughed Ben.

Next morning Elaine went straight round to see Fred, but he seemed just about the same, for which she was grateful. Nikki arrived whilst she was there, so Elaine told her to pop round to the house, as she had a little something for her, which Nikki promised to do.

Gill and Elaine had hardly got back to a normal routine when everyone was asking about Christmas. It was agreed that Liz would do Christmas Day for a change, but Elaine would do Boxing Day, hoping that Fred and Harvey would still come to Liz and Ben's house.

Just before Christmas, Elaine had a day on her own in Clitheroe, 'Sorting a few things out,' she told Gill. She had an early morning appointment for a 'well woman' check up with Sister Becky at Castle Surgery, who found everything was okay. Not having had much breakfast she popped into The Apricot Meringue café for some cinnamon toast and a cappuccino. Their cinnamon toast was the best ever she'd discovered. Then she went to the hairdressers. Unfortunately her blonde hair needed a little assistance to stay blonde nowadays and she wanted it to look nice for Christmas; there hadn't been time before the cruise to fit in an appointment. Next, she went to the bank and then it was time for her annual eye appointment. With an encouraging result and no need for new reading glasses, Elaine did some shopping for Christmas presents. By then she was exhausted and headed off home, her car piled up with lots of goodies. At least she had got most of what she wanted and the rest she would do on the Internet. She was ready for Christmas.

Chapter 22

Christmas Day was a delight. Elaine went to the Christmas morning service in Whalley, wishing everyone there a Happy Christmas. Fred and Harvey did go to Liz and Ben's and were made a fuss of. The meal was superb, the company was good and Jennifer and Fred again sat companionably together, chatting about the village in bygone times. Everybody seemed pleased with their presents and the games became more hilarious by the minute. Even Fred was laughing at some of the antics during charades.

Elaine was pleased to have no responsibilities that day and, although she was hosting Boxing Day, it was a much easier event as it was 'eat up day' with chips. Daniel, Helen, and Martin had gone to their daughter's for the whole of Christmas and New Year this year, so didn't attend Elaine's Boxing Day party, although they were sorry to miss it. So the party was quieter than usual.

New Year's Eve was also different this year as the whole family decided at the last minute to go to the party at the village hall, so that meant Gill, Liz, and Elaine could relax and not be responsible for the arrangements, although all three women had made food for the event. A disco had been organised for the party and the inevitable countdown to midnight was carried out by the enthusiastic DJ. And then everybody broke out singing 'Auld Lang Syne' and going the rounds kissing each other. Soon after the party broke up, with everyone wishing each other Happy 2019.

The following afternoon Elaine went round to see Fred, as they hadn't come to the party the night before. She found Fred curled up on the settee wrapped in a blanket. The house was untidy, with uneaten food on the table.

'Fred, what's the matter? Where's Harvey?'

'Out. Went last night. To his mates.'

Elaine was tidying the old food away as she listened to him, waiting for the kettle to boil.

'When did you last eat?'

'Can't rightly remember now. Harvey left me some food, but I couldn't be bothered.'

'Right, Fred, this isn't good enough. You're coming to my house to stay now, and I'll look after you and make sure you eat regularly.'

'Oh, I don't think I could. I don't want to be . . .' but Elaine interrupted.

'Don't you dare say you don't want to be beholden to me. You're not beholden to me; you're family now, but you're not looking after yourself either. You should have more sense. I bet Harvey's worried sick about you. Now get this tea drunk, and I'll get some things together for you.'

Fred started sipping his drink, but he didn't look happy. But Elaine was adamant. She found his pyjamas and dressing gown, got some toiletries together, and put them into the car.

'I'd better leave a note for Harvey,' muttered Fred.

'Don't bother; I've already sent a text. He knows to come to my house. Now come on, in to the car,' said Elaine, with a voice that brooked no opposition. Slowly Fred got to his feet, but it took him quite some time to cross the room, leave the house, and get in to the car. Elaine grabbed the blanket from off the settee and wrapped it round Fred's knees, then drove back to her house.

When they got through the door, she asked Fred where he wanted to go, either the sunroom, the lounge, or bed - and she was surprised when he said bed. She guided him into the downstairs bedroom and left him to get undressed and get into bed. Even though it was warm, she found an old hot water bottle and put it in the bed to warm him up, as his hands felt icy.

'Do you want another drink?'

'No, thanks. Just to sleep.'

'You've remembered the toilet is across the corridor?'

'Yes, I've not lost my marbles yet.' Elaine had to smile even though she was genuinely concerned.

'I'll leave you to sleep, then. Night,' and Elaine left him in peace. She checked her phone and saw that Harvey had sent a text saying, '*is he OK?*' Elaine said yes, but they were going to live with her for the time being. He replied just one word, '*thanks*'.

An hour later Harvey arrived back and checked in on his granddad, but he was sleeping peacefully, so Elaine made them both a meal and saved some for Fred in case he was hungry later, but he slept through the evening. Harvey said that he would go back home and get his own things and check everything was all right. He was only gone half an hour and then he sat down with Elaine in the lounge.

'Are you sure you don't mind us being here?'

'Of course not. I think it might be better if you stay here until . . . er, well for a while.'

'You mean until he dies, don't you?'

'Yes. It's not fair on you to expect you to go to college, work, and try to look after your granddad. And I'm sorry I didn't realise that before. I could see that you've been trying to make him meals and he hasn't been eating them. Well, I'm older than you and I can bully him. We'll let him sleep tonight and then we'll talk tomorrow.'

'Thanks, Elaine. I was a bit frightened on my own with him.'

'I'm not surprised. Most 17-year-olds would be. You've done very well so far, but now I'll take over. We'll look after him together, however long he's got. And afterwards, you can stay here forever.'

'Can I go to bed, please? I'd rather a late night at Oliver's.'

Elaine laughed.

'What time did you get to bed?'

'Er, I think we went to sleep about four am.'

'Go on, off to bed. I've put you in the grey bedroom. That's the first one upstairs. You'll be nearer your granddad if he needs you in the night. And I'm in the white bedroom at the far end of the corridor.'

'Thanks.'

'Night, night. Sleep tight.'

'Mind the bugs don't bite,' Harvey grinned. 'My Mum used to say that to me and Freya every night.'

'Well, I'll say it to you every night from now on, as I'm the nearest thing you've got to a mother at the moment.'

With a sudden movement, Harvey stood up and ran to Elaine and held her tight. She hugged him back and patted him on the back, like you would with a small child. Then just as suddenly, he broke away, said 'night', and went to bed.

As soon as he'd gone, Elaine went back to the lounge and spoke to Gill quietly. She updated her with what had happened, and Gill said that she would do anything she could to help her but said that it was a big responsibility that she was taking on.

'I didn't really have much option. Harvey was struggling to get him to eat and was frightened of being alone with him.'

'Are you going to keep them until the end?'

'Yes. And then I'll keep Harvey afterwards. I suppose at 17 he's too old to be taken into care, but he'll need a stable home for some time to come.'

'He'll certainly need it. To think of him going through even more loss just doesn't bear thinking about. And no word from Fred's brother?'

'No, proper waste of space, that fella.'

'Well, remember, I'm here if you need me.'

'Thanks. I'm sure I will need you over the next few months. You must come round regularly and keep Fred company.'

'I will. Night.'

'Night.'

Despite being bone-weary, Elaine didn't sleep very well. When she passed Harvey's bedroom, she could hear him weeping quietly and, although she longed to go in to him, she felt it was better if he wept alone tonight.

Next morning Elaine tapped on Fred's door and, after getting no response, walked in. He was still curled up in bed, but his breathing sounded difficult and he was red hot to the touch. She looked at her phone. It was a quarter to nine so she rang the doctor's surgery and asked if she could have a visit that day, explaining Fred's situation and symptoms. Elaine also explained that he was living with her at the moment, but gave his usual address. The receptionist said that she would put him down for a visit that day, but, if he deteriorated, to ring for an ambulance. Elaine thanked her and rang off. She went back to see Fred and, as he was stirring a little, she made him a cup of tea and took it in.

'How are you feeling, Fred?'

'I've felt better,' he said, and she put the cup of tea on his bedside cabinet whilst she got him moved up the bed, arranging the pillows so that he could sit up. His hands were shaking, so she had to help him hold the cup. She told him that she'd sent for the doctor, and he didn't look best pleased, but Elaine gave him the hard word. Harvey eventually came downstairs and went straight to see his granddad.

'How is he?' he asked Elaine.

'Not too good. I've sent for the doctor.' Harvey didn't respond but sat on the bed next to his granddad. He took the cup from Elaine and said that he'd hold it now. Fred managed to get half a cup of tea down, but then said he was tired and wanted to go back to sleep. Elaine and Harvey left the cup on his bedside table in case he woke up again and wanted another drink, and quietly left the room.

'Is he very poorly?' asked Harvey.

'He's not good, but I think it might be a chest infection. We'll have to see what the doctor says.'

'When is he coming?'

'Today sometime but they don't say when. I suppose they'll do the nearest cases first then outlying ones later, but I've no idea.'

'I know it'll sound awful, but do you mind if I go home for a while? I've got an assignment to do before Monday and I didn't bring my laptop with me last night.'

'And how long have you had this assignment?' asked Elaine, back in lecturer mode, fully knowing what students were like.

'Er, only since November.'

'It's January. You'd better get on with it. Why don't you have an hour or two at home and get it finished, and then that's one thing less to worry about.'

'What about the doctor?'

'I can deal with him.'

'Thanks, Elaine. I'll be off.'

Elaine popped in to look at Fred, but he was sleeping peacefully, even though his breathing was raspy.

She made herself a drink and had just sat down in the kitchen when there was a thundering knock on the door. Her first thought was that if she hadn't known that Fred was here, she'd have thought it was him again. Just the same knock, this doctor had. She opened the door to the doctor and stared. It wasn't any doctor that she'd met in the practice. This man was about her age, tall, very tanned, hair that was greying at the sides, and with piercing blue eyes. He must be a locum doctor. Really rather nice, Elaine was thinking, then pulled herself together.

'Thanks for coming, Doctor. Come this way.'

'Doctor? I'm no doctor,' said the man with a distinct accent. 'I've been told my brother's here. Fred Baxter. Is that right? And why's he here anyway?'

Elaine bristled. 'He's here because he is ill, and I didn't think it was fair that a 17-year-old boy was looking after him,' she said, just a little haughtily. 'I think he's got a chest infection so I've sent for the doctor. I'm sorry, I'm forgetting my manners. Would you like to see your brother now? Or would you like a drink?'

'I've just had a drink at the B & B where I stayed last night. I'd like to see my brother.'

Elaine led him into the corridor and knocked on the door. There was no reply, so she opened the door to find Fred was still asleep. They both came out of the room together.

Sitting in the kitchen-diner, the man said to Elaine. 'You're right. He doesn't look too good. I'm Richard Baxter, by the way.'

'Elaine Barnes. I wish you'd let us know you were coming.'

'I did. Wrote to Fred before Christmas. Told him I'd be in the country by the beginning of December, staying at my daughter's, and then would come up here to see him today. Didn't he tell you?'

'Obviously not, or I wouldn't have thought you were the doctor.'

Richard started laughing, his smile going right up to his eyes, Elaine noticed. A really good laugh from the heart, she thought.

'I've been called a few things in my life, but never a doctor. That's a new one. Now, where's this great nephew of mine? Is he here, or is he at work?'

'He's just gone back to the house. He had an assignment due for college, so I told him to go and do it.'

'College? What's he doing?'

'Horticulture.'

'Is that posh for gardening?'

'Yes,' Elaine laughed. 'But don't tell Harvey that. He designed my garden out front and helps me do the vegetable patch and keeps bees. He's quite an accomplished gardener. That's how we got to know each other. He came to tend the family grave, and I bought the church and acquired the graveyard as well.'

'Sounds like a good, sensible lad. I look forward to meeting him. My granddaughters are both doing airy-fairy things. One's doing Fine Arts and the other's doing Media Studies. Now what sort of job can they get with those sorts of qualifications?'

'How old are your granddaughters?'

'Nineteen. They're twins.'

'Oh, like Harvey and Freya?'

'Yes. Born year or so before Harvey, if I remember rightly. I remember teasing Fred that I was a granddad first, even though I was much younger than he. Never really knew him as a lad, you know. I was a bit of an afterthought to my parents, so Fred was away in the army before I knew him properly, and then when he left the army, I'd gone to Australia.'

'Where did you live in Australia?'

'Up the top, miles from anywhere. On a sheep ranch, with sheep my only neighbours.' But the sound of the door knocker, gentler this time, interrupted any further revelations. Elaine hurried to the door and there was Doctor Astle.

'Come in, Doctor Astle. This is Fred's brother, Richard. He just arrived less than an hour ago.' Doctor Astle smiled and nodded at Richard.

'Where's Fred?'

'In here.' The doctor went into the bedroom and Elaine told Richard to go in with him, but Richard insisted that she come in too, as he wouldn't know any answers to questions. Doctor Astle examined Fred, then she listened carefully to his chest. Fred only stirred during the examination and then went back to sleep, not even seeing Richard. When the exam was finished, the doctor said that she would talk to them outside. Elaine led them into the dining-kitchen.

'He's got a nasty chest infection, so I'll give him some antibiotics. The receptionist said that he's moved here. Is this a permanent arrangement?'

'Yes,' replied Elaine.

'But you know the diagnosis?'

'Yes, but I'm not sure whether his brother does. He only arrived a little before you.'

'I know he's got cancer,' said Richard. 'He wrote and told me. Told me it was time I came back here, so I did.'

'And are you staying here as well?' the doctor asked him.

'No, I'm at a B & B down the road for now, but I'll be buying somewhere in England soon.' Elaine wondered why her heart suddenly started beating faster but ignored it as she realised the doctor was talking to her.

'Will you be able to manage looking after him?'

'Yes, of course. I'd rather he stayed here instead of going into hospital.'

'Is he still refusing to have district nurses?'

'I didn't know he had refused. But then he's a very proud man and is always saying that he doesn't want to be beholden to anyone, so that's probably why he said no. If he's staying here, I'll accept any help I can get. I'm no nurse.'

'Good. I'll organise them to come and see you. Right, I'll be off, but don't hesitate to call me again. If he gets any worse ring for an ambulance. I'll email a prescription to the chemist. Can someone come in and pick it up for him?'

'Yes, not a problem. Thank you, Doctor,' and Elaine saw her to the door.

'I'll just ring Harvey and ask him to nip into Clitheroe to pick up the prescription,' said Elaine, 'and then I'll make us some lunch.'

'Not for me,' said Richard. 'I'm still full from breakfast.'

'Where are you staying?'

'At Buckthorn House B & B.'

'Tora's place?'

'Yes, she is called Tora. Do you know her?'

'I work as a tour guide at Browsholme Hall, where Tora is the cook in the tearooms.'

'Busy lady then.'

'Yes, she is. So where does your daughter live?'

'Milton Keynes.'

'Not in Australia?'

'No, she met an English guy who was backpacking and working in a bar in Oz, and they married eventually and moved to England.'

'And is your wife in Australia?' Elaine could have kicked herself for asking, but she had to know, holding her breath until he answered. She hadn't fancied someone so much for years.

'Not a clue, not seen her for years. She doesn't communicate.'

'I'm sorry, it's nothing to do with me. I'm just plain nosy.'

'That's alright. I suppose we'll be seeing a lot of each other for the foreseeable future.'

I do hope so, thought Elaine, but she politely replied, 'Yes, probably.'

'My wife ran off with a travelling salesman. Said life on a ranch was far too boring, and so was I.'

'Oh, I'm sorry.'

'I was at the time, especially as she took our little girl with her. I didn't see her for three years. Took a lot of work to rebuild her trust again. Think the wife had been feeding her bad things about me. I only got to see her when I stopped paying the maintenance,' he laughed. 'Knew that would bring her round. She was always greedy for money. Never had enough.'

'Did it work?'

'Oh, yes. I only continued the money if I got to have Melanie for the long school holidays every summer.'

'And what happened to your wife?'

'She just kept looking for richer and richer men. Lives on the outskirts of Perth now in a large house with a large swimming pool.'

'And is she happy now?'

'Oh, I doubt it. She's never happy. Anyway, enough about me. What about you? Is there a Mr Barnes?' Elaine's heart leapt. Is he interested in me? Is that why he's asking? Oh, I hope so!

'No, no Mr Barnes. I was married many years ago but been on my own for ages now.'

'What happened to him?'

'He married a vineyard.'

'What?'

'Well, we had a villa in France next door to a vineyard. The old couple who owned it had three daughters and no sons and had always wanted a son to carry on the business. Their youngest daughter wanted to run the business, but decided she'd like my husband to help her.'

'Ouch! So, she got your man and he got a vineyard?'

'Something like that. But I got the villa and our house in England as a divorce settlement, so I wasn't complaining, although at the time I was heartbroken.'

'I'm not surprised. Wasn't it awkward having the villa so near him?'

'It was at first but I really loved that villa, and we'd done so much to it.'

'Have you still got it?'

'No, I sold it in early 2016. I saw the way things were going with the EU referendum here, so decided that enough was enough and got a good price.'

'And you bought this place instead?'

'Not straightaway. I took early retirement and came to Dunsop Bridge for a holiday to visit my best friend Gill, and to decide where I wanted to live in retirement. As I drove in, I saw that this church was for sale and eventually bought it.'

'I don't blame you. It's a beautiful conversion. I feel so chilled here. I've never felt like this in a house before. I feel like I just want to stay forever.'

'That's exactly how I felt when I came to view it. Shall I show you round?'

'Yes, please.'

Elaine had never enjoyed showing someone round so much before. He kept stopping to ask her questions. He loved the pulpit and the stained-glass windows, stopping to stare at them for a long time.

'Jesus' eyes are really penetrating, aren't they?'

'Yes, that's what I thought when I first saw them.'

'And did you say it was a covenant, that they couldn't be taken out?'

'The pulpit and the windows. The pulpit was in memory of his wife. I think the covenants were why it had never sold. It was too restrictive for property developers to take on. I'll show you upstairs now.' Elaine had never been so relieved that she'd made her bed that morning. They briefly looked at each room and then came back downstairs.

'I've put Harvey in the grey bedroom nearest to the stairs, so that he can go to his granddad in the night, if he's needed,' explained Elaine.

'Good idea. Could I have that cup of tea now? Sorry if that's too cheeky.'

'Course you can. I could do with another one myself.' Elaine put the kettle on, glad to be concentrating on something, as the longer she was with Richard, the more she was liking him.

'I've got a graveyard and two fields as well,' Elaine said, once they were sat in the sunroom, cups in hand.

'The garden in front is beautiful. Did you plant it?'

'No, that was done by Harvey. It was his assignment from college to design a garden from scratch. He did the vegetable plot out back too and keeps bees.'

'Bees? I've always wanted to keep bees. Never got round to it. Too lazy.'

'Harvey's passionate about them and how the world will collapse if they decline any more. Don't start him on the subject or you'll never hear the end of it,' and they both laughed together.

Just at that point Harvey arrived home, clutching a bag from the chemist.

'I've got it, Elaine,' but then he stopped when he saw Richard. Richard instantly stood up.

'Harvey, this is your Uncle Richard from Australia.' The two men shook hands and Elaine couldn't stop staring at them. Now she knew who Harvey took after. He wasn't particularly like his mother or his father from the photos, but he could have been Richard's son.

'Elaine, what's the matter?' asked Harvey.

'Nothing. It's just that you look so like each other.' Both men grinned. 'Spose we do,' admitted Richard laughing. 'Elaine's been telling me all about your gardening and that you keep bees. You'll have to tell me all about it someday. I'd love to keep bees.' Elaine had to go and undo the packaging on the prescription to stop herself laughing out loud.

'Let's get this first dose of antibiotics into your granddad,' Elaine said when she'd composed herself. She went into the bedroom and found that Fred was asleep but decided to wake him as she wanted the tablets to take effect as soon as possible.

'Fred? Come on, I've got some tablets.'

He opened one eye sleepily, but then tried to sit up for her. She helped him into a sitting position and gave him the tablets and a glass of water. He took the tablet and then Elaine said, 'You've got a visitor.'

Fred's face lit up. 'Is it Harvey. Is he back?'

'No, it's someone else. I'll bring him in,' and she went and got Richard.

'Hello, Fred. I've made it at last,' said Richard, going forward to shake the old man's hand.

'Richard. You've come. Thank you.'

'Elaine thought I was the doctor. Think I gave her a bit of a shock when I told her who I was. Anyway, you need all the sleep you can get. Go back to sleep. We can talk plenty when you're better.'

'You're not going again?'

'I'm going nowhere for now.' Thank God, thought Elaine, as they left Fred to go back to sleep. Richard stayed all day and only returned to Tora's at night time. Each evening he went back, but stayed all the days at her house.

Chapter 23

For the next two days and nights there was little improvement in Fred's condition and Elaine was constantly worrying whether she should send for the doctor again. They managed to get adequate amounts of fluid into him but no food, and Elaine was getting extremely worried. However, on the third morning he sat up in bed and said that he fancied some porridge.

Elaine didn't have any, but she sent Harvey running up to the farm to borrow some from Ben, who loved it and had it every morning for breakfast. From then on, he slowly seemed to recover, and after about ten days was able to get up and sit in the sunroom. Elaine was shocked by how much more weight he'd lost when she saw him dressed for the first time, but didn't comment to Harvey or Richard until after Fred had left the room.

Fred seemed to be really enjoying Richard's company and they appeared to be making a bond that had been missing from their childhood. Elaine was glad because, besides Harvey, Richard was the only relative Fred had. And Harvey was loving getting to know this man whom he'd only heard of with derision from Fred before.

It was Harvey who took Richard to the family grave and told him a little about his family, because Richard said that he wanted to know all about them. Harvey's granny, Mary, had written regular newsy letters to Richard, whilst Fred had never written, so Richard had had no news since Mary died. Harvey and Richard appeared to get on very well together and Elaine was pleased that Harvey would have another man he could relate to. That is, if Richard stayed round here. But at any time he might go back to Milton Keynes to his daughter's. He said he was going to buy a house in England, but not where. Elaine suddenly realised how sad she would be if he left but didn't think she could do anything about it.

Although Gill had kept in touch by phone and text, she hadn't been down to the house since Richard arrived. However, after ten days, she popped in and had a good chat with Fred. She came early in the morning and Richard was still at Tora's.

'So, how are you getting on with the rogue uncle?' Gill asked Elaine.

'Rogue uncle? What do you mean?'

'That's the impression I got about him from you before he arrived.'

'Oh, he's no rogue. Quite the opposite.'

'Tell me more?'

'Nothing to tell. I wish there were. He's rather nice . . .' but the conversation stopped abruptly as the man they were talking about came into the sunroom. Elaine just prayed that he hadn't overheard their discussion.

'Richard, come and meet my dearest friend, Gill. She lives on the farm up the road.' The two said hello to each other.

'I'll go in and see Fred. Excuse me, ladies.'

Gill and Elaine looked at each other for a long time, and Elaine could feel herself getting red.

'No wonder you didn't encourage me to visit. Wanted him all to yourself, did you?' Gill teased.

'Shush, he might hear you,' pleaded Elaine.

'Elaine Barnes, I think you're smitten. Mind you, I don't blame you, he is gorgeous.' But then they heard Fred and Richard talking and knew they were coming into the room, so no further conversation could be had. They'd just got Fred settled and made him a drink when there was a knock on the door.

'Might be the doctor,' quipped Richard, grinning at Elaine, at which Elaine blushed. Gill raised an enquiring eyebrow, and Elaine explained that she thought Richard was the doctor when he arrived and knew she would never live that down. But this time it was a young nurse to whom Elaine opened the door.

'Hello, I'm Emily Yates, District Nurse. I've come to see Fred Baxter.'

'Oh, come in, Emily. You're very welcome. However, before we go in, can I warn you that he probably won't be too happy about you coming.'

'Don't worry. It'll sort itself out,' she laughed.

But Elaine was wrong. Fred Baxter took one look at Emily and beamed when she was introduced.

Gill jumped up and said that she would go and let them get on with the appointment, telling Elaine to ring her as soon as she could. Elaine saw her out and shouted to Harvey to come down, as he'd been having a lie in.

Emily got her notes out and was making sense of who everyone was. She grasped that it wasn't Fred's house, but that he was going to stay there for the rest of his life. She worked out the relationship of the three men and how they'd met Elaine. Then she started telling them about the care and what services she could offer. Emily explained that she would be one of two named nurses in charge of Fred. The other nurse was Abi Butler and she would visit next time; they would share his care between them most of the time. She explained that fewer nurses were assigned to each person, so that there would be more continuity. Emily gratefully accepted a cup of tea whilst she was doing all her paperwork and then asked if they had any questions. They all said no, as she'd explained everything very well. Fred just beamed throughout. Before leaving, Emily mentioned hospice care. That wiped the smile off Fred's face.

'I'm not going into any hospice,' he growled.

'I'll put that down as a "no" then,' she laughed, and Fred couldn't resist that smiling face and beamed at her again. 'I'll leave these notes here so that Abi can carry on with the care next week. Here's a list of phone numbers and items that can be borrowed. If you need any of them just let us know. For the time being visits will be weekly, but at any time we can increase the frequency.'

'Thank you, Emily. That's reassuring to know,' said Elaine. The men said a collective thank you, and Emily left.

'I like Emily,' said Fred.

'Good,' said Elaine, breathing a sigh of relief, knowing that it could have gone very much the other way with Fred.

That night, after Richard had gone, Elaine rang Gill. She listened quietly to Gill saying she was a dark horse, and what was happening with the lovely Richard?

'Nothing, more's the pity. I think he's just a genuinely nice guy, but I don't think he's interested in me.'

'Not many of those about, not genuine ones anyway. Well, not compared to Thomas Farnworth,' Gill laughed.

'Oh, I'm glad you mentioned him. His son has arranged for his ashes to be buried in the graveyard. He wants them as near to the war grave as he can.'

'Is there a space?'

'Yes, right in front of the Farnworth war grave, which is Square C, Plot Ten. Thomas' grave will be Square C, Plot Nine. Then his mother will go in there when the time comes. The committal is arranged for next Saturday. Jonathan and his family are coming up for the weekend and staying at the Whitewell

Inn and will bring Agnes too. He's given me a substantial sum to cover all the expenses.'

'Will you attend?'

'I suppose I'd better. It's only polite really. Especially as he's given me so much money,' Elaine added as an afterthought, laughing.

'Now stop distracting me with telling me about the graveyard. Let's get back to Mr Richard Baxter. Tell all.'

'There really is nothing to tell. He's unfailingly polite, we have a laugh together, he's interested in everything I say, but beyond that, nothing. Although he did ask if there was a Mr Barnes.'

'Oh, he's interested then.'

'Possibly not. I'd just asked him if his wife lived in Australia.'

'You didn't!'

'Well, he'd been telling me about his daughter and granddaughters in England, so it just led on from there.'

'A likely story. You just wanted to know if he was available.'

'Well, there was that as well.'

'So where is his wife? I presume she is 'ex' by now?' asked Gill, wanting to know all the ins and outs of the situation.

'Yes, she is his ex-wife now. She ran off with a travelling salesman and is very greedy for money.'

'Oh, well, we'll just have to see.' And Elaine just nodded thoughtfully, which wasn't helpful as they were on the phone. 'Are you still there, Elaine?'

'Yes, but Harvey's just come in, so I'll get going now. Bye.'

'Bye. But don't think this is the last we'll talk about this,' said Gill, but Elaine had rung off.

The following week the other nurse, Abi, arrived, and Fred was equally charmed by this new young nurse and beamed at her, too. Suddenly his life was becoming more interesting, as he had these lovely ladies dancing attendance on him, he said to Elaine, who merely smiled. Was Fred becoming a ladies' man in his old age, she wondered? Good for him. It made her life easier.

Eventually Fred was well enough to get up and about all day, but he tired soon and loved to go back to bed for a little nap. Elaine noticed that he was getting even thinner and more breathless with minimum effort. The walk from the sunroom to the bedroom was about all he could manage. And the portions of food he ate were very small. But he seemed very happy with his lot and didn't complain. He even made Elaine go and buy chocolates for Emily and Abi as a thank you for their care.

One evening Richard came in and said that he would have to find alternative accommodation as Tora had a long-standing booking for a large party.

'You can come and stay here,' Elaine replied, just a shade too quickly. But he refused.

'That's really kind of you, Elaine, but I need to be elsewhere. I'll stay most of the day here if I can, but you've enough with Harvey and Fred to cope with.'

'One more won't make a difference,' Elaine said, as lightly as she could, but he wouldn't change his mind.

'I've booked a holiday cottage up at the farm where your friend lives.'

'Greenbank Farm?'

'Yes. Near enough to get here quickly if I'm needed. Liz said that it's their quiet time in January and February.'

Bitterly disappointed, Elaine managed to reply that it was okay and smiled at Richard, but her heart was wishing he'd decided to stay as he'd be in the next bedroom to her. No! Stop all those kinds of thoughts, Elaine reprimanded herself.

February turned into March and Fred was weakening daily. Abi and Emily were coming in on a regular basis now and Elaine knew that Fred didn't have long left to live. She started trying to approach Harvey with the facts but he wouldn't talk; he just brushed her away and went upstairs. She asked Richard if he could try and he fared a little better and managed to prepare Harvey for yet another loss in his young life.

Inevitably, Fred slipped into a coma, his last spoken word being 'Mary', his late wife. Elaine, Richard, and Harvey stayed up all night with him. About four am, his breathing slowed and then finally stopped. Richard put his arm round Harvey, so Elaine left them to it. She went out to make them all a cup of tea, after ringing the surgery to tell them. When the two men came out of the bedroom, Elaine went back in to say her goodbye to Fred and lay him flat in the bed to await the doctor.

After the doctor had been, Elaine found the funeral director's number that

Fred had said he wanted to use, and they said they would call later.

Richard looked at Elaine and said that he would pay for all the funeral expenses, but Elaine told him that it wasn't necessary, and told the story of Fred turning up with £3000 in a carrier bag. At least it made them smile. She also told him the terms of Fred's will. That Harvey would be the only benefactor, but the money would be in trust until he was 18, and that Elaine would be Harvey's guardian.

'He wasn't sure you'd turn up, so he appointed me,' explained Elaine.

'He did right. I was an unknown. I'd have been here sooner, but the bloke buying my farm pulled out and I had to start all over again.'

'What will you do now?'

'I'll stay here a while for Harvey, and then I'll decide what to do with the rest of my life. I'm going down to Milton Keynes this weekend to see Melanie, Jack, and the girls, but I'll be back for the funeral. Will you be all right, you and Harvey?'

'Yes, we'll be fine,' Elaine said quietly, thinking how special her life had been since Richard had appeared. She'd got used to having him around now and would be devastated when he finally left.

Elaine kept busy during the weekend, thinking about how Richard was, but trying to concentrate on helping Harvey, who had gone very quiet again. She was glad when he went over to Tom's house for a while on Saturday night, and seemed happier when he came back. Whilst he was away, Elaine caught up with Gill, who came round for a meal at Elaine's. It gave Elaine something to focus her thoughts on.

Monday morning brought a surprise. Richard came back, but with his whole family in tow. Elaine and Harvey were introduced to Melanie, Jack, Anya, and Grace. After a drink, Elaine persuaded Harvey to take his cousins out to see his garden and bees, so that the adults could talk. It seemed to be a good strategy, as when they all came in, they were laughing and trying to work out what relationship they were to each other. Elaine was pleased that Harvey now had a new family to cling to during this sad time. The family were staying all week until the funeral, and had booked in at Tora's B & B.

The funeral was the following Friday and it was a poignant service, gathered round the familiar grave. Gill's family and a few of the villagers attended too. In the crowd was Carl, Harvey's counsellor, and Elaine was very touched by that. She noticed that Harvey had a long chat with him afterwards. Elaine had made a meal, with Gill's help, ready for after the funeral, which was appreciated by everyone who stayed behind.

Richard's family left the next day, but Richard stayed behind. Harvey went over to see Oliver and Tom in the evening, and Elaine and Richard were alone, sitting in companionable silence. But Elaine could stand it no longer. She had to know Richard's plans for the future.

'So what's next for you?' she asked tentatively.

'Not sure. Haven't finally made my mind up. Didn't think beyond Fred going. Wanted to be here for him to the end.'

'And you were. I think he appreciated it. And I know Harvey did.'

'Yes, Harvey is a grand lad. Just the lad I'd have liked if I'd had one. I'd like to keep in touch with Harvey.'

'Good. It'll help him, and meeting your girls did him good too. He feels that he still has some family left around him.'

'I've got to say, Elaine, how much I appreciate all you have done for Fred and Harvey. It made my coming back here much easier too. I can't begin to thank you.'

Elaine knew she was going to cry and got up to get a tissue from the table. Richard also stood up, caught her hand, and pulled her to him, holding her tightly against him. Elaine burst into tears and he held her soothing her and stroking her back. When her tears subsided, she lifted her head up to look at Richard and he leant down and softly kissed her, gently at first, but then when she responded, his kisses became more urgent. Eventually they broke apart, both breathless.

'I've been wanting to do that since the first time I met you. When you stood at the front door and just stared at me with your mouth open,' Richard said, still holding her close.

'I think I've been wanting you to kiss me from the same moment,' Elaine admitted. 'I was so sure it would be the doctor and then you just stood there, and I couldn't take my eyes off you. But why wait 'til now?'

'I wanted to concentrate on Fred first. But now the time is ours, if you want it to be?'

'Oh, yes, I want it to be.' Then she kissed him this time.

'But why wouldn't you stay here? Why did you insist on renting one of the cottages at the farm? It would have been so much easier.'

'I didn't trust myself. I knew the only bedroom that was available was next door to you, and I couldn't bear the thought of sleeping near to you, but not with you. So I was afraid of making a move on you when you didn't want it.'

'It's perhaps as well you didn't stay, or I might have made the first move anyway,' Elaine laughed.

'And what would Harvey think then?' - but there was no answer as they kissed again.

'Are you going to move in now?'

'No. I don't want your reputation in the village spoilt. You seem to have settled in here. Liz has told me of a small cottage that is coming up to rent in the village, as her holiday cottages are getting busy now, so I've taken the tenancy on for six months, and then we'll see.'

'Tenancy! That's just reminded me. I need to let United Utilities know that Fred has died. He worked for them from the days when it was called the Water Board, and his was a tied cottage where he could live for his lifetime, but it reverts to them now. I suppose we'd better clear it out.'

'I'll help you with that tomorrow.' And so he did, and Harvey as well. They sorted all Fred's clothes and belongings into piles for the charity shop or the rubbish and went through everything else in the cottage. Harvey said that he'd like to keep his granddad's watch and bedside clock and Elaine said that was a good idea.

In the back of the space under the stairs Harvey found a large suitcase and a carrier bag. When he opened the suitcase it was full of his own family photo albums, with lots of personal documents, such as birth, his parents' marriage, Christening, and Premium Bond certificates. In the carrier bag were two boxes; one with 'Freya' on the lid and one with 'Harvey' on the lid. Inside there were lots of personal mementoes. First teeth, first lock of hair, birthday cards, Mother's Day cards, Father's Day cards, baby bootees, first pieces of school work, school merit certificates, swimming certificates, and many more; a whole history of Harvey's and Freya's childhood. The last thing they found was a large worn envelope with two pieces of paper inside. One was Jason's birth certificate and the other was the letter written by Jason's mother and left attached to his blanket when she abandoned him. It was obvious that it had been looked at many times. Perhaps with the DNA results and this birth certificate, Harvey could investigate his father's history and get some closure.

Elaine was angry. Angry at Fred for withholding all this information from Harvey when it could have helped him so much in the early days. But it was too late for anger now and she was just glad that Harvey had found the mementoes. He would be so much more comfortable now and relive precious moments from his childhood, and perhaps he would be helped through his grief some more.

As soon as the house was emptied, Elaine rang Nikki to see if she could do a thorough clean with her the next day, so that they could return the keys to the United Utilities office. Nikki was happy to help and between them, with Gill's help, the cottage was soon pristine and ready for the next occupant. The YMCA charity shop came to collect the furniture and other equipment whilst they were cleaning. Fred's clothes would go to the Cancer UK shop in Clitheroe. It was the end of an era, Nikki said. Elaine couldn't agree more. But in her heart she thought that it was the beginning of a new era for herself, and she smiled.

Chapter 24

The summer passed quickly, with Richard and Elaine's relationship deepening. Elaine now knew what had been missing in her life and couldn't ever imagine being apart from him. He felt the same too and in June, Richard proposed to Elaine, and she gladly said yes, and, they went to choose a ring together at Nettleton's jewellers in Clitheroe. They decided that Richard would live with her rather than buy another house, as Richard loved the house as much as Elaine did. Elaine couldn't bear to live anywhere else now. They also made the decision that they'd keep their finances separate. Elaine would still leave her house to Harvey and share her estate in her will between the four godchildren and her favourite charities. Richard's proceeds from the sale of his business would go to his daughter and granddaughters so as not to complicate matters. 'But I'll make sure that you can continue to live here with Harvey when I've gone,' Elaine teased.

'Who says you're going first?' Richard replied. 'I intend living until I'm a 100 now I've found you.'

'Me too,' said Elaine. 'We've a lot of catching up to do.'

During the long college holidays, Harvey announced that he was going to France in the third week of July to visit Ethan with Tom and Oliver, and he was driving. Elaine's heart stopped momentarily as she thought of the dangers of three lads driving in France, but she was a bit happier when he said that Debby, Lily, and Kate were going too, in Debby's car. Debby and the girls were going to a campsite outside Paris, whilst the boys were staying with Ethan.

'It's the last time we'll all be together before we go to university,' Harvey explained, so Elaine had to go with it, but prayed for his safety throughout the trip. As it happened, she was worrying unnecessarily as there were no mishaps and everybody had a great time. And Harvey bought her a lovely bottle of perfume as a present. Harvey was growing up, Elaine realised, a little sadly, and was needing her less and less, which she knew was a good thing.

In the week after Harvey got home, Elaine opened her garden and graveyard to the public, after taking advice from Jean at Browsholme Hall. Richard was keen on the idea and loved it that the money raised would go to soldiers' charities, as Fred had been in the army. He took over a lot of the organising of the seating and arrangements, booking the marquee and bringing chairs and tables from the village hall, and setting out the pull-up banners from the commemorative service. That left Elaine, Gill, Liz, and Nikki to sort out the catering. They picked a weekend and opened both days and were amazed by how many people attended. Having made loads of cakes for the whole weekend, Kate and Liz then spent several hours on Saturday night baking more cakes for Sunday as they'd nearly sold out. At the end of the weekend everybody was exhausted but exceptionally pleased when the final amount came to £4000. Elaine couldn't believe it and was so pleased that she decided she and Richard would have an open day every year.

After the open weekend Richard took Harvey down to Milton Keynes to stay with Melanie and the girls. They had a great time taking him round London, seeing shows and doing all the museums, Kew Gardens, which Harvey loved, and touristy things. Elaine missed them both dreadfully whilst they were away and couldn't wait for them to come home again.

For the last week of August Richard had planned a holiday for Elaine, Harvey, Melanie, Jack, and the girls, but they also asked Gill to come along.

'What do you want me to go for?' said Gill. 'I don't want to be a raspberry.'

'I think you mean a gooseberry.'

'Whatever,' said Gill crossly.

'But Richard wants you to come. We're taking Harvey, Melanie, Jack, and the girls with us as well.'

'All of them? Oh, well, that's different. I thought you were just going on your own. Where are you going?'

'Kos.'

'The Greek island?'

'Yes.'

'Well, if you're sure? I've never been to Kos.'

'Good. I'll tell Richard. We've booked a villa with loads of bedrooms and a swimming pool, so you'll be okay.'

'Sounds great. When are we going?'

'Last week of August.'

'Great, I'll start planning my wardrobe.'

'You do that and bring a nice floaty dress because we're going to a posh restaurant,' Elaine grinned.

It was soon time to go on holiday and Gill was amazed when they got to the beach-side villa. It was perfect she said. The first evening, they went to a local restaurant and sat down with drinks, waiting for their food to come.

'Whilst we're waiting for the food to come, we want to tell you all something,' said Richard, holding Elaine's hand. 'We've got you all here under false pretences.'

'False pretences?' asked Gill. 'What do you mean? Are you abandoning us here and going somewhere else?'

'No,' said Richard, 'you're here to attend a wedding.'

'A wedding?' asked Melanie.

'Yes,' said Elaine. 'Richard and I are getting married tomorrow, and we couldn't do it without any of you here.'

'Married? Tomorrow?' gasped Gill. Richard and Elaine both nodded their heads.

'You are my dame of honour, Gill,' said Elaine.

'And you are my best man, Harvey,' said Richard.

'And are we bridesmaids?' Anya and Grace asked together.

'Yes,' replied Elaine, grinning.

'Is that why we were told to bring pretty dresses? Are they our bridesmaid dresses?' asked Grace.

'Yes,' grinned Elaine.

'Well, I never,' said Gill, and then was quiet for once.

'We'll have a party when we get home, but we didn't want a big fuss making, so that's why we decided to keep it secret. We'll probably have a wedding blessing as well. Because we are both divorced, the church might be unhappy about marrying us, but they'll often allow a blessing, like Prince Charles and Camilla did.'

Harvey was the first to recover.

'Well, I think that's great. Good for you,' he said, hugging both Elaine and Richard. Gill recovered from her shock and hugged them both as well, and then they all had a great big group hug.

'So, don't have too much to drink tonight,' Richard warned. 'We have an early start on the boat.'

'Boat?' asked Jack.

'Yes, we're getting married on a boat,' Richard replied. Then the food arrived, so there was no more chat for a while.

'Are you staying on here alone for your honeymoon?' asked Harvey.

'No, we're coming back with you. We're planning a trip later this year or next year probably.'

'Great!' said Harvey.

'Let's get back to the villa now so we can have an early start,' Richard announced after they'd finished the meal, and they all slowly walked back, lost in their own thoughts.

The wedding was perfect. The bride looked beautiful in her white floaty dress, as did the bridesmaids and dame of honour in their summer frocks. The marriage service was special and cruising on the boat made it even more magical. The boat crew provided champagne for a toast and then a meal, and when they arrived back at the villa everyone was happy, if not a little tipsy. There was much hilarity as Harvey, who was more drunk than the others, was trying to work out what relationship he now was to Elaine.

They had an idyllic five days, and then flew back to England to tell their amazed friends and families just what they had done and to plan a party for everyone. There was a simple wedding blessing at the church in Whalley first, and then the party, which they decided to hold at the village hall, which could accommodate more people. Just about everyone they knew was invited, with more people from Elaine's side than Richard's, but it was a happy gathering, nonetheless.

Insisting that there were to be no presents, a dish was put out at the party for donations to Derian House Children's Hospice, where a local child had been cared for, and an amazing donation was sent to them afterwards.

After they'd returned from Kos, Harvey asked if he could move into his granddad's bedroom and they agreed, so Harvey moved downstairs. Life for the three of them settled into a good routine. Richard and Harvey had great plans for the garden and the bees, increasing them to five hives, and they bought some chickens. They were even thinking about getting some horses for the back field, and building stables. Shame not to use it, suggested Richard, because he'd missed having a horse since he returned to England. Elaine said it was up to them but they shouldn't expect her to look after any horses or bees. Richard took on the task of researching the graves that Charlie hadn't got round to, and was making great progress in getting a gravestone, whether stone or other material, on every occupied grave. Elaine was even teaching him to play tennis. She had never been happier in her life: busy all day, either together with Richard, or separate when she was at Browsholme Hall or Whalley Abbey, or with Gill and the family at the farm, but the nights were spent with Richard alone.

Harvey decided to do his degree in Horticulture without living on campus but travelling daily. He preferred to stay with Elaine and his Uncle Richard. And it was interesting that he was spending more time at Tom's, even after Tom had gone to university. It took a while for it to dawn on Elaine that Harvey was going to see Lily, and romance was blossoming there. It was early days and Lily was quite young, so Elaine would wait and see. As far as she knew it was Harvey's first girlfriend, but only time would tell and that was what Harvey and Lily had plenty of.

It was soon Christmas again; the years just seemed to be flying by, Elaine complained. Richard said it was because she was getting older, so she threw a pillow at him, and reminded him that he was two years older than her. Elaine and Richard hosted Christmas Day, then they went to Liz and Ben's for Boxing Day, but the New Year's Eve party was at Elaine and Richard's. Melanie, Jack, and the girls came up for that party, and Helen, Martin, and Daniel came too.

An added bonus was that Lindsay, Tim, and baby Sophia came for New Year's Eve. Sophia was spoiled rotten by everybody there, with the females fighting as to whose turn it was for a cuddle. Gill was delighted that Sophia was wrapped in a shawl that she had knitted and she was wearing an outfit that Liz had bought. Tim and Lindsay had spent time with Lindsay's mum and dad on Christmas Day and had decided to alternate each year, to keep the peace between the two families, as many other families decide to do at Christmas.

During the evening, Elaine was telling Gill that they had booked their honeymoon for next March. Their itinerary was to go to Australia first, hiring a camper van in which to travel. Richard wanted to show Elaine the land that had been his home for so many years, and she had never seen. Then they were to go to New Zealand, China, and Thailand. They were booked to travel on March 23rd, so only three months away. They would be away for three months in total, and Gill promised to keep a check on Harvey, and make sure he didn't have too many wild parties whilst they were away. At last the clock got to midnight and they all wished each other a Happy 2020.

Elaine got up to make a speech, a little tipsy by now. 'Here's to 2020. This is going to be the best year of my life; I can feel it in my bones. And my lovely husband is taking me on a trip of a lifetime. So a toast to my lovely husband, our trip, my friends and family, and my special son, Harvey.' And everybody else raised their glasses. A perfect end to a lovely party.

It was during January and Elaine and Richard were sharing a coffee together in the sunroom before going to Gill's for lunch, when a text denoting breaking news pinged into Elaine's phone. She took it out to have a look.

'What does it say, Elaine?' asked Richard.

'Oh, it's just about some new virus in China. They're calling it corona virus. Probably won't affect us. Probably all be over by the time we go on March 23rd.'

'Yes, probably,' replied Richard. 'Let's get going to Gill's. I'm starving. I hope she's made cheese and onion pie today.'

About this book

Going on holiday to Pocklington, travelling down the A1079 towards Hull, I noticed a 'For Sale' sign on a church set back from the road. It was surrounded by a graveyard. That got me thinking. If you bought the church to convert it, would you own the graveyard as well? And would the relatives of the graves be allowed access to their graves? So that is how this book started. It celebrates friendship and love, grief and loss, and some of the things that are special to me. It is unusual for me in that it is set in modern times, when I usually write books set in history. I've set it in Dunsop Bridge in the Trough of Bowland, an Outstanding Area of Natural Beauty. But if you visit Dunsop Bridge don't be looking for the church, as it is all a figment of my imagination and doesn't and has never existed. But some of the people and places in this book are real. My husband Jim and I visit Dunsop Bridge regularly, always calling at Puddleducks café, of course!

During the corona virus lockdown, I've listened to daily broadcasts by the Christian writer and comedian Adrian Plass and his lovely wife Bridget. He asked 'What is your legacy of the lockdown?' I suppose you could say that this book is my legacy of lockdown, as it was written entirely during the lockdown period, although the idea for the book had been in my mind for a couple of years.

About the author

Linda Sawley is a retired senior lecturer in children's nursing, having worked with children for all her career. After having to re-write a 40,000 word dissertation for a Master of Philosophy degree, Linda decided to try non-academic writing. She set up her own publishing company in 1998. A committed Christian, Linda is a member of the Association of Christian Writers and an Associate Member of NAWG (National Association of Writer's Groups.) Linda loves her friends, family, knitting, classical music, reading, talking, singing, eating out and buying shoes – not necessarily in that order! She hates cooking, cleaning and all things domestic.

Linda is a founder member of the charity 'Petal' which was formally known as Ribble Valley and White Rose Ladies Luncheon Club, which raises money for childhood cancer in the north of England. She supports the charity through a donation made from the sale of each book. Her other charity, who also receive a donation from the sale of each book, is Derian House Children's Hospice, in Lancashire.

In 2004, she was awarded two prizes at the David St John Thomas Self-Publishing Awards for her third book 'The Key'. One award was the Community Cup for self-publishing for charity, and the second award was the Overall Grand Award, for the person showing the most promise in self-publishing.

www.linricpublishing.com